Moira

Encounters With the Holy Spirit

Book 5 of the *Buddy* series

Arthur Perkins

SIGNALMAN PUBLISHING

Moira
Encounters With the Holy Spirit
by Arthur Perkins

Signalman Publishing
www.signalmanpublishing.com
email: info@signalmanpublishing.com
Tampa, Florida

Scriptures are taken from the King James Version of the Bible unless otherwise noted.

ISBN: 978-1-940145-88-4

Printed in the United States of America

Also by Arthur Perkins

Fiction

Buddy
(Book 1 of the Buddy series)

Cathy
(Book 2 of the Buddy series)

Jacob
(Book 3 of the Buddy series)

Home, Sweet Heaven
(Book 4 of the Buddy series)

Nonfiction

Marching to a Worthy Drummer: A Christian layperson speaks out about the Holy Spirit

Uncle Art's Bible Favorites

Family of God Revised Edition

DEDICATION

As in my previous Christian novels, **Buddy, Cathy, Jacob, Home, Sweet Heaven** and my books on the Holy Spirit, **Marching to a Worthy Drummer, Family of God**, and **Uncle Art's Bible Favorites**, I dedicate this work to my wife, Carolyn, the joy of my life. We both dedicate this work, above all, to our God, and to our four daughters and their families.

ACKNOWLEDGEMENTS

I wish to extend a grateful, heartfelt thank-you to the following people who have been instrumental in the production of my books. First, to my God, whose loving character elicits my devotion and the thrill of learning and writing of His beautiful nature. Second, to my wonderful wife Carolyn, whose loving support in all matters of our happy marriage have given me added incentive and the freedom to pursue my writing endeavors. Third, to my brother Jon, whose support has been extremely helpful. Fourth, to my friend and publisher, John McClure of Signalman Publishing, for his enthusiasm and professionalism. I'm truly fortunate to be associated with him. I also wish to thank our pastor, F. David Lambert, ThD. While we don't always agree on every theological matter, we do agree on much, particularly on the divine inspiration and inerrancy of Scripture. I have learned much about God and the Church through his very thorough exposition of Scripture and Church doctrine.

The title of this book is given in honor of a special lady who came into and out of our lives many years ago. Our brief encounter with her has contributed much to the shaping of my character.

INTRODUCTION

Mankind just never seems to learn from the past. Like in the days of Noah, affairs on Earth continued to progress downward into violence and depravity. The majority of humans had become the embodiment of the person that Paul had so bleakly described in 2 Timothy 3:1-9, and those Christians who remained faithful were afflicted with the fulfillment of the following verse 12:

> *This know, also, that in the last days perilous times shall come. For men shall be lovers of their own selves, covetous, boasters, proud, blasphemers, disobedient to parents, unthankful, unholy, without natural affection, trucebreakers, false accusers, incontinent, fierce, despisers of those that are good, traitors, heady, high-minded, lovers of pleasures more than lovers of God, having a form of godliness, but denying the power of it; from such turn away. For of this sort are they who creep into houses, and lead captive silly women laden with sins, led away with various lusts, ever learning, and never able to come to the knowledge of the truth. Now as Jannes and Jambres withstood Moses, so do these also resist the truth, men of corrupt minds, reprobate concerning the faith. But they shall proceed no further; for their folly shall be manifest unto all men, as theirs also was. . .*

> *. . .Yea, and all that will live godly in Christ Jesus shall suffer persecution.*

There was some reason for persons of those latter days to fail to profit from the past. They were denied the knowledge of it by corrupt educators who had the gall to excise such failures of character from our common history. Nevertheless, that was a poor excuse for the excesses of the time, for the common person was so mean-spirited and self-centered that he would have ignored the past anyway even had he full access to it. The leaders and educators that they installed to control them were simply reflections of the person on the street;

they got what they deserved.

For decades God had warned them of their continuous descent into corrupt and harmful behavior. The people pinned the blame on those warnings to mother nature, not understanding that a very personal and loving God was watching over them, pleading with them to return to Him. The time eventually arrived, as He knew was destined to happen, when all possibility of a remedy was gone for the collective wrong that people had imposed upon themselves. The world and its inhabitants had fallen into an unmitigated hell, darkly inspired by a satanically-directed government that sought to suppress all independent thought. Suffering was ubiquitous.

In this horrible environment God had brought all but a few souls who were written in the Book of Life into His gentle, benign and loving fold as citizens in the spiritual realm. Earl and Joyce were happy participants in this near-final collection, viewing with astonishment the beauty of their new domain and their new bodies in which all the parts that had been torn away by violence were completely restored. Having courageously and selflessly fulfilled the Will of God in their lives on Earth, they were welcomed with loving arms by their Lord Jesus Christ.

Jacob and his beloved wife Moira remained on Earth during this transition, having been asked by God to perform a special task intended to strengthen a marginal segment of society toward endowing them with the ability to be worthy elements of God's domain. For the sake of those people, Jacob and Moira were required to endure the deprivations of a world that had been so devastated by wholesale destruction that it was universally called Earthchange. In the process their own nobility was strengthened, to the immense delight of their Lord Jesus Christ.

The Earthchange was violent beyond comprehension, having been initiated at the level of the cosmos, in which an errant planetoid ran amuck through our solar system in a re-enactment of cosmic billiards, much like the event that caused the Great Flood millennia before, and its catastrophic aftermath during the Exodus of the Israelites from Egypt.

This story is a record of their trials and triumphs.

PART ONE: BEFORE

PART TWO: EARTHCHANGE

PART THREE: AFTERMATH

PART ONE

BEFORE

Preface to Part One

Earth as it existed just before the Earthchange suffered greatly from the continuing mismanagement of mankind's various forms of governance. Air quality steadily worsened to the point of affecting the lungs of all but a few inhabitants who were fortunate enough to live in the ever-dwindling areas of relative purity. A rash of earthquakes, severe but not even close to the enormity of the superquakes attending the Earthchange, nevertheless had caused widespread poisoning due to the large number of nuclear power plants that had spewed out radiation on their travels downward toward the center of the Earth. On top of that, the solar windmills and panel arrays that covered much of the planet as part of the ill-conceived attempt to reduce the perceived global climate change littered the planet, making more of a mess than the plastic and paper that already trashed much of the ground.

That was just a small portion of the physical damage wrought upon the Earth by man's inability to handle the technology for which his mental capacity was ill-prepared. The rampant corruption of governments worldwide led to mass starvation, deadly diseases, continuing strife and warfare, and a general malaise and hopelessness of the population that was periodically interrupted by episodes of mass rage.

Mankind's answer, as God was fully and painfully aware would happen, was a fear on the part of those with the ability to do something about it that society was collapsing into indifference and sloth. Unless humanity could be controlled, it would release unbridled, irreversible destruction. They acted in haste driven by their fear. A sudden, massive move of overwhelming strength was initiated on the part of the world's elite to create worldwide governance, a one-world government in which every person on Earth was required to participate on the threat of torture and inevitable annihilation. The move was indeed intended to correct the deteriorating environmental desecration, but it wasn't entirely altruistic. The elite controllers saw enough personal incentive to their rigid management of the population that the acquisition of power ended up eclipsing the desire to improve the planet. Satan, of course, clapped his hands in glee over the base mindset that he had so successfully inculcated in them. It was a long time in coming, but the reward was vast.

Control over the masses of humanity was virtually complete: cameras everywhere assured compliance with the dictates of the self-adoring, ignoble elite. Most people accepted this new regime, having lost any true knowledge of world history, any notion of morality, any concept of selfless nobility, or even the ability to think for themselves. All they wanted was a continuation of food, comfort-inducing drugs and pornography. In essence, they wanted the ability to survive with the illusion of comfort without having to work for what they received. But there was a segment of society, temporary in nature, that adhered to the more noble statutes of their Judeo-Christian God, to whom they remained steadfastly loyal.

Among the demands of the evil cretins was the command to replace the worship of God with the worship of the head controller, a person who had willingly given up his soul to Satan. The full-scale slaughter of Christians rivaled the killing of innocent but unwanted babies through abortion, both inside and outside the womb.

It was in this environment that Jacob and Moira found themselves increasingly embroiled in the warfare that beset their beloved country Israel. In a kibbutz perched on a mountainside they were in a position to see the spectacular but terrifying destruction of nations and armies.

CHAPTER ONE

"Here, here! What's this?" Catherine Trey-Ellis said in alarm from the seat of Charlotte's carriage.

"I thought we were friends," Charlotte replied in a husky voice.

"Not that kind!" Catherine responded, attempting to distance herself from her companion.

Charlotte opened the privacy window. "Martin, please drop Mrs. Ellis off," she said to the chauffeur in a voice that had sharpened considerably. "You know where."

Mrs. Trey-Ellis left the carriage abruptly, her exit having been assisted with the heel of Charlotte's left foot. As the horse clopped down the cobblestone street, she found herself alone and terribly afraid in the middle of a poverty-ridden district. Her fear was well-founded, as this area in the late-eighteen hundreds was a hotbed of working-class unrest and hatred toward the robber barons whose fortunes were acquired at the expense of human misery. Mrs. Ellis' elegant dress and demeanor invited unspeakable conduct from the miserable inhabitants. She shivered in the cold misty air, the wet cobblestones reflecting the hazy glow of the gas lamp mounted on the pole above her. Her eyes darted about, looking for some shelter or a passing carriage, but the street remained empty of travelers, and the storefronts were dark.

As the world passed the midpoint of the nineteenth century, emerging technology was opening paths for opportunity. Industrial barons came into being, but at the time, technology was insufficiently developed for wealth to be acquired without the back-breaking labor of the exploited masses. Therefore, those with an acquisitive nature also required the possession of a shocking indifference toward the welfare of their fellow man.

Alone now in her seat, Charlotte herself seethed with an unquenchable rage. She had misjudged the woman, thinking her to be weak and pliant, to be easily overcome by her aggressive behavior. Domination in that direction being off the table for now, she smiled briefly at the likely consequence of the creature's rejection of her advances and turned her speculations toward domination of a different kind, the acquisition of Mr. Ellis' corporate holdings and the humiliation and poverty that would inevitably follow.

This thought process proceeded without the slightest twinge of conscience. Her ego, like those of her peers, refused to accept her predatory nature, telling her instead that she was self made, cut out of cloth of a superior quality representing the cream of humanity.

As the world's elite, other people of like minds came together frequently to reinforce their belief that the state of affairs which they so thoroughly enjoyed should remain inviolable, guaranteeing the comfort they possessed to the generations of their offspring who would follow them. Or, failing to possess such a high-minded objective, gratifying their lust for ever more comfort and control.

And who could blame these would-be masters of humanity? God didn't exist to them, a situation that they liked just fine. They didn't need an external influence to curb their enjoyment of the pleasures their wealth afforded them.

"What's that, Ronny?" asked Franklin Langerholt. "Doesn't sound good, whatever it is. You need another drink, and let's forget what you thought you wanted to say." Franklin placed his cigar in an ashtray and grabbed Ronford's empty glass. He poured four fingers of a priceless single malt whisky into the glass and handed it back to him. That task completed, he picked up a little silver bell and shook. As it tinkled, a door opened and his houseman Malcomb rushed in. "The fire needs tending, Malcomb," he said petulantly. "As a matter of fact, it's almost out. See to it. Build it back up until we have a little warmth in here." Malcomb responded immediately, striding to the huge fireplace enclosed by massive river rocks. He pulled out a log from the stack on the left side and thrust it into the gaping hole. He repeated the process until the flames emanating from the fireplace rivaled the firebox of a steam locomotive, the warm light filling the room and enriching the color of the dark mahogany walls.

The others looked on passively as Malcomb finished and left the room to obey Franklin's command to fetch more wood. When he had disappeared, the conversation resumed as if there had been no interruption.

"I really can't let it go," Ronford replied. "We know that God doesn't exist. It was simply a panacea to comfort a primitive, underdeveloped people stuck way back in the evolutionary struggle."

"Of course," said Randolph Eagleton, who had been sitting back comfortably in his overstuffed chair. "So what's your point?"

"The point is, gentlemen, that given God's nonexistence, this mythical creature can't solve any truly large problem that might threaten our world. It would all be on our own shoulders to take care of."

The others looked at each other blankly, puffing on their cigars. Franklin took a sip of his drink and sat back. "That's somewhat of a Pandora's Box, Ronny. Let's not go there, especially as our good old world has already survived billion of years without coming to an end. Try to be a bit more optimistic, won't you?"

"But come to think of it, he does present an idea that we may be able to exploit," Randy offered.

"What would that be, Randy?"

"Have you heard about this new theory of Charles Darwin's? It has received much favorable commentary within the scientific community. If we could continue from there to indoctrinate the masses with this information, a general decline in religiosity would quite probably follow."

"So?" asked Franklin.

"Don't you see?" Randy remarked rather sharply, offended by his lack of comprehension. "If the masses stop believing in God, they'll start feeling responsible for the future. We can feed off that fear, use it to increase our control."

With that statement the concept of a global community began to form and harden among the elite.

The recent publication of Darwin's Theory of Evolution had been enthusiastically received by those who spoke the most eloquently in behalf of science. Well this tome should have enjoyed such favorable opinion among those who mattered, as it drove a stake, perhaps the final one, into the persistent myth among the rabble that a God truly existed. It didn't take long for the elite to perceive that the time was ripe for that myth to be shattered completely, and to their collective advantage in furthering the fruition of their desired objective of obtaining a government capable of controlling the entire planet. They knew, however, that such a profound change in the organization of society from its current nationalism would involve events of earthshaking magnitude. That prospect caused the discomfort of many, who preferred to leave the problems of the future to the next generation and beyond. Others, however, saw the prospect in a more encouraging light.

"Why, yes, Randy," Franklin added with growing enthusiasm. "Even if no such actual situation should come to pass, we may be able to create on our own the prospect of doom of one sort or another. It could generate enough fear on the part of the masses to give us absolute control over them."

Randy stroked the end of his moustache in pleasant approbation of Franklin's approval. "Now that's something quite soothing to the ear," he said with a complacent smile. "I do like the sound of that."

"But there's a problem with that," Ronnie replied. "America."

"Yes, America," Randy assented, taking a deep drag on his cigar and tamping down the smoke in his airway with a large dollop of liquor that hadn't seen the light of day for centuries. "America, the epitome of nationalism. They have God, guns and grit. It won't be easy getting them to acquiesce to socialism."

"Not all that hard," Franklin countered. "Might take a bit of time, but certainly doable."

"How?"

"Do it in steps. Universal education is already under way. Push hard for its completion by mandating laws requiring it in the name of social improvement. Once that's in place, acquire control over the curriculum, best done by forming a teacher's union headed by a representative who answers to us. I doubt if it would take much to buy the loyalty of an appropriate leader. At the same time, achieve absolute control over the teachers' colleges. Indoctrinate these future teachers with viewpoints that will wean them away from all notions of God. Darwin's evolutionary theory would be an ideal example of this – a good start. The process will have to proceed slowly and gently, like putting a frog in a pot of water and turning up the heat. By the time people catch a glimpse of the intent behind the process, it will be far too late for them to do anything about it. Turn history and civics classes into leisure time. As time goes on, introduce notions that will appeal to the hedonistic instincts of the masses, eventually making them so morally weak that even if they see the end of their unique values, they won't have the will or grit to resist."

"Not bad," Ronford said, scratching his chin in a gesture of delighted approval. "Not bad at all. I think, among us gentlemen, we can proceed with a detailed plan to implement these thoughts."

Except for their plans for mass public indoctrination toward a unified world government, the attempts of the budding globalists to formulate future disasters didn't amount to much at the beginning of their efforts. Although some did address the potential of large-scale warfare as a means of furthering their new objective, most were simply too busy enjoying themselves to delve into future situations, helpful as they may have been, that would in all probability never occur. But their focus on the rearrangement of government was more fruitful. To that end, they defined the nature of a government that would permit a small number of like-minded and supposedly conscientious individuals to have absolute control over the great unwashed masses. The government would be a centralized dictatorship, the only form that would fit in with their plans of dominating the insignificant little ants that formed the majority of the world's population. Bending them to their will would not only be necessary for the continuation of their civilization. It could actually be enjoyable if done in the right way.

Charlotte periodically redirected her lust away from her preferred mode of gratification sufficiently often to conceive and bear a child, a daughter whom she promptly named Charlotte in a tasteless display of vanity. Most of those who came in contact with her called her Junior, a label that she accepted with grace. Unlike her mother, this Charlotte was sweet and kind, even bearing her mother's venom with resignation, including the time that her mother threw her beloved kitten out the third-story window in a fit of rage.

For the most part, unlike Junior, those of the ruling class followed in the path taken by their forebears, preferring to embrace acquisition and power over the more honorable qualities that one might hope for in one's leaders.

"Even if we foresee nothing on the horizon in the nature of a threat to the world," Charles intoned, "perhaps the introduction of diesel locomotion, along with this new automobile, and now the aeroplane, may just create some situations nobody has considered. We must be quick to exploit whatever comes our way, as I'm certain that something will."

"The situation in Europe may give us that opportunity," Warren offered. "It looks like war clouds are peeking above the horizon."

"Splendid!" Grant said with enthusiasm, rubbing his hands in glee. "Perhaps we can speed things along in that area."

"Don't get too hasty about it," Charles countered. "It hasn't been half a century since the Civil War. That was a slaughter. If something like that actually ignites, the entire world might get involved. A lot of lives will be lost."

Warren and Grant looked at Charles in astonishment and then at each other, shaking their heads. "Let me explain something to you," Grant said, frowning at Charles' inappropriate outburst. "Or ask you a question. How many people do you think live on this planet?

And how many people will live if a war doesn't happen sooner or later? Would you like to live on an overcrowded planet?"

"Yeah," Warren spoke up. "Do you think you'll have anybody you know on the front lines? On the other hand, what do you think will become of your manufacturing plant with massive infusions of government money to support the war effort? Are you going to complain about that?"

The next generation of elites took up the baton of control over the world with ever more energy, pushing forward as if the outcome could be seen with sufficient clarity as to involve them personally in its warm embrace.

In line with this new vigor, it was proposed to pursue an alteration of the system of education to the elites' advantage. Its corruption leading to a general moral decline would be a necessary feature, as only by that means would the people be made to be compliant. Their main targets were the teachers' colleges and the Christian seminaries, both of which had already been infected with secular myths, the most prominent of which promised to be Darwin's new evolutionary theory. This useless and rather scatterbrained concept had already begun to undermine the prevailing faith in the accuracy of the Judeo-Christian Bible. Other falsehoods were added that supported the notion that the God of the Bible was a creation of man rather than the other way around. These first institutions had already produced teachers and pastors of progressively lesser faith and wisdom to create widespread influence on the understanding and moral character of the population in general.

As time went on, the impact of world wars, social upheavals, atom bombs, nuclear meltdowns, economic reversals, weather changes and earthquakes had a profound impact on the complacent attitudes of the later generations of elites. Planetary destruction was a very real possibility. As God continued in His nonexistence to these people at the top of the food chain, their responsibility to maintain the existence of the planet was now very real and foreboding.

The creation and use of armies of goons out of the dregs of society caused chaos and destruction within those nations that needed to be pruned back into compliance with the wishes of the elites. The people of those targeted countries actually begged for the imposition of harsh measures to gain back law and order. The formation of the actual one-world government was easily accomplished after that softening-up process.

The actual government, of course, had been anticipated over a millennium before the elites were even born. The prophet Daniel had much to say about it, as did Jesus a half millennium later, first to His disciples, and then in greater detail to John, who had been incarcerated for a time on the island of Patmos.

There were some Christians, not a great many but an ever-growing number, who perceived the budding trend toward godlessness. The Book of Revelation began to be examined more closely than ever before. Prophecies began to rise in number and specificity as strong Christians saw glimpses of the fulfillment of Scripture. The world now enjoyed, for the first time in human history, mechanized transportation and other clever inventions, and recognized those innovations as signs of the approach of the end of the age.

Charlotte Junior eventually married and gave birth to a daughter of her own. Despite her weak protests, the child was given the name of Charlotte as a result of her mother's sometimes violent insistence. Her husband, having impregnated her and then left for greener pastures with the announcement that she was with child, was not available for support, so she had no choice but to acquiesce. The daughter was called Three to her face but those who knew her gave her darker names behind her back. These epithets were well-deserved, as she rejected her mother's personality in favor of her grandmother's, but with additional traits that placed her firmly in the category of sociopath. As she grew into adulthood, her craving for wealth and domination drove her to claw her way into the world of masculine control.

CHAPTER TWO

Within God's spiritual domain was the ability to access the interplay of characters of interest who influenced future issues. The corresponding events ranged from trivial to momentous during times extending from the distant past into the distant future. A conversation among the very top elites as the world passed beyond the twenty-first century was recognized as uncommonly important. Their dialogue advanced their project of forming a universal government at an accelerated rate. That event itself caught the attention of numerous watchers in the angelic community, the term "watcher" referring to an angelic observer and communicator as mentioned very briefly and enigmatically in Daniel Chapter 4.

Watchers observed with interest a new generation who inhabited the elegant mahogany-paneled room with the enormous, rock-faced fireplace. Wood continued to burn fiercely within its gaping maw, casting a warm glow onto the walls and the intricately carved molding that bordered them. The priceless oriental carpet and the elegant furniture responded in kind to its cheerful light. The house had been upgraded with a central furnace, but its new master Dwight preferred the comfort of visible flames. So did his several guests, who continued to enjoy their precursors' generous stocks of rare wines and spirits.

Vance poured a generous portion of his late father's priceless whisky from a cut-glass decanter into his exquisite crystal tumbler, and from there to his expectant lips. "You know, friends, I have one-upped my father at last. To him this whisky was ancient. For me, it's older yet." He grinned smugly and took another sip, leaning back in his father Ronford's overstuffed chair, allowing the liquid to drool down his throat.

"It gets even better," Franklin's son Dwight said. "We're going to outdo them all. They dreamed up a world more to their liking, but they never had a chance to see it actually come to pass. Despite their frantic attempts to extend their longevity, they all died. Now it's our generation that'll see the whole thing come together as they'd planned."

"I'll drink to shat," slurred Randolf Junior, the son of the late Randolph Eagleton. Randolph had been drinking to that for over an hour now, and was well on his way to incoherence. His demeanor irritated the others. "Careful, Randy," Franklin cautioned. "I think you've had quite enough."

"It's Randolph to you," Randolph shot back. "How many times do I have to tell you?"

"As if it matters," Dwight said. "You are what you are, and to me you're Randy."

Randolph's reply was cut short by his sudden descent into slumber. He snored loudly, infuriating Dwight. Dwight let it go, returning to more important matters. "We need a different kind of president. One who's pliant enough that he'll do our bidding."

"I know the perfect man," Vance said. "He has no credentials to speak of, but an ego so huge that he thinks he has the ability to control the world. He's presidential in the sense of his looks, and his race automatically puts him at the top of the heap. If he got the office, we could manipulate his ego to put forward our agenda of socializing America."

Dwight spoke up. "Don't forget congress. It's there for a reason, that being a check on the executive branch."

"Yes, but we'll be working on them, too. And besides, the president can get a lot of things done through executive orders. What I'd like to see the chief executive do for starters is divide up the country, create sides, polarize people to hate the other side. We'd get a lot of mileage out of that if race was involved. And then get the masses used to handouts, like universal health care. Nip their high-sounding moralism in the bud, downgrade religion, overload them with drugs, get them hooked on porn."

"Yes, well, Dwight, aren't you kind of hooked on porn yourself?"

"We're not talking about me. We're talking about the masses, so shut your face. What about you and coke, if you want to go down that alley?"

"Okay, okay. What about congress, then?"

"We have plenty of money to throw around to buy elections for anybody we want in. I have my eye on a particular woman in California who's so hungry for wealth and power that she'd do anything we told her to do."

"Anything?" asked Randolph, who'd awakened at the hint of porn. The question caused an uproar of laughter.

"Careful," Charlotte said, giving Randolph the stink eye. Charlotte was the viper in the room, not being the daughter, spouse or relative of anyone in that inbred financial circle, and not particularly welcome. A CEO of a highly-successful corporation, she'd clawed her way into the group through her intelligence and predatory behavior. Her ruthlessness was legendary, as the rest of those in the room knew from experience. To the man, they'd been on the receiving end of her blackmail. Each of them had something in their pasts that they would prefer to keep under wraps, but the information fortresses they'd erected for that purpose were no match for her cunning ability to ferret out the disgusting things in other peoples' lives. Her own past wasn't any cleaner. It was known among the men in the room that she was a sexual predator. She knew they all knew, but she also knew that nobody there had the guts to call her out on it.

"You can have that piece of cow flop if you want, Charlotte Three," Dwight sneered in an uncharacteristic display of hubris, emphasizing his opinion of the singularly ego-driven use of the same name over three generations.

Charlotte turned to Dwight and narrowed her eyes into a vicious glare. "Not that you could have her anyway, you pathetic little pussy. You wouldn't even know what to do with her."

"In California, people like her are low-hanging fruit," Randolph said, pretending that the exchange hadn't happened. "Same with New York. We've got that in the bag."

"What about the judicial?" Vance asked, eager to redirect the conversation.

"No problem there," Dwight replied. "We have some excellent goons on the payroll. A few threats here and there, and those softies on the bench will cave in no time flat."

"That's how they reached the Chief Justice," a watcher said.to his companion, commenting on the gist of Dwight's implication in this turn in the conversation. "Abducted his beautiful trophy wife and threatened to use her in unspeakable ways if he didn't acquiesce to their judicial agenda. Those who thought they'd installed a conservative on the bench were surprised and very disappointed in the negative influence he had on the court. They got to the congress too, getting quite a few very unqualified people elected. The moral depravity and just plain idiocy that came out of those hallowed halls is beyond belief."

The result of all that was the headlong plunge of the country into factional hatred, corruption of every sort, and debauchery so extreme that the ancient Sodomites would have been embarrassed. By that time, the younger generation had been brainwashed to such an extent by a corrupted educational system that they neither knew of the more noble generations that preceded theirs, nor cared about what they were missing.

"Time to get aboard for the end game," Charlotte spoke up as the watchers in the spiritual domain continued to witness the conversation. "They're ripe for the picking, so let's pluck."

The watcher shook his head in disgust.

"What do you have in mind?" Vance questioned.

"Disease. Put fear into their minds with an epic pandemic, something deadly like the plague. If it's done right, they'll be afraid to go outside their homes. Their economies will collapse into stinking piles of garbage. They'll beg for some relief and give up anything they called unique to get on the bandwagon if it will help them to survive. Our dream, a universal government under our direct control."

"But where will the disease come from?"

"Seriously? You can't be asking that. Every major government in the world is playing with deadly bugs. Some of them have been at it so long that they've slacked off on their security. Others are so greedy they'll give up the bugs at the drop of a coin. Still others can be shown how good it will be for them if the rest of the world suffers. It's like kids with their first chemistry sets, doing everything they can to blow up the basement. So choose your poison. It's not like our governments are burdened with nobility."

Charlotte continued to think over the implications of such enormous power, and of what she could do with it. She had to force herself to prune back an incipient orgasm. "I want a piece of this," she told the others, daring them to challenge her. "A big piece. A very big piece." Not particularly fond of alcohol, Charlotte reached in her jacket and extracted a plastic bag. Shaking white powder onto the table in front of her, she arranged it into a line and, with a straw, inhaled it into her nose. The others looked on passively, avoiding her defiant eyes and wondering whether to follow her lead.

The watchers gasped in surprise. "A female antichrist?" one asked.

"Why not?" answered another. "Their gender may influence the character of women against wholesale savagery, but, as we've seen more than once, the very worst of them are right up there with the menfolk. Even beyond. This poor excuse for a lady would make an excellent candidate for unrestrained evil."

"But what about our Holy Spirit? A female antichrist would confuse those on Earth, many of whom are just beginning to understand Her as feminine. Wouldn't they pull their heads back into their shells and insist on a Holy Spirit who had nothing to do with femininity?"

"Possibly. But that's exactly what our nemesis satan is hoping for, and that's precisely why most humans will have to wait until they reach heaven to get a true understanding of the Godhead."

"I don't know. I still think a female in the antichrist role is too dangerous to the welfare of many Christians. It might be too easy for them to get suckered in."

"Perhaps. We'll just have wait ourselves and see what God will do about it. But make no mistake – Charlotte is every bit as evil as any man could be."

The passage of time transformed technology far beyond what had existed a mere century previous. A host of mechanical labor-saving devices came onto the market to make life less physically strenuous. Electricity came into homes. Vacuum cleaners, refrigerators, washers, dryers, hair dryers and a huge variety of appliances were made available to the consumer. It took some time, but diesel engines replaced all but a very few of their steam predecessors. New forms of transportation eclipsed the old, revolutionizing travel by automobiles, fast ships, and airplanes. Communications were enhanced first by telephones and radios, followed by satellites placed in space through rocket technology. Next, television, computers, and especially cell phones came to the general public.

All this astonishingly rapid development of technology brought the prophetic elements of Scripture into much sharper focus. The baffling verse 4 of Daniel Chapter 12 was now exposed and plain as day.

> *But thou, O Daniel, shut up the words, and seal the book, even to the time of the end; many shall run to and fro, and knowledge shall be increased.*

What earlier Church greats like Augustine couldn't possibly understand of the trappings of end-time society, despite their arrogant insistence that they could, the man on the street now saw as commonplace. Those who knew their Scripture knew exactly what John was talking about in Revelation 13 when he described the mark of the beast. John was obviously giving details of the end-time economic system that employed digital cash. The user of that system would have some kind of identification, a mark, that could be picked up electronically to carry out a financial transaction. Embedded credit could be added or deleted at will by the system controller. This meant, of course, that whoever controlled the economic system could add or subtract credit at will to the individual consumer at any point-of-sale terminal. The very life or death of the person on the street was in the hands of those in charge. The political implications were staggering.

The denial of truth, unfortunately, proceeded in lockstep with amazing technological developments. Paul said it well in Second Timothy 3:7, when he spoke of modern man as *"Ever learning, and never able to come to the knowledge of the truth."*

The technological innovations didn't apply just to the benefit of society. In other areas, advances in the capability of electromechanical devices transformed the nature of warfare. Ever more monstrous engines of destruction proliferated. A vast assortment of such devices, including submarines, battleships, tanks, helicopters, fighter and bomber aircraft arrived on the scenes of conflict. These were topped off by nuclear weapons in such numbers that there was now a threat that they could erase all life on Earth. The destructive capability became ever more deadly. Another neglected prophecy came to light: Second Peter 3:10. Skeptics of the Bible used to scoff at the phrase *"and the elements shall melt with fervent heat,"* claiming that it was impossible to melt atoms and molecules. But they were terribly wrong, as nuclear explosions vividly demonstrated.

CHAPTER THREE

"**D**on't you understand?" Pastor George yelled at his congregation. "Are your hearts so hard that your eyes are unable to see and your ears are dull of hearing?" He held his Bible high over his podium. "Can't you read? We have a problem in this country just like the Bible said would happen, and it's so serious it will affect us all."

By the time that George Connelly had graduated from a Christian seminary and was looking for a Church in which to preach, the escalating deterioration of world society had become so extensive as to constitute an irreversible condition. Disease threatened to run out of control in America, on the verge of overwhelming the health care system and causing a severe downturn in the economy. On top of that, civility suffered. Tempers flared, bursting out in uncontrolled riots and unthinkable damage to towns and cities, causing such chaos that the public gave less attention to the sharp uptick in natural disasters and other depressing problems, the mass focus turning inward toward the immediate fulfillment of their baser desires.

Worse yet, the change wasn't accidental, as George well knew. Much of the impetus for this enormous and rapid movement toward depravity was intentional, its source the desire on the part of a few extremely wealthy self-styled elites to form a single government that would embrace and rigidly control the majority of the world's populations. George recognized the darkening situation as fitting in quite thoroughly with John's narrative in the Book of Revelation: America and the world at large had been spiritually and morally weakened, and technological developments made the time ripe for the elite to make a final push toward the formation of a global world order.

George decided to preside over a highly conservative Church in Kansas that was in need of a like-minded pastor. It was well-attended, his rural constituents being in the midst of flyover country with a well-deserved skepticism toward a technology-rich but wisdom-poor media that daily spewed out falsehoods, trash and depravity.

Having had their brains toyed with to a lesser extent than their fellow citizens closer to the coastal areas, they were both more noble and wiser than them. Unfortunately, they weren't as noble and wise as they needed to be. There was a certain torpor that prevailed over attitudes, and the pastor desperately feared that it would worsen. George leaned toward the reactionary, being somewhat more extreme than was appropriate even for the conditions the country was descending toward. His services were much closer to the theology of Martin Luther and his Reformation than those of the more contemporary Churches, even in his area of the country. There is much to say about Luther's courage and what he had accomplished through it. In his day, the Church was truly corrupt, and needed to be pruned back to a better and, particularly, a more noble understanding of God. Luther was the man of the hour in that matter. But, like everyone else, he had his faults as well, among them being his temper and rigidity with respect to certain misunderstandings of God that remained uncorrected in the commotion that he left in his wake.

Despite George's tendency toward overkill, he might have taken a path toward a reasonable form of worship had the world about him remained as it was. But he lived in a world that had been undergoing such a profound change in societal conventions that its effect had crowded them into his mind, creating their own sharply-defined space therein.

While the secular world was planning in lockstep with the elite to exploit Darwin's theory toward the discrediting of the Bible to American schoolchildren as a major component of their general dumbing-down, George, to his credit, attempted to explain to his congregation the flaws of the evolutionary notion.

"Wake up, people!" he shouted. "You're being lied to!" Noticing a tendency toward disfavor on the part of his audience, he attempted to tone things down.

"We find ourselves in the middle of spiritual warfare," George told his congregants quite sternly but in a more reasonable tone of voice. "We're fighting the secularists, who insist on forcing on our children in their schools and just about everywhere else the false claim of science that the theory of evolution is not only a truth, but is the only notion of our origins that is worth embracing. Do you know what that does to our understanding of the Creation Epic in the Book of Genesis? Permit me to tell you: it trashes it, and with it our understanding of Scripture as both inspired by the Holy Spirit and inerrant. How does it do that? It explains the existence of man as the upward development of life through the lowliest creature to the ultimate presence of man, whose brain some of us adore and worship. It takes God completely out of the picture and replaces Him with random mutations operated on by natural selection, which amounts to the ability of an improvement in function to improve the chances of reproduction. It may seem reasonable on the surface, but only to the most shallow examination. The theory had been pushed in schools for a long time, long enough for a whole host of Christians to have been raised with the false certainty of its truth. Some struggle with it and attempt to accommodate their faith to its teachings. Let me tell you now, without any hesitation," George said with an angry glare to his audience, "that any such effort is doomed to failure. Either the Christian will have to admit the wrongness of Darwin's theory, or he will be forced to forsake his Christianity. It may happen slowly, first with his admission that the Bible is not really inerrant, but it will always proceed to one of those ends unless the individual is so shallow that he will refuse to think about the inherent contradictions. But if he does that, he's not an actual Christian to begin with."

Despite the harshness of George's presentation, his message was correct. The secular community was winning this battle. Churches were devolving into apathy and self-interest. With the change in the communities' general awareness and beliefs, people were leaving the Churches in droves. In one sense, the public forsaking of

Christianity was a positive event, as those who remained were actual Christians and stronger in their faith. In spite of this, the general abandonment of Christianity opened the door for Jesus to walk out of American society altogether, leaving the country to its own devices. The degeneration of secular society followed immediately thereafter, descending to the point where Paul's caution in Second Timothy Three became startlingly accurate. It bears repeating:

> *This know also, that in the last days perilous times shall come. For men shall be lovers of their own selves, covetous, boasters, proud, blasphemers, disobedient to parents, unthankful, unholy, without natural affection, trucebreakers, false accusers, incontinent, fierce, despisers of those that are good, traitors, heady, high-minded, lovers of pleasures more than lovers of God, having a form of godliness, but denying the power of it; from such turn away. For of this sort are they who creep into houses, and lead captive silly women laden with sins, led away with various lusts, ever learning, and never able to come to the knowledge of the truth. Now as Jannes and Jambres withstood Moses, so do these also resist the truth, men of corrupt minds, reprobate concerning the faith.*

The entire world became a third-grade playground, complete with the ubiquitous bully.

CHAPTER FOUR

Jacob Perlman lifted his bicycle up the steps onto the white plank porch and chained it to a rail. He opened the front door and stepped inside. "Hi, honey," he called to his wife. "I'm home." Receiving no answer, he called out again, louder this time.

"Out in back," Penny replied. "I'm in the yard getting some sun." Jacob gave her a kiss, patted her bulging tummy and pulled up a chaise lounge next to hers. "I'll be back in a second. I'm going to get out of these clothes and put on some shorts. Want anything?"

"You can get us some more iced tea," she said, handing him the pitcher. When he returned, he kissed his wife and filled her glass from the pitcher in his hand. He filled his own glass and sat down. He sipped the tea and looked with contentment over the neat little yard with its patch of grass and the flower-lined privacy fence.

Long before the Earthchange, and even before the United States had been integrated into the ten-region world government; yet even before the U.S. had been fundamentally transformed into a socialist state preliminary to the formation of the three-nation North American Region, back when this vast change in society had been kicked into gear by the rejection of their Judeo-Christian God, Jacob was a happy, productive and proud citizen of the United States. He had a lovely wife who was expecting. They both were excited over the prospect of the new addition to their family, particularly since they were able to afford a child. They lived in a two-bedroom house on a quiet, tree-lined street in a suburb of Sacramento, California. He mowed the front lawn on Saturdays while his wife Penny tended the flowers that bordered the house. When they'd finished their chores before the heat of the day, they'd sit on the swing on their front porch sipping iced tea and chatting. They were the best of friends. In fact, their cheerful, outgoing personalities attracted many friends, some of whom they would invite over on Sunday evening for entertainment. Their favorite game was Mexican Canasta.

They had no issues with their mortgage, and often indulged in expensive restaurants, because they could afford these amenities as well. Jacob had a decent, well-paying job as an aerospace engineer with a large company not far from their home, close enough, in fact, that he often rode his bicycle to work. The fact that he was Jewish was not an issue at all, not then. He was comfortable with his religion, and they attended their local synagogue frequently. He was proud of his knowledge of both his Jewish God and cutting-edge aerospace technology.

He had a friend at work, Sidney Cohen. Sid was a technician and they often worked together when lab work was called for. The lab itself was as clean as a hospital operating room. In fact, it somewhat looked like one, with a long sterile bench filled with electronic equipment and bright overhead lights. Outside the lab were desks occupied with other workers in a rather crowded common room.

Sid was Jewish as well, which tightened their bond. They went to the same synagogue, and often conversed with each other about the nature of God. Sid was a bit less polished than Jacob, and sharper of personality. He looked down on the other workers in the crowded common room, considering them to be mindless robots, shallow serfs who were interested only in the next hamburger and the next sexual experience, perfectly suited to the fast-food outlets that they favored. The conversations he often overheard gave him ample reason to view them with such disdain. "If we ever were so unfortunate as to be threatened to be taken over by a dictator," he told Jacob one day, "they'd fall over themselves to get in line."

"Why'd you say that?" Jacob replied. "We're in America, Sid. That'll never happen."

"Look around you. Don't you see the corruption that's beginning to infect our Congressional leaders? Sometimes they behave as if they were in a third-grade playground."

Sid increasingly fretted over what he thought to be a decline in the collective character and morals. "Some day we won't be adult enough for the privilege of possessing guns. Then they'll take them away from us."

"You're starting to sound paranoid," Jacob responded.

"Sure. Just because I'm paranoid doesn't mean they're not out to get me."

Jacob laughed at that, taking Sid's cautions as over-the-top expressions of his combative nature. Sid was Sid.

One day Sid came into the lab and sat down next to Jacob like he usually did. The lab was almost full of others who were occupied with their own projects. Sid glared at them. "Looks like fun," he said to a worker next to him. "But what did you do with the play-dough?" he needled.

Jacob, who was examining a circuit board of his design that had just been fabricated, thought that Sid's dig was a bit harsh, although he had to admit that the other workers were acting like kindergarten kids in play session. He expected to hand his board over to Sid for a look-see. Sid ignored the board, to Jacob's surprise. Instead, he reached into his jacket and extracted a military model 1911 .45 caliber pistol, which he proceeded to brandish around the lab, accompanied by a dramatic glare of feigned outrage, as if to dare anyone to challenge him. He placed the weapon on the table and proceeded to disassemble and clean it. As he worked on the gun, he glared meanly at his companion workers, openly defying them to speak out. They were too horrified to do anything but lower their heads like alarmed turtles and focus on their projects. When he finished his own task, Sid pulled out a magazine and a bag of rounds, which he thumbed into the device one by one, continuing to sweep the room with angry eyes. Finished, he slammed the magazine into the gun and cocked it. After a significant pause, he stashed the gun back into his jacket and left the lab.

Jacob stared after him, laughing at the outrage to convention. He told Penny about the event that evening, laughing again. Penny refused to join in the mirth. She considered Sid to be a loose cannon.

He mentioned to Sid once that perhaps he should tone down his comments, at least when he was around Penny. "Just wait and see," Sid had said to that.

Life back then for Jacob and Penny was like a wonderful dream. Back then.

Pastor George had begun his next sermon to his Kansas audience with an angry shout, failing to notice that attendance had dwindled somewhat since the previous Sunday. "Appeasement never works!" he told those who remained. "And evolution isn't even good science! Have you heard of Professor Michael Behe?" Seeing no response, George continued. "He's a biologist committed to the proper application of scientific principles. He conducted a study of the interaction of humans with malaria-bearing mosquitos, finding that the human body responded to that threat in Africa where it was most prevalent by altering the nature of blood cells. The result was the sickle cell, known for its debilitating effect on a large African population. Under certain conditions sickle-cell anemia, as it's called, can be dangerous, even deadly."

"He's right, you know," one man whispered to his wife. "I've read some of Behe's works, and they make sense – a lot more than what the evolutionists have to say." His wife patted an arm and squeezed it, signaling him to listen to the pastor.

"How did the sickle cell come into being?" George asked and continued without pausing after his purely rhetorical question. "Through possibly one, or at most, two mutations in the body's DNA, a tiny, almost insignificant change that took place over hundreds of generations. Yes, it did succeed in lessoning the effect of malaria, but at the expense of a net loss of information and damage to the body as a whole. Even though it did succeed with regard to malaria, it was an incredibly weak response, certainly not capable of creating a new species, even over the span of billions of years. Its overall effect was negative, not positive as the materialists would claim. In addition, it supported the Second Law of Thermodynamics, which without exception, including the red-herring 'open system' attempt at rebuttal, claims that all processes tend to disorder. The bottom line, people, is that a perpetual motion machine is nothing but a myth. So is evolution, for anything but miniscule changes."

While he was completely accurate in what he was saying, George had not correctly read his congregants. Some actually listened, accepting the information he was giving. Most, however, had no idea of the violence that was soon to visit them. To them, their attendance at Church was intended to produce comfort, not a university-level lecture. The apathy of those so-called Christians was palpable, with some squinting in an attempt to keep their eyes open and others, having given up on that struggle, faced downward with chins resting on their chests.

Ignoring the general malaise, George proceeded on. "Dr. Behe," he shouted, startling one member of his audience awake, "also established a very important and general concept, which he called 'irreducible complexity'. Darwin, he noted, claimed that unless it could be demonstrated that the pattern of evolution is a long sequence of very minor changes, it was a false concept. In essence, he claimed, evolution did not take place in large leaps, with many beneficial changes happening at once. In reality, Dr. Behe noted, and in contradiction to this restraint, many living systems show clear evidence of multiple elements coming together simultaneously to create a well-defined function. That could happen only under the direction of a Designer who had a specific goal in mind. Evolution, being by definition a mindless and therefore a blind process, is utterly incapable of looking ahead. Evolution does not, and cannot, anticipate."

A loud snore startled George, who looked around at the congregants, realizing for the first time with a shock that the assembly wasn't hanging on to his every word. He bravely began to wind up his sermon with an example, hoping that its graphic nature would perk them up.

"Imagine this," he said. "A land animal that walks on legs and which is eventually going to achieve the ability to fly as a bird. Evolution says that's what actually happened. But to bring that goal to reality, the animal's bones need to become hollow to save weight.

It also has to develop the unique eyesight of a bird, which is so necessary to its method of hunting from the air at great distances from its prey. The bone structure of its chest and elsewhere needs to be rearranged as a proper scaffold for its flight-specific ligaments and muscles. Its arms need to change into airfoils, keeping in mind that the evolutionary process has no clue as to why that is necessary. The same goes for its feathers, with their intricate ability to form shapes that support different modes of flight. Its respiratory system needs a complete makeover, as does its entire nervous system, including the numerous reflective responses that must be performed too quickly for cognition.

"We know that, despite Dr. Stephen Gould's false notions of 'punctuated evolution', evolution requires large amounts of time, even under the equally false assumption that such species changes are possible. Keeping this in mind, picture such a creature midway through the process of changing from a four-legged land creature into a bird, perhaps able to flap its developing wings but not achieving flight, being pursued by a hungry bird or an equally hungry land animal. How long do you think such a creature would survive? I rest my case for now."

A man toward the end of the room suddenly learned forward, his projectile vomit spraying on the pew in front. Gasping in horror, those nearest him jumped up and fled the Church. The woman in front of him, the man's breakfast clinging to her hair, stood up, touched her polluted head, and fainted from fright and disgust. Most of the others in the congregation rushed to follow the others, causing the aisles to be blocked. Others, more noble than those who were attempting to flee, stayed behind to comfort the sick man and the terrified woman, and to clean up the mess.

George looked on, proud of those who remained but saddened by the panic that held most of the congregation in its vicious grip. He realized that the world was very near the time of the end spoken of by John, and he got down on his knees to pray fervently that the Rapture might take them today. Immediately.

The world was indeed approaching the end of the age. The

pandemic and the violence that went with it had caused such economic turmoil that physical cash had been replaced by digital currency as the only solution to maintaining financial order. Every person had been required to accept the insertion of an electronic chip with which he could buy and sell. Universal health care had been adopted, which gave the chip the additional utility of maintaining the person's health history and a record of his medicines. Most of the population, including many in George's Church, accepted this chip willingly, even eagerly, counting on the government bonus of an initial deposit to help them out. But others who were committed to following Jesus Christ as their Lord, recognized its danger. It was too close to being the mark of the beast, described in Revelation 13, whose consequences were deadly, as warned about in Revelation 14. Perhaps it even was the mark of the beast.

CHAPTER FIVE

The turmoil last Sunday in Church caused many of George's congregants to re-examine their commitment to him. They already thought of him as a reactionary. In fact, he was too over-the-top reactionary for their liking. Why was it necessary for George to blast Darwinian Evolution the way he did, which made him completely out of step with pretty much the rest of society? Everybody knew that evolution worked. It had to, or else why would the scientists be so adamant about it working? They had to know a lot more than the rest of us. Or George. Particularly George.

If pressed to answer, most would admit that George knew his Bible, and he knew how to preach. Because of his other qualities, his congregation put up with his reactionary excesses for quite a long time. But that ended when he started trashing Darwin. Several people left after his first rant about it. The number increased after his second sermon on the topic. Not long after that, George was forced to face the fact that most of his audience had left. But he failed to admit to himself that he actually was reactionary. In fact, having convinced himself that those who had left had been influenced so greatly by the secular society that they had abandoned their faith, George grew even more intransigent.

Actually, George was correct in his negative assessment of all the evolutionary theories, from the Greeks through Darwin and those who followed in their neo-Darwinian revisions. They all were bogus, as ascertained by the few biologists who had actually applied scientific principals correctly in their attempts to understand the true limits to evolutionary progress. What they found was a mechanism so restrictive that it led to the term *microevolution* to express the miniscule ability of the theory to accomplish change. Even then, the changes were found to always result in the loss of information, forcing evolutionary change to work regressively rather than progressively. The evolutionists should have expected that, claiming themselves to be scientists, as one of the most fundamental principles of science is the Second Law of Thermodynamics, which essentially asserts that all natural processes tend not to greater order, but to the opposite.

Right or wrong, George was left in an unpleasant situation, the loss of much of his congregation. If he'd looked around at what was happening in other Churches, he might have known that he had lots of company: other Churches were experiencing the same difficulty, but for a variety of specific reasons, most of which had little to do with reactionary attitudes. They had in common one fact: secular society had claimed the hearts of most of the population. In its unjustified complacency, the Christian leadership had failed to notice the godless direction that the scholastic community had taken. Even some highly-respected Christian seminaries, having been infiltrated by secularists posing as Christians, had blatantly compromised the Word of God in Scripture. Pastors who graduated from such schools went out in the community, further secularizing a host of Churches.

Those who remained in George's Church were more noble than those who left, but they were almost as reactionary as he was. They remained with him while the country turned ever leftward, repudiating every principle upon which the nation was founded. On the edge of becoming a cult, the Church was primed to adopt a fortress mentality when George brought up another subject, the rampant sexual chaos that had descended on the country. Virtually every possible permutation of sexual expression was not only condoned, but thrust upon the public at large as proper. Any reaction against the attempt of women to become men, and of men to change into women, or of men to love men and women to become romantically involved with other women was met with angry accusations of bigotry. While evil was now claimed to be good, good became evil. The Christian Church bore the brunt of this upside-down philosophy, the persecution against it turning ever more overt and violent.

George responded by focusing his sermons more toward sexual

purity, claiming that an attitude of sexual discipline set the Church apart from the depravity of society and was blessed in the sight of God. While refraining from the time being of suggesting anything drastic like abstinence, he kept equating purity with chastity, as if the two very different concepts were equivalent in God's mind.

He lost several more congregants with his intransigent attitude toward the evils of sex. Finally coming to the conclusion that perhaps he should back off a little on that, he returned to his old standby topic of evolution. He had been reading up on the latest issues regarding the subject of evolution's intellectual bankruptcy, and his sermons reflected his increasing understanding of it.

"You probably don't realize it," he began one Sunday morning, "but the basis of all life is found in software. Did you hear me? Our physical being is defined not by molecular machinery, but by code. It's the same with every animal on the planet, and every plant besides. Even algae and bacteria are built and operate according to that code. It's called DNA, deoxyribonucleic acid. Every one of the trillions of cells in our bodies encapsulates this personally unique code and uses it to construct, operate and repair the intricate machinery of our bodies. Again, every one of the trillions of cells in our bodies contains in the DNA a string of data amounting to several billion bits of information. And that's what it is – pure information. Some people think that science has discovered all there is to know about DNA. They're very wrong. In decoding the genome, they've uncovered the means by which proteins are made out of amino acids. It's a very complex process, but it's only one small part of the entire workings of the molecule we call DNA. Even with what little we know yet about it, we've already come up against a serious conundrum, a chicken vs. egg issue that speaks rather loudly against the creation of life through evolution. It turns out that a special protein is required to read the subroutine that specifies how to make a protein. The bottom line is that with a protein required to interpret the protein-manufacturing code, the protein had to exist before the instruction that was required to make it. A naturalistic process like evolution is simply not up to that kind of task. In addition to that, there's a little factor called 'chirality' that flings a monkey wrench into any possibility that life could have been created by chance. It turns out that the backbone of the code, its carrier, is made up of sugar and phosphate molecules. But these molecules can be oriented in two directions, called for convenience 'left-handed' and 'right-handed'. Each of these directions is equally likely to occur in nature, like a coin that can fall on the ground in the 'heads' or 'tails' position. Now, given the multiple billions of sugar-phosphate elements in the DNA string, all living things have a single orientation, the right-handed one. Can you begin to imagine the astronomical odds against such an occurrence, even once in the history of the universe?

"And then there's even more complexity on top of DNA and the molecular machinery required to utilize the information it contains. This higher-order system, called 'epigenome' has several different features. Listen to me: how can anyone believe in evolution with such unimaginable complexity?" He left the podium in a huff.

Chapter Six

As Jacob rode his bicycle home from work, his usual route took him past the public park that he used to bring his little son to. He'd gotten good enough on the swing to ride on it without Jacob's help. They'd given up this activity when homeless people began to squat there. It wasn't the people so much as their disgusting habits. He used to feel sorry for them, and even gave them money to eat with from time to time. No more. He couldn't abide their open drug use and their general shiftlessness. When they started pooping on the grass and going around without clothes on, he stopped donating to them, considering them to be useless, mindless animals. He knew that they weren't all that way, but he couldn't tell the difference. He simply asked God for the discernment to tell the good from the bad. So far he hadn't received a response to that. Now he couldn't help but notice that the park was nearly full of tents. As he continued on, a naked man jumped into his path and grabbed a handlebar. He stared boldly into Jacob's face with bloodshot eyes. "Gimme your wallet," he said, shaking the bicycle. There was no way Jacob would do that and give the creep access to his ID and home address. Overcoming his revulsion at the prospect of touching him, Jacob jumped off the bike and delivered a roundhouse to the man, dropping him to the ground.

"Hey, man," the cretin whined. "Why'd you do that? I only wanted to eat."

"Yeah, sure," Jacob said. "Besides your stink, you reek of pot. Get out of my way." He got back on his bike and pedaled away, lamenting the loss of decency, the work ethic and respect of others that used to be common in his city.

As Jacob fretted over what had become of his city, Charlotte glared meanly at her underling. "What did you do with it?" Charlotte's

47

voice wasn't particularly angry. It was low, almost soothing, but the very lack of emotion emphasized the implacable hatred behind the words.

Kathy gulped in terror. "I've been looking for it everywhere, but I just can't seem to remember. I'm so sorry. I'll have to keep looking."

The item in contention was a paper that Charlotte wished to reference in her latest dictum. It was almost insignificant to her, but a point was a point, and it had to be made. She disregarded the offense in her excitement over the prospect of the punishment to follow. She rose from her elegantly simple glass desk and came over to Kathy, confronting her face-to-face. "And waste the time and good money I pay you? It's too late, Kathy." She pushed her secretary against a wall, grasping a nipple and crushing it in her fingers.

"Uhhh." The involuntary moan escaped Kathy's lips. This wasn't the first time she'd faced a situation like this. She knew what was coming next, and the thought of it disgusted her. But she also knew that if she failed to comply, Charlotte would get rid of her and make sure she never got another job. That she might be left homeless and starving was a very depressing possibility.

"Take off your blouse," Charlotte demanded. Kathy complied, submitting again to the utter humiliation and pain to come. *Just another rodeo,* Kathy thought to herself in an effort to prevent a total meltdown.

"I have a new edict I want to get out. Take it down," Charlotte told Kathy later, all business now as she resumed fulfilling her position as Attorney General. "This will be to the general public: Due to the worsening nature of the pandemic that has afflicted us, you will remain sequestered at home for the indefinite future. Non-compliance will be dealt with harshly. Only tasks absolutely required for the conduct of essential commerce will be exempt. A specific list of such jobs will be issued shortly.

"Next I want you to contact one of the cable news outlets," she added before Kathy could catch her breath. "The big one. And do it now. Chop Chop."

What an inhuman cretin, Kathy thought to herself as she typed the dictation and made a mental note to call Manfred. Electric shocks coursed through her body as damaged nerves complained, but she dared not show her distress. *If only God would do something about this sadistic monster. She's on her way to controlling the world. Unless God intervenes, she'll be unstoppable.*

"Patience, darling," a watcher said, but Kathy wasn't tuned in to the spiritual realm. "It will be soon now," the watcher told her companion, who nodded enthusiastically.

"Get Vance on the phone," Charlotte told Kathy after she signed her latest edict. "You should have completed the universal ID by now," she told Vance when he responded. "The cattle have to be branded before we proceed further. What's the holdup?"

"We're almost done, Charlotte," Vance replied deferentially. "There's a group of people who refuse to accept the vaccine. They insist that the inoculation includes a chip. They're Christians all, and there scattered everywhere."

I wonder who spilled the beans about the chips? Charlotte asked herself, searching her mind for possible leakers. "Arrest them all," she told Vance. "Why do I have to explain the obvious to you?"

"Then what?"

"Are you completely stupid? What do you think?"

Overhearing Charlotte's side of the conversation, Kathy shuddered in revulsion, knowing full well from her understanding of Charlotte's basic nature that the solution she had in mind would involve wholesale slaughter.

"Manfred," she said to the well-known owner of a cable news outlet when he called in response to Kathy's request. "I have an issue with you. You don't want to have that, do you?"

"No, of course not," he replied. "What's the problem?"

"You know what it is," she accused. "Your lead talking head decided to jump off the res and call an apple an apple. He told the truth about our increase in public surveillance, and stuck in some very convicting details. You know the guidelines I sent over to you. You'd better know, Manny. Truth or not, we want pure indoctrination in support or our policies. Am I going to have to remind you every day about what we want over here? Or do I have to find a better use for you, Manny? Well? Maybe something using Big Bob that I'd find entertaining?

"I'll do something immediately, Charlotte," Manfred said in a voice that quavered in fear. "Start out with a stern dressing-down."

"And finish by firing his sorry ass. Then send him over here for an exit interview with Big Bob. And remember who's giving you your real paycheck. And keeping you alive. For now."

CHAPTER SEVEN

"Get outta here, Jewboy!" The epithet shocked Jacob. *Where did that come from?* he asked himself. But he knew. The news lately had made a turn, back to the time of Hitler's Germany. It had started subtly, as such things do.

The anti-Semitism had become stronger lately, more harsh, insulting and demanding. This time around it included Christians and the elderly as well. Jacob and Penny were beset with increasing anxiety about it, their discomfort morphing into dread as they tucked their son into bed at night. It began with slightly disparaging comments on the nightly news. They brushed that off rather quickly. After all, the Jewish community had been facing slurs for most of their history. But then as the comments began to be more strident and marginalizing, they began to worry a bit more, and yet more when their neighbors began to avoid them. It seemed that they were becoming full-blown pariahs.

Jacob, Pastor George, and a host of other Christians and Jews were facing increasing discomfort as their rejection continued to expand. George wished to delve further into the issue of God and gender, but he couldn't help but see the prevailing attitude about his harangues over sex within his flock. Having once seen the movie *Mutiny on the Bounty*, he thought the wisest path forward might be to select another topic for his upcoming sermon. He fell back on his old standby.

"They're all fakes!" he screeched the next Sunday morning. "Every last one of them! Evolution claims that the fossil record will show that the tree of life has a single trunk that branches outward from there. No, it does not. Are you listening? No! The record actually shows a sudden proliferation of life from one era to the next. It's called the Cambrian Explosion, and it demonstrates the exact opposite of what the 'experts' want you to believe. It's the same story with the 'missing links' that supposedly connect the ape with us. The 'experts' failed to find any such link between Darwin's time and ours. That didn't stop them from foisting a bunch of frauds on the gullible public. Have you seen the actual skull of a 'missing link'? Of course you haven't, because there isn't one. What they did to justify their assumptions was to cherry-pick bone fragments from areas that were too large to rationally represent the same animal. Java Man was artistically assembled from a fragment of a skull cap, a fragment of a thigh bone, and three molar teeth. The skull of Piltdown Man was a composite of a fragment of a human skull and a jawbone of an orangutan. Not content to merely stretch the truth, the creators of this farce intentionally went over the edge into blatant fraud by chemically aging the result. And how about Nebraska Man? It was the product of a single tooth of an extinct pig, to which much imagination and artistic skill was applied. A single tooth was again responsible for another abject fraud, the Southwest Colorado Man. Ramapithecus was next to be discovered. Rather, some fossilized teeth of another orangutan were discovered and applied to its creation. A few bone fragments and misinterpreted data were assembled into Lucy, who was later determined to have walked on all four feet like the ape she was found to be. Peking, Neanderthal and Cro-Magnon 'links' were later admitted to be the remains of modern human beings. As for other animals who were supposed representatives of 'missing links', the archaeopteryx was just another sordid attempt at manufacturing a link out of nothing of the sort. National Geographic Magazine was caught with its pants down for its hasty and unjust depiction of a dinosaur with feathers.

"I could go on about all this false evidence of missing links. But I'll end with the famous so-called Biogenetic Law that "ontogeny recapitulates phylogeny" from another fraud, the eminent Doctor Ernst Haeckel. This phony 'law' claimed that the various stages of embryonic development (ontogeny) revisit the history of evolutionary change (phylogeny). More sophisticated research established with certainty that nothing of the sort was true. What Haeckel did was to use artistic imagination, like what was done for the bogus missing links, to cook the books on this supposed correspondence to make it appear as if his wild overreach was actually the case."

George was right about the frauds, although his speaking style could have benefited from a little more empathy with his congregation. Nevertheless, his claims were generally accepted by the congregation.

At home like most of the rest of the country, the people of George's Church tuned their TVs to what was supposed to be an important talk from their new leader.

"As your newly-positioned director," Charlotte said without preamble, "I'm forced to curtail the seditious activity that has come upon us of late. Your obedience to me and to every command I give you is both necessary and mandatory. As of now, the use of your embedded chip will be expanded to monitor your compliance with my administration. Any person who refuses to willingly and openly display this commitment to me will have his credit automatically cut back. Further disobedience will eventually result in the complete removal of credit from your embedded chip." *There it is!* Jacob thought, his adrenalin level rising. *Now it's right out in the open.* "You will be an outcast of society, no longer able to buy or sell," Charlotte continued to speak. "You will be forced into thievery, which will result in your quick incarceration and loss of life.

"Furthermore, until the virus that caused the recent pandemic is completely eradicated, and by that I mean that until there are no such bugs remaining on Earth, our population as a whole will be restricted to their homes and their places of work. If any person in a household needs to go outside these boundaries, to shop or whatever, the household will be restricted to that one person leaving. Beyond that, the person who leaves the household or place of work will be limited to a three-mile distance from his household or place of work. Again, any violation of this restriction will be met with the immediate removal of credit from his embedded chip. The amount deducted will factor in the number of previous violations the individual has committed."

This 'talk' troubled George greatly. He knew that neither he nor his Church would survive under those conditions. After much thought and input by Wisdom, he planned his next sermon. This would amount to proposing preliminary plans to emigrate to Israel. The preliminary part would occupy a very short time. They had to leave, and they had to do it fast. The first words that he said the next Sunday were "Does anyone know how to sail? What amazed Charlotte after her talk to the public was the ease with which the people on the street accepted her increasingly harsh methods of controlling them. *Are they really that stupid?* she asked herself. It wasn't the first time she'd asked that question. She knew exactly what she was doing, and knew that it was basically very wrong. *No,* she thought to herself after more reflection. *They're not idiots, at least some of them. They're just scared, little scared rabbits. Cowards. Maybe some of them are just naïve, preferring to ignore the increasing intrusion of government over their lives, looking instead for something else to distract them from thinking about their sorry state. Shallow. But still cowards. Gives me* carte blanche *to do anything I want to the spineless jellyfish.* The thought of such power over others was almost a sexual experience.

That evening there was a knocking on the front door of Jacob's house. When Jacob opened it, two large and unfriendly men in military uniforms brushed past him and entered the living room.

"What do you want?" he asked, indignant at the rude violation of his home.

"Bring your wife and son here, please." It was the polite "please", said so indifferently, that struck fear into his heart.

When his family was with him the larger man spoke. "Bring me your phones. Don't try anything, because we'll check, and if you hold back we'll know and deal with you accordingly."

They remained silent and watchful as they retrieved their phones. "We'll remain here while you pack your bags," he told them. "But only if you do exactly as you're told and don't try any funny business."

They were allowed only a bag apiece. When they'd finished this dolorous task, they were rushed out to the waiting black SUV. A plane trip and another long ride afterwards in a car similar to the one at their home, they arrived at an extremely hot, dry and desolate plot of land in the Arizona desert. Surrounding the entrance guard house was a barbed-wire fence that extended around the plot into the far distance. He saw a familiar face among the new arrivals, his friend Sid.

Agonizing days later, his wife and son could take no more of the inhuman abuse. He lost them to the vicious barbarians. Still other torture-filled days after that, he and Sid met Earl Cook under life-changing circumstances.

CHAPTER EIGHT

"No!" Charlotte yelled, her rage uncontrolled. "How can this be?" She smacked a fist on her desk at the news of the Pope's demise, causing it to reverberate just short of shattering. The messenger was Kathy, who now stood before the desk almost catatonic in her terror.

After the passage of very little time since her days as District Attorney a few short years ago, Charlotte had risen to the top of the filthy governmental heap, having recently assumed the position of President of the Western European Region, one of ten regional governments controlling the world. This failed to satisfy her power: she wanted it all, and she wanted it now. She thought she had it in the bag, having curried the favor of the Pope, who had indicated that he'd be content as second in command. He wouldn't be content with that, she knew, but she'd already made plans to counter his inevitable attempt to assassinate her. Just one more step and she'd be home where she belonged as leader of the entire world.

But the Pope's murder had intervened. As the prophet Daniel had foretold two and a half millennia earlier, the ex-president of the old United States, POTUS, had deposed his successor and immediately rid himself of the presidents of his immediate neighbors to the north and the south and installed himself as President of the North American Region, POTNAR. Not content with that power grab, he placed himself in Charlotte's sights as a contender for world leadership. This usurper, Charlotte mused, had the effrontery to declare it done, calling himself the Grand Leader of the World, GLOW.

He had a comeuppance in his future, Charlotte vowed meanly. It would never happen.

"Come here," Charlotte demanded. "Get me Vance. I want him here, and I want him here NOW."

Kathy crept over to her tiny little cubicle in the corner of the room. She sat and operated her telephone, wishing desperately for Vance's secretary to answer. If Vance failed to show up, Kathy faced another rodeo with Charlotte. With the connection made, Kathy almost wept on the phone in her plea for Vance to come and redirect Charlotte's rage away from her.

When the man arrived, Charlotte thrust her chin toward him as he sat dejectedly in front of her desk prepared for an extended dressing-down.

"Why do you think it's my fault?" he questioned, in full defensive mode. "Maybe I did know about GLOW. We all did, including you. I remember you telling us that the Pope would keep him in place. How were we to know that the Vatican would be torched with the Pope inside?"

"Stop your whining, you little wet brown cylinder of stinking crap. Get your head on straight and start thinking. We need to do something about this character before he turns on us as well."

"There's only one thing we can do, Charlotte. He needs to go. Not a big deal. Just do the same as with all the others we've removed from the table as we've needed to. Big Bob's still in the game. I'll get hold of him and the problem will go away like always."

"Get on it now, before I sic Big Bob onto you."

The problem with that was that Big Bob was already employed. He had been hired by one of GLOW's underlings for the same purpose, the difference being that the target was Charlotte. With his own goons having brought the building under complete control, he was now just outside her door at that very moment. He barged inside her office, heading for her desk like a freight train out of control as Vance watched in horror.

As Kathy saw that his undivided attention was on Charlotte, she took the opportunity to slink out of the office. Job or no job, she still had her life.

Big Bob clasped his huge hands around her neck and squeezed as

Vance stared in stupefied immobility. After her desperate struggles subsided, he threw her off her chair, reached over the desk and clasped his hands around Vance's neck until he, too, stopped breathing.

"Looks like God decided that a male antichrist would be preferable to a female," a watcher told his companion. "It does seem to fit a little better."

"I don't agree," the other said. "Charlotte was so vicious you could hardly call her a woman anyway. But our God knows what's best. I wonder who will replace Charlotte as POTNAR?"

The most urgent of POTNAR's new tasks was to respond to GLOW's edict to implement a new function in the chips embedded in most of the masses. This amounted to the subject's acceptance of a loyalty oath that recognized GLOW's worthiness to be worshiped as God.

Anticipating the outcome of Big Bob's excursion into Charlotte's domain, GLOW had already selected her replacement. The new POTNAR was another ex-United States president, one of the worst in his effort to remove the country's exceptional values and open it up to a fundamental transformation into a socialism that made it compatible with global domination.

POTNAR approved of Charlotte's egregious trampling of the rights of American citizens, observing that through her the fundamental transformation of America had made significant strides towards completion. But not quite. It was time, in his opinion, to do some housecleaning, particularly with those who had refused to accept the chip. The garbage needed to be taken out, and he had the men to accomplish that task. Men who actually enjoyed the prospect of doing so.

Jacob and Sid came into contact with Earl and Joyce Cook during a distressing circumstance. They'd found themselves, along with Jacob's wife Penny and their toddler son, behind barbed wire enclosures that represented POTNAR's effort to clean house. The reason they were there was that Earl and Joyce and their adopted daughter Cathy were Christians and Jacob and his friend Sid were

Jews, all of whom had refused to accept the chip. It was also the reason why Jacob no longer had a wife or a son, these two having been violently killed at the hands of the prison guards. Cathy was also gone, and Joyce was on her way out as well.

But Joyce survived the ordeal, as did her husband Earl. Jacob and Sid also survived, along with a number of fellow Jews. God, who would have preferred for them all to come back home to heaven where they belonged, decided to hold them back in the material world for some important missions they would fulfill first to His glory. Having a different mission, Earl and Joyce ended up in a recreational vehicle in Texas where Earl preached the Word of God to an enthusiastic remnant. God split Jacob and Sid off from the couple near Ozona, Texas, where they wound up in Houston, and from there to Israel in a roundabout, hazard-filled route.

With the aid of his beloved Holy Spirit, Earl had filled Jacob with many insights into the nature of God during their brief time together. Jacob and Sid became Messianic Christians. In the process Jacob met Moira in Israel, a lovely lady who eventually became his wife, returning him to a semblance of happiness. His life was very different from what it had been. Leaner and more aggressive to suit his new circumstances, he joined Moira to spread their insights into the nature of God wherever they went, finally settling in a kibbutz near the thick of fighting between Israel and her enemies. He and his new wife received rifle training by an ex-U.S. Marine, and acquitted themselves well in clashes that followed. He often thought of how prescient his friend Sid was in his complaints about the way their old government and society in the States were deteriorating. He had been right about his concerns, terribly so.

Sid himself linked up with Mary, a darling young girl who gave him much happiness. They settled elsewhere in Israel, meeting again from time to time.

PART TWO

EARTHCHANGE

Preface to Part Two

The earth is utterly broken down, the earth is thoroughly dissolved, the earth is moved exceedingly. The earth shall reel to and fro like a drunkard, and shall be removed like a booth; and the transgression thereof shall be heavy upon it, and it shall fall, and not rise again. Isaiah 24:19, 20

It happened again, this time by another strike from the cosmos. Angered beyond patience by the multitude of man's arrogant, ego-driven cruelties against his fellow man and against the Earth, God decreed within Himself that enough was enough and it was time to put satan in his proper place. It was time again to demonstrate that not only was God Himself relevant to humans, but that these unjustifiably bigheaded, self-worshiping creatures were puny, undersized and thoroughly weak, particularly in the tarnished nature of their self-serving characters. They needed to know that the greatness defined by their outsized egos were no match for Him. Their evil devices were enormously outclassed by their Creator and the time had come to point out the fact to them that they were actually tiny and inconsequential in a way that they wouldn't forget.

The first hit came upon Jupiter rather than the earth, like it did with Noah's flood and its multi-century aftermath, and once again Jupiter expelled a planet-sized mass that came very close to colliding with the earth before wandering off like a drunkard to other parts of the solar system. The water canopy surrounding the earth having been destroyed during the Great Flood, this new earth-threatening disaster didn't directly cause the waters of the seas to rise, nor did the close approach of the new proto-planet to Roche's Limit on Earth cause water bound in the Earth's crust to spew forth. Nevertheless, the seas themselves, greatly troubled by massive earthquakes, generated enormous tsunamis that overflowed the continents, adding to the devastation from the trembling earth and screeching tornadic winds that accompanied a new polar shift. Geologic columns of layered soil dissolved back into the encroaching sea and were re-deposited elsewhere to create patterns defined by new geologic columns. The Mount of Olives east of Jerusalem was bisected by a gigantic chasm, its depth exceeding that of the old, no longer existent Grand Canyon in Arizona. Much as the village of Tiahuanaco in Peru was elevated from the level of the sea to a stupendous height surpassing ten thousand feet during the previous planetary catastrophic event, the cliff on the east side of this valley rose up several thousand feet, elevating Jerusalem to a lofty altitude of seven thousand feet. In line with this grand elevation, Jerusalem now stood as the capital of the world, presided over by Jesus Christ, along with His Church, an entity that bore little resemblance to the enclaves of self-serving would-be Christians that had sparsely dotted the planet before the Big Strike. The Dead Sea merged into the Mediterranean, contributing to massive changes to continental boundaries. Huge rafts of dead plant and animal life and rotting human detritus drifted aimlessly until finally being submerged to begin again the process of forming coal and oil. The poles underwent substantial relocations, permitting the emergence of Antarctica as an ice-free continent that would eventually support life. Jerusalem itself, having transited forty-seven degrees to the south, occupied a latitude fifteen degrees below the new equator. The city basked in a hotter sun, the greater heat compensating for its higher altitude.

The devastating upheaval visited upon the Earth was a necessity. Appreciating that the time of the Father's end game had arrived, Wisdom responded to the Father's will in that matter. She knew as well as He that there was no longer a choice. In addition to the progressively evil innovations his hatred-driven inventions of torture were practiced against his fellow beings, mankind had pretty well converted the seas into plastic-filled cesspools and the land into junkyards even before the Grand War began and ubiquitous zones of radioactive poison emerged to render even less of the planet habitable. The war essentially spoiled the planet. Worse yet was the hatred-filled savagery that afflicted the secular population.

Demonic possession had become commonplace, having been invited into godless lives by excesses of greed and lust. Through unrelenting anger and fear it drove its victims into horrible acts of brutal violence against each other.

Something far more destructive than mankind's puny efforts at control had to be done, and the cosmic catastrophe did the job wonderfully, completing the task of ending miserable, meaningless lives and thrusting much of the blight deep into the earth's mantle. Yet there remained isolated pockets of filth and junk that would require more precise work to remove.

The planet was still reeling from the extraordinary disaster when Earl and Joyce finally were taken from Earth to merge with other loved ones and, as components of the Church, to marry their divine Lover, Jesus Christ, as foretold by Paul in Ephesians 5:31 and 32. Their extraction from Earth was anything but benign. The enormous tsunami that had hit the Rushmore region of South Dakota swept them along with it until they were rammed into a tree. They were saved from drowning by the violence of the collision, which was merciful in its abruptness. In one instant they found themselves in heaven, there to remain in joyful wonder over the spectacular richness of this grand new domain.

Halfway around the world and situated in one of the very few nodes of minimum disturbance, Jacob and his bride Moira found themselves alive and remaining on Earth. This awareness was accompanied by mixed feelings: on the one hand, they remained joyfully united to each other. On the other hand, they suspected, rightly so, that the marriage between Jesus and His Church had already taken place without including them.

CHAPTER NINE

The earthquake shook them awake. Moira rose first, looking down gratefully upon her husband Jacob. He looked up at her, then spread his arms to enfold her, planting a kiss on her lips.

"Thanks for the kiss," Moira told him, caressing a cheek. "I needed that. At least I have you." She wrapped her arms about his back and clung to him. She looked toward the mountain in the distance, Jerusalem at its top gleaming in the sun. "But I'll bet that Jesus is up there right now, with His Church alongside."

"How so?" Jacob asked her.

"It's in the Book of Zecharia. Chapter 14, I think. It says that when Jesus comes down to Earth to straighten things out, His feet will stand on the Mount of Olives, splitting the earth and creating a huge valley, like maybe the Grand Canyon. I think we're looking at it now. If that's the case, He brought His Church with Him as His bride. So as I look at it I wonder why we've been left out of that picture."

"I don't know, Moira. It doesn't feel right. I'm pretty sure that we haven't done anything so bad that we'd be excluded. At least I can't remember anything like that. And if we did, I'd think that Wisdom would have let us know loud and clear."

"You're correct on all counts," a soft, melodious voice said to their rear. Startled, they turned sharply to see the gorgeous apparition they recognized as Wisdom standing behind them. "Right now, you're more useful to Us here than over there. It's about your attitudes and skill set, which are quite unique."

"How can we still be alive, with all the upheavals and torn earth that we've been surrounded with? And is Jesus up there in Jerusalem now? If He is, how come we're still having earthquakes?"

"As for the violence, Jacob, you and Moira are alive because you happen to be in a node of relative quiescence. There are such nodes scattered around the earth. The math is a little complicated as to how I managed to place you near one, but then I am God, after all, and there are some perks to that position. I'll admit that your location wasn't enough to save you, though. The worst of it happened while you were asleep, when I could remove you from the action. Think of the violence as a healing process, which it is. Much of it was necessary to get rid of all the mess you humans have made of yourselves and the Earth as well. A good part of all that trash and radiation is now safely under the crust, where it won't be a danger. I was particularly fond of thrusting the windmills into the Earth's mantle, where they melted down to almost nothing. The remaining earthquakes, and there will be more of them, are smaller, surgical operations to remove pockets of trash and radiation. Even then the process is too coarse to remove what remains without adding to the collateral damage. That's partly where you come in."

"I have a question, Wisdom," Moira said. "Maybe more than one. Was this tremendous violence really necessary? I mean, I hear you on the need to heal the earth of the problems we caused, but don't you think that maybe it was a bit over-the-top? Overkill comes to mind without a whole lot of mental prodding."

Wisdom laughed, a rich multi-harmonic melody. "At least it was quick. It would have been much more painfully drawn out had it been less violent. In thinking only of its enormity, you underestimate the destruction you caused on your own and were about to make much worse. I'm speaking collectively, of course. You two weren't so bad. But others were. Daniel said it correctly in his Chapter Seven when he spoke of the final kingdom of mankind, the fourth beast, as dreadful and terrible, and strong exceedingly, with great iron teeth that devoured and broke in pieces and stamped the residue with its feet. This beast of iron was indeed different than the kingdoms that preceded it, because it acquired its vast power by fashioning machines of iron and steel that could move by themselves. Steam locomotives and steam tractors, wonderful devices for freeing man of limited travel and backbreaking work. But not content to create mechanical contrivances to ease the burden of manual labor, they put this new knowledge to use creating engines of war – trucks, tanks, artillery pieces. Then came the airplane, first for travel and next for bombs, and after that the nuclear bomb. Think of the American civil war, with its horses and primitive cannons and foot soldiers who had to march long distances to engage their enemies. The only means of land transport other than the horse and the foot was the steam locomotive, which itself was rather primitive. Less than a hundred years after that war, the Second World War was fought in the air as well as land and sea. The red badge of courage fell upon bomber crews and fighter pilots, where eighty years before the skies were entirely free of human intrusion. Even rockets were put into play. Finally came the computers with their ultimate purpose of stripping man of all vestiges of the freedoms he once enjoyed. All this happened very quickly, over less than a third of the span of a Patriarch's lifetime, and it all was associated with the fourth kingdom, the iron beast.

"Daniel foretold that one day Jesus would come to Earth to destroy this last government of man and replace it with His own. It's not as if mankind had no way of knowing where he was heading as corruption followed upon corruption. A remarkable feature of man is his inability to learn from the past and the warnings of his earlier failures and the reminder of them from Scripture. After the Second World War, Winston Churchill paraphrased a warning made earlier by a fellow Englishman by saying that "Those who fail to learn from history are condemned to repeat it." As time went on, the dreary fulfillment of this warning came to pass as man forgot the lessons of Scripture and History and, having lost even his limited and imperfect understanding of God, tossed Him away as well. That's when things really began to go south. Having replaced the wisdom of God with the wisdom of man, he became profoundly foolish, being subject to all kinds of false notions and harmful character traits. God had to put a halt to his folly, as man was about to destroy himself and destroy God's other creations along with him."

"So what we did to ourselves and the Earth was so terrible that God had to take the extreme measure that He did?"

"You can answer that one yourself. Can you imagine living on the surface of an Earth that was so saturated with nuclear fallout that you'd have to live as primitives in caves for your entire lifetimes? Which would be so short as to preclude your children's ability to reach maturity because they had no uncontaminated source of milk or other necessities of life? The Earth, polluted already by mountains of plastic and chemical waste, would be hostile to life after being ravaged by unlimited nuclear warfare. Existence would have been short, brutal and miserable."

"Oh."

"As for your second question, the one you and your dear husband were talking about when I showed up, My Jesus has indeed married His Church, and at long last, I might add. He and His Church are over there now. Actually some of them are. Others are busy getting people like you ready for the Big Move. But you won't be left out for much longer. In fact, when the time comes to join the rest, you'll enjoy a special place in His heart. But right now there are more people remaining on Earth whom We'd prefer would join Us in Father's great plan for mankind, but cannot because they worship a different God than Us. They simply don't know Us well enough to justify being more than strangers."

"So they're not Christians, then."

"They're not really, Moira. That's the issue – they think they are Christians. They claim to worship Jesus as their God. They actually think they're the best Christians of all, as they're committed to being defenders of the faith, showing no tolerance for any deviation from Scripture as they know it from their versions of the Bible. But sincere as they are, they're close to being eternally separated from God, as their versions, along with their traditions, stray very far from the original Scripture that portrayed Us with accuracy. What they need, but don't realize yet, is a restoration of Scripture from man's misplaced deviations to what I originally gave to My prophets. We don't want to lose them to their devotion to their egos. That's another element of where you come in. We need actual humans, people that they can relate to as among them, to give them some badly-needed insights about Us. You need to reach them with your knowledge of Us, the Godhead, so that they might actually love Us and allow Us to return that love."

"That's a tall order, Wisdom. Are we up to it?"

"Not entirely yet. But you will be when the occasions arise. And remember, I'll always be here with you, having you say what you need to say. As for now, put your things into your backpacks, as you're going to be doing some walking.

"At least we're well-armed to challenge their view of You, particularly Your gendered relationship with the Father. Thank you so very much for having showed us such an abundance of Scriptural passages that define that aspect of your relationship."

Wisdom gave some thought to Moira's assertion. "Just one passage, being so clear-cut, should have been sufficient to arouse some deeper thought into the matter."

"Which one?" Jacob asked.

"Which one would you have picked?" Wisdom responded.

"Probably Genesis 1:26 and 27," he replied.

"Yes, right there at the beginning of Scripture. It's difficult to justify their omission of Our gender when it's plain as day that the passage declares that mankind was created male and female *in God's image.* It takes a lot of mental gymnastics to parse out that relationship from the passage. Nevertheless, they do just that, and your job is to get them to start thinking more for themselves and less about themselves. First, you need to gain their trust. Given that you're still in your material bodies, they'll think that you may be in the same situation as they are. You don't want to lie, but you also don't want to discourage such an attitude, as you need to let them feel that you belong in their group. You need to delay your approach to the subject, and when you do get around to it, do so gently."

"What happened to Sid and Mary?" Jacob asked Her. "Are they up there now with Jesus?" he added, pointing to the mountain.

"They are, and very happily so. But you two will be even happier when your time comes."

"So where do You wish us to go?"

Wisdom pointed down to the northeast, where the pattern of disturbed earth indicated a community of sorts. "That's the ground where Ephesus once stood. It's located in what once was Turkey, on the eastern coast of the Aegean Sea. It was originally settled there by Greeks hundreds of years before Jesus walked the Earth the first time. It became a Roman province around the first century A.D. and was known for its pagan Temple to Diana, which was considered one of the wonders of the Earth. Paul had quite a time there bringing Christians into the fold, and those who opposed him in the name of the goddess Diana created something of a tumult in the city. We made certain that Christianity prevailed, but for a while it was a bit of a go. When you stop for the evening, read about it in Acts 19. It will help give you some background for your visit there. After Paul's little to-do there, John was the next in Scripture to get involved. In Revelation Chapter 2, as part of Jesus' discourse regarding the seven representative Churches, He described Ephesus as having grown cold in her love for Him. I'll quote the passage, as there are some interesting implications in it for the people there now:

> *To the angel of the church of Ephesus write: These things says he who holds the seven stars in his right hand, who walks in the midst of the seven golden lampstands. I know your works, and your labor, and your patience, and how you cannot bear those who are evil; and you have tried them who say they are apostles, and are not, and have found them to be liars; and have endured, and have had patience, and for my name's sake have labored, and have not fainted. Nevertheless, I have somewhat against you, because you have left your first love. Remember, therefore, from where you are fallen, and repent, and do the first works, or else I will come quickly, and will remove your lampstand out of its place, except you repent. But this you have, that you hate the deeds of the Nicolaitans,*

which I also hate. He who has an ear, let him hear with the Spirit says to the churches: To him who overcomes will I give to eat of the tree of life, which is in the midst of the paradise of God.

"Wow. That's kind of coincidental, given what you implied about the rigidity and coldness of the group there now."

"Actually, Moira, it isn't all that coincidental, with My propensity for nudging people. But there's a definite parallel between Jesus' forecast to John about that Church, and the present inhabitants. John, by the way, was heavily involved in that Church after his release from Patmos.

"The most interesting thing about this situation," Wisdom continued, "is that Paul's letter to the Ephesians was the most direct in all of Scripture regarding the love between Jesus and His Church, and of His eventual marriage to Her. The entire letter was indeed a prenuptial counseling discourse for the Church, not that many Christians have viewed it as such. Ah, well. Do read the letter when you get a chance, particularly Ephesians Five."

"I have one request, Wisdom."

"Yes you do. You're hungry and thirsty as we speak. Don't worry. When you reach your resting places, you'll find food and water there. You might have to hunt for it, but I promise you, you'll have it. Enough for the evening and noontime meals. A word of caution before you set off: don't expect too much in the way of accommodation when you reach your destination. Okay, so off you go."

"Are you going to be close by?" Jacob asked. But She was gone.

"Jacob, that was kind of a silly question," Moira shot back. "By this time, you don't get it that She's *everywhere?*"

"Yeah. Let's saddle up."

As they trudged down the mountain, they saw that the landscape had changed drastically since the return of Jesus. The Mediterranean Sea below was significantly wider near the area of the Dead

Sea, which no longer existed as a separate entity. The Jerusalem Mountain, as they called it, rose abruptly from the water. In places, sheer cliffs prevailed almost to the vegetation-covered top, which in the distance appeared lush, almost tropical to their eyes in its green profusion. Jerusalem dominated the very top like a storybook castle.

The countryside closer to hand was rather harsher in appearance, as most vegetation hadn't returned yet to the uprooted soil. But Jacob and Moira were happy that they didn't have to contend with radiation or trash laying about. As evening approached, they started looking for a place to stay as they continued walking.

"Ewww!" Moira cried. "What is that stink?"

"A dead something," Jacob replied. "Over there. It looks like a rat. A very big one. And very dead. I wonder if this is what Wisdom had in mind for our supper – roadkill."

"Of course not, silly," Moira said, laughing. "More like this isn't where She wanted us to bed down for the night. Keep going, and let's make it fast."

A half hour after they continued down the hillside, they rounded a bend to encounter an amazing sight. Here there was a beautiful oasis, with a crystal-clear pool surrounded by large palm trees. "These trees look decades old," Jacob said. It's strange how they survived all the turmoil."

I don't think so," Moira said. "They may look old, but I'd be willing to bet that this is a new creation. For us. It's too perfect. Look at the sand next to the water, soft and inviting, begging us to lay our bedding there. And look at all the dates lying around! I feel like we just entered the Garden of Eden, Jacob. How wonderful is our Wisdom!"

"It looks beautiful. I suppose it's free of scorpions as well." His chuckles broke out into laughter.

"Where'd that thought come from?" Moira asked, frowning. "And why are you laughing about it?"

"Just remembering something. I had a friend once, back in the

States. He said when he was in high school, he and his friends went out for a hike after drinking a little too much. He lived in Arizona at the time, and he got halfway up a hill when a rattlesnake bit him in the ankle. He went back down the hill fast as he could with all the pain, yelling for his friends for help. When he got back to the car, he got in on the passenger side and sat there waiting for one of the others to drive him to the hospital. He let his arm drop down to the ground, where his hand was stung by a scorpion. He said the sting was more painful than the snake bite."

"Wow. I don't think I'd be laughing about that."

"He was good natured about it. He laughed as he told me. He said it was kind of cosmic."

The tale gave Moira a delightfully wicked idea. Later that night as they lay snuggled together so comfortably on the soft sand, she slowly extracted herself from his sleeping arms and went over to a palm frond that lay on the ground. She tore off a piece and wrapped it around a fuzzy piece of bark, carefully preserving a sharp end, and returned to where Jacob slept. She cuddled him, thinking of how he used to smile in his sleep when she did that. Positioning the assembly above his side, she jabbed it into him, shouting *scorpion!* in his ear.

Jacob erupted in a tornado of motion, shouting "AAAggh!" After some time, he noticed that he wasn't in pain. He also heard his companion giggling in the dark. "Sorry, Jacob," she said. "You're so easy to tease that I couldn't resist it. Come here and let me make it all better."

He complied, almost instantly forgetting the incident in her comforting arms.

They set off the next morning after a breakfast of dates, refreshed and happy, their trust in God heavily reinforced by their experience at the oasis. "I wonder what Wisdom has in store for us tonight," Jacob speculated.

"I wouldn't mind if we came across a place like the one we had last night. As a matter of fact it could be exactly the same."

But it wasn't the same. At their next stop for the night, Jacob and Moira discovered an even grander oasis, stocked this time with orange trees and coconut palms. The water was more extensive too, being the size of a small pond. A warm, gentle breeze rustled the palm leaves, creating a melodious background as it caressed their bodies. They decided to take a swim to wash up.

This place looks lush," Jacob said, "but I don't know if I'm up to eating the coconuts."

"Why? Are you allergic?"

"It's not that. I used to love coconuts. Too much, as a matter of fact. Back when I was a little kid and didn't know any better, I grabbed a handful of shredded coconut my mother had on the counter and squirreled it away in the drawer of my little desk. I suddenly remembered about it a few weeks later. I was hungry, and jumped out of bed to eat it up. The next morning, I looked in the drawer and the few shreds that were left were green. I was green too, and rushed to the toilet to puke. I had an aversion to coconut from that time on."

"Wisdom must have known that when She stocked this place with food. Maybe it's time you made a stab at trying it." Moira picked up a coconut off the ground and handed it to him. With great effort he finally cracked it open and put his mouth over the dripping milk. "Hey, not bad, he said. He picked at the white meat and chewed it. He gave half the coconut to Moira and devoured the remnants of his. "I guess I'm over my aversion," he said after he'd finished his portion. Let's get some more."

By the end of the week of traveling into increasingly comfortable oases, they neared the region where the community was supposed to be located, almost disappointed that their journey was reaching an end. They approached a hill of sorts, mostly house-sized rocks.

"I don't see anything here," Jacob muttered, looking around. "No houses, no nothing. Where are the people?"

"I don't know." Moira squinted, searching for signs of civilization. "Oh," she said as they moved in a circle around the rocks. "Over there – looks like a garden." Jacob's eyes followed her outstretched arm.

"Kind of puny. I see some women there with baskets on their backs. They're picking what looks like squash."

And there," she pointed in a different direction. "There is a lone house, but it looks abandoned. No wonder – it could fall apart any second."

"Look at that, Moira," Jacob said, pointing up at the rocks. There's a cave up there with a ladder down to the rock below. And some lines down to the ground." Two of the lines were actually a single loop of a strangely-fashioned rope, obviously handmade, connected to a pulley system, like an old clothesline. A third was tied off to a wooden cleat. "I think I saw movement inside, but it's hard to tell with the shadows. The cave may be hiding some people inside."

"Cave?" They live in a cave like man did a million years ago?"

"Don't get carried away by the old uniformitarian myths our old society tried to pass off as truth," Jacob corrected her. "What do you think those who followed Noah had for living quarters? As you know yourself, the real cave persons were forced into that life by the Flood's desolate aftermath. It happened just about five thousand years ago, not a million. It looks like they're having a post-catastrophic hardscrabble existence like our post-Flood ancestors did."

"We sure had it better coming here. I guess we got the luxo treatment from Wisdom."

"Right. I think these folks have had to settle for the basic plan. Wisdom doesn't seem to be cutting them any slack."

As they stared up at the cave, a shabbily-dressed man came out into the opening, looked down at them, and with an animal-like skill, clambered down the ladder and the rocks below and approached them. Other faces peered out of the cave.

The man carried a long pole, sharp at the end. His stern look was matched by an abrupt, almost rude, tone of voice. "What are you doing here?" he said suspiciously. "If there's something you're wanting, we don't have much to give. And we're Christians," he spat out, as if daring them to speak against God.

Jacob swallowed his repulsion. "Hello, sir," he said. My name is Jacob, and my wife's name is Moira. We're Christians too." His reply appeared to cause no change in the man's attitude. His hostility was palpable, evidenced by his frown and his refusal to shake Jacob's extended hand.

"What kind?"

"What kind of Christian? Is there more than one kind? If you want to know whether we believe that Scripture is inspired and inerrant, yes we do."

"Homer!" a feminine voice called. "Be nice!" A far more cheerful woman stood up from her labor in the garden. She walked over to them and put out her hand. "Hi! I'm Elizabeth, and this is Homer. Welcome to our little community."

Elizabeth responded to Moira's kindly smile by taking Moira by the hand and leading her toward a long bench, apparently a community structure. Homer stared meanly at them and turned back toward the cave. He untied the rope from the cleat on the pole and yanked at it. Another man responded by coming to the front of the cave and looking down. Homer impatiently retrieved a pad from a pocket, ripped off a sheet of paper, and penned a short note. He attached it to the bottom rope of the pulley system and cranked the pulley until the paper reached the man at the mouth of the cave. The man read the note, scribbled something on it, and cranked it back down to Homer, who read it with disapproval and stomped away.

"You've just witnessed our high-tech communication system," Elizabeth said with a snort. I'm afraid that Homer's greeting skills need some work," she said as they walked. "Homer's an elder in the Church and takes his position a little too seriously, I fear. The man's suspicious of any and all people that aren't part of this little town."

"Even fellow Christians?" Jacob asked.

"Mostly fellow Christians. Other Christians, not of our ilk, have generally been disposed to argue with our Church leaders about policy and dogma. As self-proclaimed defenders of the faith, the leaders here take that position very seriously. In fact, any opinion that differs from theirs is automatically placed in the category of heresy."

When Jacob came over to them, Elizabeth beckoned for them to sit. "Where are you heading?" she asked.

"We, um, aren't sure. We don't even know how we've survived so far. We hope that we might stay here long enough to collect our thoughts and think out some kind of plan for the future."

Two men were sitting at another bench in front of them before a long table. They were holding coffee cups, and they'd been listening in. At Moira's mention of wanting to stay, one of them got up and walked over to them. He extended his hand to Jacob. "Jack's my name, he began. "Come over and sit with us for a spell. Want some coffee?"

They assented to his offer with enthusiasm. Elizabeth joined them at the table. "Careful about the coffee. It takes a little getting used to. It's not really coffee, for starters – just burnt seeds. And you don't want to know where the seeds came from. But it's better than nothing. Here's Bill," she said, turning towards another man. "Hi," he replied with a smile, shaking their hands. "Are you willing to work?"

"First things first," Jack broke in. "Are you Christians, or are you Jews?"

"We're both," Moira said. "Is that a problem?"

"Maybe," Jack said, "maybe not. "Depends on what kind of Christians you are."

"What kind of question is that?" Jacob shot back at him.

"Yeah, Jack, how about playing nice for the first few minutes or so?" Elizabeth gave him a glare. Two other sets of narrowed eyes stared back at him. Bill stared off into space, willfully noncommittal.

"A Christian is a Christian," Jacob continued. "At least one who believes in Scripture as inspired and inerrant in the original as both Peter and Paul wrote. That's the kind of Christians we are. There is no other."

"Okay," Jack said without apology. "I'll let my brethren elders know. Back to Bill's question – are you willing to work?"

"Yes, of course," Moira told him. "You can tell by looking at us that we're no strangers to hard labor."

"We'll call a meeting of the elders and talk about it. But if they say you can stay, you'd better bet that you'll be tired at the end of the day. As you've seen, there isn't much growing around here. It takes a lot to keep us fed. There's a Bible study Monday, Wednesday and Friday at five. We'll expect you there tomorrow. As for now, Elizabeth will see to a place to stay. For tonight."

"We'd be more than willing to carry our load, Jacob said."

Neither men replied. "Let's go, Bill," Jack said, rising from the table. "We've got things to get done."

When they left, Moira looked at Elizabeth. "Not exactly a welcome mat," she said.

Elizabeth nodded in assent. "You're the first strangers we've seen in quite a while. We've all had it pretty hard up to now just surviving. We're in the same boat you're in, and the uncertainty of a continued day-to-day existence on top of our question about why we're still here has had our teeth on edge. Still, that's not an excuse to be rude. Things will get better after you've been here a while and they get to know you." "If they let you stay," she added under her breath.

They followed her up into the cave, where she extended a welcoming arm. "Our community quarters," she said unnecessarily. "There's a few empty spaces. You'll each get a mat."

When they'd climbed up the ladder and gotten their first look into the cave, they were surprised at how large it was. Not only that, but it was homey as well. The women had obviously been hard at work to make it livable. There were large mats woven out of palm fronds scattered about the rock floor, and where other large rocks created nooks of relative privacy for the occupants woven mats hung from the sides. These wall hangings were colored with red, yellow and green dye. Other rock walls were also painted with murals depicting hunting scenes. As the pictures showed, these people had successfully made spears and bows. The paintings were rather primitive, but then the artists had not had access to courses in painting, nor to paint and brush supplies. All things considered, they did rather well at it. The two also noted several fires scattered about the enclosure. Judging from the pungent smell, the fuel within the clay pots was animal fat. Most of the smoke, they saw, rose up through the ceiling of the cave. Obviously, there were openings through the cave to the air above. As they moved farther into the interior, they saw that this enclosure wasn't a true cave, but rather a void covered by a number of very large rocks. The void included another opening on the opposite side of the enclosure, but it was blocked off by smaller rocks and more woven mats to keep the wind from blowing into the area.

"Pretty good for what we had to work with, wouldn't you say?" Elizabeth said. "Come. I'll introduce you to Mary, who'll get the ladies working on your mats."

Mary, another friendly person, sized them up and told them that the mats would be ready for them by the time they would return to sleep for the night. "You'll each have one," she commented.

"But we're married," Moira challenged. "We sleep together."

"Not here you don't. Here nobody sleeps with anybody else, even the ones who are married. We're trying to keep as close to Jesus as we can, no distractions. We've been expecting to be raptured for a long time now, before all this destruction came down. It can't be that far away. It just can't." She squinched her eyes in a frown. Unbidden tears trickled down her cheeks.

They were assigned sleeping places, fortunately next to each other. They were given bedding, which they arranged head-to-head. "Jacob," Moira whispered after they'd eaten, attended the evening prayer and turned in with the others. "I can't believe this – this rigidity! They're living like monks! Maybe we'd be better off hitting the road tomorrow."

Jacob reached over to hold her hand. "No, Moira. We've had clear marching orders. This is where Wisdom wants us to be, no matter how terrible it may seem. Elizabeth seems to be reachable. Let's see how the Bible study goes tomorrow. Maybe we'll find others there we can start to befriend. In the meantime, we'll have to give thought to how we can approach them. The first order of business is to live by their rules."

After a time of silence between them, Moira spoke again. "Wisdom said to begin gently," she whispered. Maybe we can start out with the women. Tell them that if the Trinity is composed only of masculine Members, as the "He" in their versions of Scripture probably say, Genesis 1:26 would have to mean that only the menfolk were made in God's image. That, in turn, would suggest that a good half of the world's population has been left out in the cold. Perhaps, then, at least the womenfolk would get riled to the point that they may start thinking a little more deeply than they have been."

The next morning, as they waited for the Church elders to tell them whether or not they could stay, Jacob and Moira walked together outside the compound. "Maybe if we do eventually reach the women with the message of a gendered masculine-feminine Godhead, and the women try to get that across to the men, it might cause quite a stir. We could get booted out on our ears."

"On the other hand," Jacob countered, "conditions here may just work in our favor. I imagine that the anxiety level is pretty high right now. They appear to know by now that Jesus has returned, and here they are with no rapture having happened yet. I'm fairly certain they've been searching the Scriptures to see what they might have missed in their interpretation, being incapable, I'm sure, of perceiving that they might have been left out of the picture."

"And," she said with the hint of a grin, "don't forget the beast in the room, the celibacy issue. I'll bet that a portion of the menfolk must feel that their abstinence has been forced upon them. Can you imagine how eagerly they might receive that information if they found that their wives had suddenly pulled their covers back and jumped into bed with them?" Her grin turned into a snort and they both laughed.

CHAPTER TEN

That afternoon after the noontime snack Jack approached them. "The Church committee has reached a tentative conclusion," he told them. "You've been allowed to stay, maybe temporarily, subject to a more thorough evaluation next week. We'll be looking at how you fit in with our Bible study and work schedules. Remember the Bible study tonight at five. We'll have your work assignments posted on the bulletin board before then, so check that out too. Do you have Bibles?"

"Yes, we do," Moira answered. "They're pretty ragged, having gone through so much lately, but the pages are all there and readable."

"What version?"

"King James."

"At least that's good. I'll see you at the study."

At the Bible study, which was held in the bench-filled clearing, Elizabeth came their way and sat next to them. A tall, sturdy man trailed behind. "Hi," she said, her face cheerful. "I heard that you're going to stay a while. I'm happy for you. And for myself. As far as I'm concerned we could use a little fresh blood around here. Meet Carl, my husband."

Elizabeth's friendly attitude gave Moira a big lift. After the introductions, Carl sat next to his wife. Moira was about to reply when a man walked over to the podium, Bible in hand along with another book. "Today," he began, "I'm going to continue with a message that I feel is very important. This one will address the purity issue again." Moira could tell from his expression that he was worried about their present situation, maybe even desperate about their having remained on Earth in the face of their expectation of being raptured. Having been forewarned by Wisdom, she knew that his worry was fully justified. She also knew that in his desperation, the man at the podium would probably go further off the rails. "What's his name?" she whispered to Elizabeth.

"George." She frowned, but failed to elaborate. Apparently, Moira thought, the two weren't very close. As George began to speak, she began to understand why.

"As you well know," George began, "in our voluntary celibacy, we are following the will of our Lord Jesus Christ." At this pronouncement, there was an uneasy stirring, not limited to the menfolk. "For a reminder of this," he went on, "open your Bibles to Matthew Chapter Nineteen and verses 10 through 12. Here Jesus is responding to his disciples on the matter of marriage and adulterous infractions of the marital pact:

> *His disciples say unto him, If the case of the man be so with his wife, it is not good to marry. But he said unto them, All men cannot receive this saying, except they to whom it is given. For there are some eunuchs, who were so born from their mother's womb; and there are some eunuchs, who were made eunuchs by men; and there are eunuchs, who have made themselves eunuchs for the kingdom of heaven's sake. He that is able to receive it, let him receive it.*

"Paul said much the same thing in his first letter to the Corinthians. In Chapter Seven verse 1 he says:

> *Now concerning the things about which ye wrote unto me, it is good for a man not to touch a woman.*

"Paul continues to say in verses 29, 32 and 33:

> *But this I say, brethren, The time is short; it remaineth that both they hath wives be as though they had none . . . But I would have you without care. He that is unmarried careth for the things that belong to the Lord, how he may please the Lord; but he that is married careth for the things that are of the world, how he may please his wife.*

"Did you catch that, brethren – that the time is short? We are all daily – no, hourly – expecting Jesus to bring us into His Church through the rapture." George scrunched up his red face to heaven in pleading expectation at that. "And hear the essence of what Jesus and Paul both said: that celibacy will bring us closer in our relationship with our God. In confirmation of that, I'll read to you what a giant of a Christian, Church Father Justin Martyr, had to say about that same subject in his first apology. I'm reading from a wonderful book entitled *Early Christian Fathers*, which was edited by Cyril C. Richardson. I'll make it available for any who would like to pursue this topic further. But to continue, I'll read from selected passages of Justin's apology, beginning with his quote from Matthew 19, which we addressed above:

> And: *"There are some who were made eunuchs by men, and some who were born eunuchs, and some who have made themselves eunuchs for the Kingdom of Heaven's sake; only not all are able to receive this."*

"Justin elaborates on the implications of this on proper Christian behavior:

> *But to begin with, we do not marry except in order to bring up children, or else, renouncing marriage, we live in perfect continence. To show you that promiscuous intercourse is not among our mysteries – just recently one of us submitted a petition to the Prefect Felix in Alexandria, asking that a physician be allowed to make him a eunuch, for the physicians there said they were not allowed to do this without the permission of the Prefect. When Felix would by no means agree to endorse the petition, the young man remained single, satisfied with the approval of his own conscience and that of his fellow believers.*

"Did you hear with the man said? And no less than Justin Martyr, a pillar of the Church. There you have it, brethren. Should we ask any less of ourselves than to follow the example of this rock-solid Christian who went way back as far as the middle of the Second Century A.D.? Turn now to your Bibles. Carl, please read First Corinthians 7, verses 1 and 8."

Carl stood at the command and read verse 1.

Now concerning the things about which ye wrote unto me, it is good for a man not to touch a woman.

He skipped to verse 8 as he was requested and read:

I say, therefore, to the unmarried and widows, It is good for them if they abide even as I.

"See there?" George screeched as Carl sat back down. "Did you catch the meaning behind that – the utter depravity of sex? But there's more, and much more. Jacob, you're our new man here. Stand up, please, and recite verses 32 through 35."

Jacob stood as instructed, reading the passages as pastor commanded:

But I would have you without care. He that is unmarried careth for the things that belong to the Lord, how he may please the Lord; but he that is married careth for the things that are of the world, how he may please his wife. There is difference also between a wife and a virgin. The unmarried woman careth for the things of the Lord, that she may be holy both in body and in spirit; but she that is married careth for the things of the world, how she may please her husband. And this I speak for your own profit; not that I may cast a snare upon you, but for that which is seemly, and that ye may attend upon the Lord without distraction.

With a frown directed toward George, Jacob closed his Bible and sat back down.

George returned the glare, exposing the whites of his eyes in outrage. Nudged by Moira, Jacob backed down and stared at the ground. Satisfied, George commented on the Bible passage. "You see clearly, don't you," he said, his eyes sweeping over the tiny crowd, "what the point is, here? We need our focus to be laser-sharp on God. Only then can we please Him. Pray together now that God will give you the necessary mind and discipline to live in obedience to that. I know you women are married, and so are no longer virgins – he spat this last out in disgust – but you certainly can behave like you are. The same goes for you men. I leave it to you to ponder over what you have learned today, and to back it up with your fervent prayers." George left the podium and self-importantly stalked off.

Moira was shocked at how George had cherry-picked those passages. When placed in the context of the surrounding verses, she knew, the message came out very different – softer by far, and, in places, virtually the exact opposite of how George intended to interpret this Scripture. Paul himself acknowledged that marriage was not sinful. Indeed, in that same text he had urged those who were married not to deny their spouses. He had even said there that it was better to marry than to burn. She looked around her, convinced that the faces of the others were depicting their burning. She arose to speak to them, but Jacob placed a firm hand on her arm, motioning for her to sit back down. "It's too early yet," he whispered in her ear. "Give it some time."

"Time? Do you see their faces? I don't think there's any time left!"

"Just a little patience, darling," he said. They both remained quiet until Elizabeth spoke up. "George is really depressing," she said to Moira.

"That's an understatement!" Moira replied. "And the bad thing about it is that George is not entirely wrong. He does have a point in calling out the depravity of sex. Back just before the Earthchange, sex was misused in the worst possible way. Women were treated like animals, as nothing more than sex objects for the gratification of men, many of whom were animals themselves. Human trafficking was rampant, enslaving girls and destroying their lives right and left. Kids were taught to explore their sexuality at an inappropriate age by a depraved educational system, removing their ability to pursue more normal childhood interests. The world was no better than Sodom and sinking beyond the capability of society to recover a semblance of normality."

"In his rants George is correct," she continued, "but only partially."

Like all truly vicious lies, it has an element of truth. But it isn't the complete truth. He speaks of the misuse of sex, not the manner that God intended for us to apply and enjoy this wonderful gift He created for us. God never intended us to live in total abstinence. If we did that, the human race wouldn't survive, of course. But there's more to it – much more. There's bad sex, but there's also good sex, and God Himself set the rules for making it good in the laws He gave Moses. In a one-man, one-woman relationship, sex fosters intimacy, cementing the loving bond between life partners. It also upholds the way we were designed in the image of the Holy Trinity, which is complementary otherness, where the partners operate as a well-oiled system without getting in each others' way or attempting to compete with each other. And then it supports the most basic of social relationships, the family. Did you notice the byproduct of all the sexual craziness that took place, the disintegration of the family?"

"Tell me more. Please."

Elizabeth's obvious interest in hearing about something that contradicted the Church policy surprised and encouraged Moira. Despite what she'd said to Jacob, she didn't expect to have it happen so quickly. Now she needed time to think, to get her ducks in a row. "Not here. Can we meet somewhere we'll have a little more privacy? Maybe after we've been here long enough to get accepted by most?"

"I hate to break this to you, Moira. You and Jacob have an uphill battle there. George and some of his cronies like to think of themselves as ultra-godly, but, truth be told, they seem kind of mean-spirited, at least to our friends. George for sure has no sense of humor. Tell him a joke and he'll frown, like you urinated on his shoes. To him, anything remotely funny is obscene."

Carl broke in, attempting to lighten up the conversation. "Don't worry. Elizabeth and I'll run interference for you, break the ice with our friends. If enough of us like you, George and his pals won't have much say in who stays and who doesn't. Won't we, Elizabeth?"

"I guess. Of course. I know – let's find out what your assignments will be. And where. Then we can show you around wherever it is."

The four of them went together to the bulletin board, where Moira found that she was assigned to the garden. "That's wonderful," Elizabeth spoke. "But we'll have to be careful. Privacy is in short supply there."

While she said that, Jacob looked at his assignment. "Looks like I'm going to be working out in the garden with a hoe," he said. "But Moira, you've also been given the task of carrying water up to the cave. That's hard labor. I promise that I'll help you with the job."

"Have you ever looked at an old National Geographic magazine?" she retorted. "Taken a look at the primitive men carrying spears, then looked at the primitive women with pots on their heads? You figure it out."

Elizabeth laughed at Moira's comeback while Carl frowned at Jacob's assignment. "I could sure use some help in the shop. I'll try to get that assignment changed. I have a feeling we'd work well together."

CHAPTER ELEVEN

The next day Jack approached George. "I'm not sure that new couple are keepers. I saw them talking with Carl and Elizabeth, and I have a feeling it was about your sermon. I don't think they were heaping praise on you. Carl's been more skeptical lately. I've been watching him and Elizabeth closely and I've seen them both frown at what I'd consider inappropriate times when you were delivering a sermon. I even saw Carl put his hand on Elizabeth's thigh, and he did it more than once. Now they look like they're getting tight with the two newbies."

"You could be right. I don't have such a good feeling about them either. But we may want them around a while to check out something on my mind. I have this terrible suspicion about the mountain over there," he said while pointing with his arm, "the highest one with what looks like a jungle on top."

"About what?"

"That maybe Jesus is there right now. Maybe He came back already."

"Why do you think?"

"I don't know. Just a feeling. No, more than that. There've been lots of changes to this world of ours, some not so bad. Look at the sky. Pretty clear. Clearer than before the shakeup. And when things started to get rough, remember that huge pipeline oil spill? That dismal event covered a lot of ground. And all those fires! Reminds me, as a matter of fact, of an old Calvin and Hobbes cartoon I came across once. It was a real sicko, I don't know how people could laugh at that kind of thing. The little brat was playing in his back yard, imagining an epic disaster that was being visited on Farmer Brown or whoever. As I recall, a train had derailed on the tracks next to his house, an airliner was diving out of control, and a huge earthquake was splitting the ground, creating a chasm that was heading directly toward his house. The poor farmer was going to get clobbered by everything at once. Talk about overkill. But look around. Do you see anything happening now? Or a lake of oil?"

"Yeah, but we've moved around some. We may not be close to it any longer."

"I know. But what about all those nuclear power plants that melted down? There was a huge number of them. I think by now we'd have run into at least one. But there again, I don't see anybody with symptoms of radiation. The world seems to have gotten better, if anything."

"Is that why we're grubbing around for food and living in caves? Thanks to you, we've been getting real close to God. I think He'd treat us better if He's really back."

"Perhaps. Maybe we can find out more from the newbies. If they have nothing else to offer, we can send them packing."

As Jacob was heading out to the garden, Carl came up to him with a beaming smile. "You're in, fella," he told Jacob. "I was able to get things changed around so that you'll be working with me. Come with me – I'll show you around your new digs."

The two men approached the lone, derelict-appearing shack that Jacob and Moira saw as they had first come into the compound. Carl opened the door for Jacob and closed it after they entered. The hovel consisted of one large room with a matching outsized fireplace in the middle of the far end. A stack of what looked to be galvanized water pipes covered the top half of the cavernous opening. A large clay pot was situated below. One tube came out of the fireplace piping and branched off into three smaller tubes, the ends of which were connected at the top to what appeared to be an old four-cylinder automobile engine. A complex-looking contraption sat on the top of the engine. An odd woven belt ran from a pulley attached to the engine to another pulley on the mechanism on top. Another pulley arrangement ran from the engine to an alternator. Electrical wires ran from the alternator to what looked to be an automobile headlight and from there through a hole in a wall to the outside.   Various smaller mechanical contraptions littered the room, some being faced with short benches.

"As you can see," Carl said as he walked over to the engine, "we're not quite finished with this baby." He pointed to a hole in the fourth cylinder that originally housed a spark plug. "We've built a lathe of sorts to marry the piping to the spark plug holes, but it's very hard work getting the threads right. We're doing okay so far with using just three of the four cylinders until the last coupling gets built. That's John's job, and it's a full-time one until that chore's done. You can hear him getting salty with his language from time to time."

"What's that tangle on top of the engine?" Jacob asked.

"That's our greatest achievement," Carl said proudly.   "For a while we were able to run the engine off the gas remaining in the tank, but that only lasted for a little while. We couldn't find any more gasoline, so we had to use a more primitive fuel – body fat from the coyotes and other little critters we've managed to kill for food – and switch from internal to external combustion, which means steam. "In order to convert the engine to run on steam, we had to remove the built-in camshaft and re-fashion it into a suitable shape before replacing it. The new profile of the cam lobes opens the intake and exhaust valves at the same time, on every upstroke of the pistons, which makes both valves for each cylinder act as exhaust valves for the steam. The pipe connected to the old spark plug port does the job of inputting steam to the cylinders during the downstroke of the pistons. Those T-valves at each port operated from the mechanism open to shove steam into the pistons at the beginning of their downstrokes. The mechanism is driven from that wheel that's connected by belt from the engine's crankshaft."

"Remarkable," Jacob murmured. "But does it actually work? And that's a pretty interesting belt. Where did you get that?"

"As for the belt, a few of the women have learned to weave those, and the ropes you saw, out of palm fronds. They've had to work very hard to get it right, but now they're very good at it. And yes, it does work. I'll show you." Carl went over to one of the small devices and sat down on its bench. He pedaled the treadle to turn a rock wheel. As the wheel turned, he held a stick against it. The end presently got hot enough to smoke, and then broke out into fire. He abruptly got up from the bench, went over to the pot in the fireplace, and thrust the burning torch onto the surface of the liquid inside. Presently the contents of the pot burst into flame, and Carl stood back, waiting for the fire to heat up the pipes.

After some time had elapsed, Carl touched a pipe, withdrawing it quickly in obvious pain. He opened a valve at the pipe's head. As Jacob watched, the pulley at the end of the engine's crankshaft began to turn. A hiss came forth from both sides of the engine, and dual clouds of steam escaped. The crankshaft began to turn more rapidly, accelerating until Carl tamped it back down by partially closing the valve at his hand. The headlight shone brightly.

"Amazing!" Jacob exclaimed.

"Only problem is," Carl responded, "we can't use it that often. It takes a bit of time-consuming work to extract the fat from the animals and we don't get all that much out of them. Sometimes we can use the wood from a palm tree, but I'm sure you've noticed that there aren't that many of them around, either. I'll shut it back down again till something important comes up." He grabbed a thin metal lid and placed it over the clay pot, dousing the flames.

"Come over here," Carl said, walking toward another wooden device with a bench seat and a foot-operated treadle that connected to a large stone wheel. "This is where I have in mind to put you to work, if you're up to it. We broke our only saw blade last week, and need to make another."

"Good," Jacob said. "I'll be more than happy to do something useful."

"Okay. Let's get the raw material." He went to a corner of the room and returned with a strip of sheet metal. "This came from the same car as the engine did. You'll want to cut teeth lengthwise along one edge. Too bad this metal's so soft, but it's all we have. Your work will be primitive and more irritatingly boring than if we had the proper tools and raw material, but we do what we can do with what we have to work with."

"I'm fine with that. I take it that while my feet make the wheel go round, I hold the edge of the sheet metal against the edge of the rock and make a triangle-shaped bite."

"That's the idea. Don't worry about making the teeth evenly-spaced like the saws you've seen before – before all this happened. The saw will be for cutting wood. Just do your best."

"I'm ready to do it. Thanks for the job."

"No—thank you. Oh, I forgot. Soft as that sheet metal is, it'll still wear out the rock pretty quickly. You won't be able to work with that rock if its corners are rounded. See that pipe over there?" he said, pointing to another corner of the building. That used to be the car's drive shaft. We've roughed-up the surface some. Every once in a while you'll need to put it on the edge of the wheel and dish out the rock to give it an edge."

"Got it." As Jacob set to work, Carl went to another device with a seat and a treadle, and went to work on some process that was obscure to Jacob. A few minutes passed in companionable silence, but a thought intruded upon Jacob's mind that moved him to speak to his new friend. "Hey, Carl," he called over to him.

"Yeah?"

"So your Church has started a new tradition."

"What's that?"

"Celibacy, as if you didn't know. Probably as if you haven't thought about it every minute of the day. There's a lot more to the issue than we've spoken of, particularly the implications of the direction your Church has taken. Have you given any thought to what the end result of that will be? If you maintain that tradition, guess what? Your Church will become extinct."

"Well, there is that. I never did go along with it. Elizabeth didn't either, as you know from her response to what Moira had told her. It's insane. The prevailing thought, though, is that we'll be raptured sooner than we'll die off. You witnessed yourself how our leadership has interpreted Scripture as saying that God would be pleased with our abstinence."

"I wouldn't be too sure about that interpretation, Carl. Have they ever thought that creation was designed to require, for continuity of life, a position in opposition to that notion? By the same God who gave us His Word in Scripture? Remember something: by the time of Jesus' first advent, Jewish tradition had gone so far off the rails that they didn't recognize Jesus as their long-awaited Messiah, despite the crystal-clear Scriptural representation of Him. They refused to understand the story of Joseph, and how his life had foreshadowed Jesus, or the real meaning behind the Passover that they so religiously observed, or David's Psalm 22, which spoke of crucifixion several hundred years before it became a punishment known by the Jewish people, or – and this is the most important of all – Isaiah 53, which identified the Christ who suffered on the behalf of mankind. And Isaiah was a prophet whom they revered.

"But getting back to the gender issue," Jacob continued, "you yourself know from Ephesians 5 that Jesus will marry the Church, and that the way Paul stated it, the marriage won't be trivial. Common sense tells us that if Jesus is sufficiently gendered as to enter into a marital relationship, and if Jesus is a Member of the Godhead, it directly follows that the other Members would be gendered as well. That's particularly the case since Jesus in John Chapters one, eight and elsewhere represented Himself as the image of the Father."

"I don't know, Jacob," Carl said, scratching his head. "It's hard for me to wrap my arms around the thought of God Himself being gendered. It goes against what we've been taught to think about God."

"Which is a terrible misunderstanding, Carl. First off, think about the way you and Elizabeth complement each other. You each have different tasks to do that are compatible with your different natures.

You don't get in each others' way and you don't get jealous over what the other is doing. Doesn't it make sense that the Father would want it that way between Himself and the Holy Spirit? Why should there be any confusion about what role each of them should play? You need complementary otherhood to grease the axles."

"That does make sense, I guess. But that's not enough to convince me that they're gendered."

"There's more. When you have time, pick up your Bible and read Exodus 40 and First Kings 8. Those passages speak of a cloud that came down and rested upon the wilderness tabernacle and Solomon's temple at their dedications. It was an indwelling of the temples by God, Carl. This manifestation of God was called the Shekinah Glory. But it was a precursor to another indwelling, that of the Holy Spirit on those who accepted Jesus Christ as their Lord and Savior. John spoke of it in his Chapter 3 as being born again."

"I understand that, but what does it have to do with gender? And what does the temple have to do with us?"

"In One Corinthians 3 and Ephesians 2, Paul claims that our own bodies are indwelt by the Holy Spirit as temples of God, so the Shekinah Glory and the Holy Spirit are one and the same. But the Shekinah Glory was always perceived as being feminine. If you look up the first verse in Proverbs 9, you see Wisdom as feminine claiming that She built Her house and has hewn out her seven pillars. Her house is the one built without hands, the temples of our bodies that are indwelt by Her. Revelation Chapter One reveals the Church as having seven spirits - pillars. This identifies the obviously feminine Wisdom with the Holy Spirit as well as the Shekinah Glory."

"That's deep, Jacob. Deeper than George."

"You can't put all the blame on George. By the time he went to seminary, they were handing out all kinds of misleading information to pastors-to-be. They were also redirecting the thrust of sermons from Gospel support to support of the Churches – things like Church growth and practical advice to the flocks for being healthy, wealthy and wise. But there's a lot more evidence in Scripture to suggest a feminine Holy Spirit.   What about Proverbs 8, where Wisdom tells us that She was at God's side as the world during the creation of the world?   Beyond that, several prophets in the Old Testament spoke of God in gendered terms as well. You've read Hosea. You know that God spoke of Israel to Hosea as being a harlot to Him – as an unfaithful wife. The allusion there to unfaithfulness is more than trivial, as can be seen by the graphic nature of the parallelism between illicit sexuality and the turning away from God. The same goes in passages found in Isaiah and Jeremiah."

CHAPTER TWELVE

While Carl and Jacob went off together to the derelict shack, Elizabeth took Moira's hand and, looking earnestly into her face, told her to say more in defense of her attitude about George's Bible study. Looking about for prying ears and peaking confidentially in a soft voice, she played the devil's advocate. "I haven't been very happy about this rule of ours, but I guess if Jesus Himself said that, it has to be true and we'll just have to live with it."

"No!" Moira responded quietly but vehemently. Despite Wisdom's caution to start out gently, she couldn't control herself over this misrepresentation of Scripture and of some early Christians' wrong interpretation of Jesus' words. And of their misinterpretation of Paul as well. "From my perspective, those cherry-picked statements from Scripture, isolated from the background context, say pretty much the opposite of what God intended. Particularly when they're applied to our Trinitarian Godhead. Have you ever wondered why, when God told Moses in Genesis 1:26 and 27 that mankind is made male and female in the image of God, that facet of our makeup is never discussed? Or why nothing is said about the nature of our beloved Holy Spirit? Or how the three Members of the Holy Trinity all seem to be the same – so much so that for centuries the modalist heresy continues to crop up, where the Holy Three are really a Holy One?"

"Are you saying that there's a better way to look at the way we are made in the image of God?"

"Of course! Go back to your Bible, to Matthew Chapter 19 again. God may have given some people the ability to treat their gender with such indifference, but He certainly didn't do so for most of us. Here, let me read to you verses 4 through 6:

And [Jesus] answered and said unto them, Have ye not read

97

that he who made them at the beginning, made them male and
female; and said, For this cause shall a man leave father and
mother, and shall cleave to his wife, and they two shall be one
flesh? Wherefore, they are no more two, but one flesh. What,
therefore, God hath joined together, let not man put asunder.

"Doesn't that sound like marriage is more God's Plan A for us than Plan B? As a matter of fact, to prove what I'm saying, let me go back further in Scripture all the way back to Genesis 2, verse 18:

And the Lord God said, It is not good that the man should be
alone; I will make him a help fit for him.

"Oh," Elizabeth said. She paused to think. "But there was a change in the New Testament. Remember George's quotes from Paul."

"The change from Old to New Testament never negated the earlier Scripture. Jesus promised that. George didn't tell the whole story by any means. As I said, he was cherry-picking to misdirect Scripture. Let me go to First Timothy Chapter 4. I'll read verses 1 through 4:

Now the Spirit speaks expressly that, in the latter times, some
shall depart from the faith, giving heed to seducing spirits,
and doctrines of demons, speaking lies in hypocrisy, having
their conscience seared with a hot iron, forbidding to marry,
and commanding to abstain from foods, which God hath
created to be received with thanksgiving by them who believe
and know the truth. For every creature of God is good, and
nothing is to be refused, if it is received with thanksgiving; for
it is sanctified by the word of God and prayer.

"Wow!" Elizabeth exclaimed. "That pretty much says the opposite of what George was trying to get across."

"Pretty much," Moira agreed. "It isn't the fault of Scripture. In being over-selective of what he quoted from the Bible, George failed to supply the context in which those passages were embedded. That's been a favorite ploy for centuries for those who wish to make the Bible say what they want it to say. For those of us who are healthily gendered, it is my belief that God intended for us to enjoy how He made us. If He made us that way, why should we turn our backs on our very natures?"

"There's more from Paul," Moira continued. "If you go back to First Corinthians Seven that George quoted verse 1 from, I'll continue from the very next verse:

> *Nevertheless, to avoid fornication, let every man have his own wife, and let every woman have her own husband. Let the husband render unto the wife her due; and likewise also, the wife unto her husband. The wife hath not power of her own body, but the husband; and likewise also the husband hath not power of his own body, but the wife. Defraud ye not one the other, except it be with consent for a time, that ye may give yourselves to fasting and prayer, and come together again, that Satan tempt you not for your incontinency. But I speak this by permission, and not by commandment. For I would that all men were even as I myself. But every man hath his proper gift of God, one after this manner, and another after that. I say, therefore, to the unmarried and widows, It is good for them if they abide even as I. But if they cannot have self-control, let them marry, for it is better to marry than to burn.*

A brief laugh escaped Elizabeth's lips. "Looking around at the men around here, they're real close to burning! And not just a few of the women as well."

"Paul puts it in perspective in Ephesians Chapter Five. There, he has much to say about the beauty of the marital relationship, and of its rightness. He then compares it with the Church's heavenly marriage to Jesus, which is of an even grander scale. It's that difference in greatness between the heavenly and material domains that Jesus and Paul implied in George's quotes."

"To tell you the truth," Elizabeth responded after looking around again to ensure their privacy, "this – enforced – abstinence is a recent thing, coming after that change in Jerusalem. We were all much happier before that. I think the real reason behind this rule is that our leaders are beginning to panic about our still being here unraptured. They're desperate to be obedient to God."

"I'm not sure you'll be so happy to hear this," Moira whispered back, "but taking the approach you people did was probably the worst thing you could have done as far as appealing to God is concerned."

"Yes, but the nature of Jesus is important. Don't you think our treatment of sex is less so? Jesus Himself, according to Scripture, abstained from having a relationship with a woman."

"The exercise of gender is absolutely not of little importance to God. The reality is quite the opposite. The reason that Jesus abstained from exercising His gender is that He was already betrothed to His wife-to-be, the Church. Paul made that very clear in Ephesians 5."

"Oh. That's a surprise. I don't think many people, pastors included, have thought about that." Elizabeth stopped talking to consider that new understanding. Then a frown clouded her features. "But we know that gender will be absent in heaven. Jesus made that clear in Matthew 22, and Paul did too, in Galatians 3. In our spiritual form, according to them, we won't marry and we won't be male and female any more."

"Oh, really? You, and I'm really talking about your Church here, have no understanding of what Scripture was really saying about gender in those passages. Take Matthew 22, for instance. Why did Jesus directly couple His statement that we won't marry in the spiritual domain with the statement that they didn't understand the power of God? Why would the loss of an attribute represent power?"

"Golly, I'd never thought of that. What's your take on it?"

"The answer is in Scripture. Specifically, in First Corinthians 12, as well as in other places. Of course, Paul's account of Jesus' marriage to His Church in Ephesians 5 utterly contradicts the notion of God being genderless. The Church simply failed to think things through. Does your ankle possess gender? How about your toenail? Or the hair in George's nose that needs quite badly to be plucked? Are those things sexual?"

"No, of course not. What does that have to do with God's view of sex?"

"Nothing. And everything. As Paul takes pains to tell us in First Corinthians 12, in our spiritual form we're just components of a much bigger body. We might not be gendered at the individual level, but as a composite, the Church is definitely feminine. It's probably the same situation with angels. Individually they're not gendered, or at least they aren't supposed to exercise it, because together as a multitude, they comprise the feminine Holy Spirit who Herself is married to the divine Will, the Holy Father."

Elizabeth paused again to think about what Moira had just said. Her head shot up suddenly. "Oh, my!" she exclaimed. "I just had a thought that fits in with what you said. Do you think that's why Solomon had seven hundred wives? Was he trying to represent the Jesus who will marry the Church?"

"Bingo. Remember that Solomon was given more wisdom than any person on Earth. That wisdom included the foreknowledge of Jesus and the Church. But what led to that foreknowledge was his understanding of that same relationship that existed between the Father and the Holy Spirit."

"Wow. I can't wait to pass on this information to Carl. Maybe it'll get things going again with us, despite the attitude of our Church." She looked at Moira with a hungry expression. "Maybe you or Jacob will stand guard outside his building on occasion while I come in to see what Carl's been working on."

Moira laughed. "Of course," she responded.

That night as they lay uncomfortably beside each other, separated by their individual pallets, Jacob leaned over to Moira. "Have you noticed something about this community?"

"What's that?"

"I don't see any children."

"What?" Moira raised up from her pallet and turned to him. A deep frown line bisected her forehead. "Well, duh. Kindly explain to me how this terrible sleeping arrangement supports the production of children."

"Oh. Yeah. But shouldn't there be some older children?"

"That depends on how long George has been holding sway over this community. Who knows how long he's been messing with their minds?" The question was purely rhetorical. She thought he'd been at it for a rather long time. While Moira thought about George, Jacob's thoughts went in an entirely different direction. His thoughts were occupied with the discomfort of their very basic bed, and of how he might improve things for Moira.

CHAPTER THIRTEEN

"Hey there, fella!" George called out to Jacob as he walked toward the shed. "Hold on a second, I want to talk to you." Jacob stood, waiting impatiently for George to catch up. *The man thinks he owns us all*, he thought to himself. *Like he's God's designated leader.*

"I'd like to know where you and the girl come from," George said when he came close.

"Why?" Jacob responded rather abruptly. *Condescending too. Moira wouldn't particularly care to be called a nameless girl.*

"Well, you sound like an American. Are you? I mean, were you?"

"I was. I was also an Israeli more recently. Moira always was. An Israeli, I mean. See that mountain over there?"

"The one that looks like a jungle on top?" *What does this man know about it?*

"Yes. Apparently, we haven't moved very far since the Earthchange. We could see it then, and we can still see it now. It's different than it was, of course."

George cut to the chase without additional preamble. "What do you know about it?"

"Not much. I never went there, before or after. Moira had been there, but only before. We kind of get the feeling that Jesus is there."

George's stomach dropped. "You mean right now?"

"Yes." A voice intruded in his mind. "Don't tell him yet. He's not ready for that," Wisdom cautioned in a wordless communication.

"I don't know for sure," Jacob continued with George. "Moira and I are still here. I'd like to think that if Jesus had come back, we would be up there instead of here."

"Amen," George breathed, somewhat relieved by Jacob's equivocation. "Well, continue with what you were doing," he said, and left. He had his doubts about whether Jacob and Moira would fit into the community, but sensed that they had made so many friends by this time that it might be unpleasant for him if they were to be told to leave.

George had indeed been preaching to his congregation for a long time. But that itself was but a tiny fraction of the time it took to cause his obsessive pursuit of purity in the worship of God. For him, the most urgent task of achieving that purity was to remove all thoughts involving gender from the people he led.

Perhaps George's wrong notion that purity was equivalent to chastity was an influential factor in taking his mental engine off the rails and down the cliff into the lowlands of false worship. But he got a big push in that direction from other causes, one of which was the desire on the part of godless intellectuals to create a global government, and the evil nature of the one-world governmental system that fulfilled their passion for control.

CHAPTER FOURTEEN

Jack came back beaming with pride. He held an ersatz sack in his right hand. It looked empty, but his face said otherwise. "I got something!" he said to the nearest people. He reached into the sack, extracting a tiny creature, and held it up for all to see.

Bill looked at it skeptically. "Back in the States before the big blowup, I'd recognize that as some rich woman's rat dog," he said. Several of his friends started laughing.

"What is it?" another asked. "Looks like a mole to me. A tiny underfed one. It might as well be a beetle."

"Which I'd rather eat than that ugly thing."

"Can you cut it with a knife?"

"Only a real sharp one."

"What's the point of cutting it?"

Jack was crushed. Never a good hunter, he was more than happy to have gotten anything at all.

"If it wasn't so disgusting looking, I'd be tempted to eat it myself," a female onlooker said. "On the other hand, I doubt if it would be more than a little swallow." The laughter grew louder as Jack's face grew redder.

Jacob turned to Moira. "Actually, there's not much of a selection of food around here," he said out of the side of his mouth. "I'm so hungry for something different, I could eat a snake."

"Funny you should mention that," she replied. "Remember Jerry, back when you first met me?"

"How could I forget? The guy thought he owned you. A creepy sort, he was."

"He did end up that way with me. But there was a time when I felt compassion for him. I think that's what got him to thinking we had a special relationship."

"What does that have to do with snakes?"

"It was what brought on the compassion. One day we took a day off and decided to get away from the crowds. We rode out to the countryside in a bus and got out in the middle of nowhere. We climbed into our backpacks and started hiking up to a nearby hill. We got about halfway up when Jerry got bitten by a viper. His health went downhill faster than we could, but we finally managed to get back down to the bus stop. He didn't get stung by a scorpion like your friend did back in the United States, but this snake bite had a neurotoxin in it, so it was very dangerous. I kept praying that he'd have a miraculous healing like Paul did in his perilous journeys. But it wasn't to be. In fact, what happened next was quite the opposite."

"What happened?"

"He sat on a big rock, all miserable and swelling as I tried to shade him from the sun. As he sat on the rock another snake came up and bit him on the finger."

"You have to be kidding!"

"No, and we had to wait like it seemed hours before the bus came. All the while we waited his pain got worse and worse. Then he passed out. I thought he might be dead."

"That must have been a long ride back to civilization."

"That's the only good thing that happened that day. The bus driver had a radio, and he called in an emergency. A 'copter met us within fifteen minutes and rushed Jerry to the hospital, where they quickly gave him a dose of antivenom. A doctor told me later that it was a matter of minutes whether he lived or died. During his recovery we became closer. But apparently not as close as he expected."

"I thank God for that," he breathed.

"So do I," she murmured.

"How's that?"

"It kind of quickened the pace with you," she said laughing.

CHAPTER FIFTEEN

As Jacob and Moira had discovered earlier, the Earthchange had taken pastor George over the cliff into full-blown cultism. He and his little herd were primed for the rapture. Fortunate as they were to endure the violence the Earth had wrought against itself, they correctly perceived from the beauty and activity in the mountain in the distance it was a revamped Jerusalem and that Jesus had come again and was residing there. They were keenly disappointed that they apparently had missed the rapture, and George took steps to regain the grace of God upon his community. He attempted to do so by prohibiting any and all sexual communication, forcing the community into abstinence. He had enough supporters to carry out this drastic edict.

The first Sunday after the arrival of Jacob and Moira to their primitive community, standing in his little cube in a corner of the mess hall defined by thatched, withered palm fronds, Pastor George looked up to heaven once more and scrunched up his eyes with all the might that his soft facial muscles could muster. *Please, Lord,* he begged. *Let it be today.* Our rapture *must* happen soon, he thought. He vowed that today's message would be more serious than the last, perhaps finally evoking from his people the necessary fear to make things happen with God as they should.

At the appointed hour, Pastor George stood behind his makeshift podium and looked out at the congregants with grave intent. To Moira on the audience side of the podium, his demeanor was a wet, red-faced pout. He looked like he was about to whine for a pacifier. At that moment she had a clear understanding of the difficult work with this crowd that lay ahead for Jacob and her.

"People," he began loudly. Intended as a bark, the high-pitched voice turned it into a yap. "We are sinners in the hands of an angry God." He continued the plagiarism of Jonathan Edwards by thrusting out his palms and turning them downward as if to drop the people down to hades. "You may be maintaining your celibacy as I'm certain you are, but I know your filthy minds. You think daily, no, minute by minute, of sexual indulgence." Moira thought that she had a pretty good idea where that condemnation came from. She leaned over to Jacob and whispered in his ear, "Pastor is pretty sure he knows our thoughts. Doesn't that speak volumes about his own thoughts in that regard?" Jacob snickered as George continued to speak.

"Remember the words of our Lord Jesus in Matthew 5: 'Ye have heard that it was said by them of old, Thou shalt not commit adultery; but I say unto you that whoever looketh on a woman to lust after her hath committed adultery with her already in his heart. And if thy right eye offend thee, pluck it out, and cast it from thee; for it is profitable for thee that one of thy members should perish, and not that thy whole body should be cast into hell.'"

He paused for effect. "Obedience!" he squeaked with fervor. "We must bring even our thoughts into obedience to God! How else will we attain that happy state of heavenly companionship with Jesus?"

The expected fervent concurrences of "Amen, brother" never arrived. His audience remained grim-faced and restless. Without realizing it, he had brought their present distress to the forefront of their minds. Hoping to verbally beat them into submission to his message, he continued to harangue them with their obvious disobedience, which, he was convinced, would cast them into hell unless they repented immediately. The problem with that, of course, was that he was an integral part of "them". At the completion of his lengthy sermon, the congregation breathed a collective sigh of relief, an action that he failed to notice.

Elizabeth moved to rise from her seat, but Moira grasped her arm. "Stay here for a while," she said. "I have something important to say to you both," to which Jacob confirmed with an "Amen, sister."

"I want to continue with the conversation Elizabeth and I had a little while back," Moira began. "Pastor's kind of correct, but not entirely. Jesus does ask for our obedience, and He did indeed talk about lustful thoughts and adultery. Where pastor is very wrong is that this 'lust' doesn't extend to the perfectly acceptable, even encouraged, sexual feelings between those who are married to each other. What I'm trying to say is that for millennia the Church has misled Christians – celibacy between married couples is acceptable to God only if they both agree that their voluntary devotion to God is so infinitely more important to them than their feelings for each other that such feelings need to be cast aside. Of course, that implies that they never should have married in the first place. I can't speak for God, but – oh, wait, I guess I can do that – yes, I can indeed tell you that God would prefer you to exercise your marital rights in the manner that He designed you as male and female. Remember what God said in Genesis 2:18:

> *And the Lord God said, It is not good that the man should be alone; I will make him an help fit for him.*

"I think that Moira just heard from our Wisdom," Jacob broke in. "Wisdom being God and all."

"Are you telling us that not only is our celibacy not only not helpful, but that it may actually be hindering our relationship with God?"

"I'll let you answer that yourself, Elizabeth. Does your present devotion to God take away your feelings for Carl?"

"Oh, boy, I don't think so. In fact, all I can think about most of the time is what Carl and I are missing."

"I think that answers your question. You weren't made to be celibate. I don't think Carl was either."

"Amen to that, sister! So where did that disparagement of sex come from?"

"The short answer is the Church. Ever since that attitude was cast in concrete at the Council of Nicea, we've all been misled about it. And look what happened with all the sexual abuse of children that's been going on in the Church for the past how many years. But the long answer is deeper than that, and goes way back to the Garden of Eden. It involves the role within the Godhead of the feminine Holy Spirit, and the way God designed mankind in His image as male and female, just as Moses said in Genesis 1:26 and 27. The role of the Holy Father within the Godhead is that of the initiator, the divine Will. The corresponding function of the Holy Spirit is to respond to that will by giving birth to its implementation. The result is the glory of Creation, Jesus Christ, the Son of the divine Father and the divine Mother. Our own gendered natures are patterned after that attribute of God."

"Well, that's a revelation," Elizabeth mused. "It puts God into an entirely different perspective. A much warmer one."

"Yes. There's more coming, the root of the problem: the real sin of Adam and Eve was a role-reversal. In responding to the serpent instead of her husband Adam, she instantly committed adultery. Almost as bad, in giving the fruit to Adam to eat, she played the role of the initiator rather than the responder. Adam wasn't clean in this either. In accepting Eve's offer of the fruit, Adam became the responder rather than the initiator, another role-reversal. Of course, the overlying shadow of evil in this is the disobedience of Adam and Eve against God in their obedience to Satan. The fruit itself was the punishment. In partaking of the tree of the knowledge of good and evil, something caused them to be ashamed of sex. Perhaps they were able to see into the future and, to their horror, observe how greatly mankind deviated from the way God designed sex to be enjoyed, and consequently how evil that deviation became. That's only my own opinion, but I think it holds water, because look at how Moses described the difference between their attitudes before and after they took of that fruit."

"Here's the bottom line," Jacob broke in. According to Genesis 2:23 through 25, God tells us through Moses that before their temptation, they had no shame of sex:

And Adam said, This is now bone of my bone and flesh of my flesh; she shall be called Woman, because she was taken out of man. Therefore shall a man leave his father and his mother,

*and shall cleave unto his wife; and they shall be one flesh.
And they were both naked, the man and his wife, and were not
ashamed.*

"According to Genesis 3:7 through 11, after they took of the fruit,
their attitude changed dramatically:

*And the eyes of them both were opened, and they knew that
they were naked; and they sewed fig leaves together and they
made themselves aprons. And they heard the voice of the Lord
God walking in the garden in the cool of the day: and Adam
and his wife hid themselves from the presence of the Lord God
among the trees of the garden. And the Lord God called unto
Adam, and said unto him, Where art thou? And he said, I
heard thy voice in the garden, and I was afraid, because I
was naked; and I hid myself. And [God] said, Who told thee
that thou wast naked? Hast thou eaten of the tree, whereof I
commanded thee that thou shouldest not eat?*

"The tragedy of this," Jacob said, "is that for the several thousand
years since that time, even to today, the shame of sex has been with
us. It was formalized in the Church by the Church Fathers at the time
of Constantine, even to the extent that Scripture itself was tampered
with by the switching of the Holy Spirit's gender to either weakly
masculine or neuter. And the result? It alienated us from God."

"And we're suffering because of it, and because of our misguided
pastor. I think Elizabeth and I'll take a walk. A long walk. Come
along, Beth." She complied with a smirk, and they left rather
abruptly.

After they were gone, Jacob and Moira remained in the mess
area, strategizing on their next move, particularly on who they
would contact next with their message. They didn't realize it at the
time, but their further involvement wasn't necessary. One quick
glance at the faces of Carl and Elizabeth after they returned from
their walk was sufficient for the rest of the community to grasp what
had happened. All they needed to know next was how to reconcile
Pastor George's stern message with the couple's content demeanor.
Pastor George grasped this new reality rather quickly, and demanded

Carl and Elizabeth's presence in his "office".

"Explain yourselves," he croaked. "Not ten minutes after my sermon, and you caved in to your baser instincts. Utterly without shame."

"You're absolutely correct, pastor," Carl said. "We are without shame, because there's no reason to be burdened with it. The shame is on you for getting it all wrong. God never wanted us to deny what is a natural attribute of ours."

"What?" Pastor George shrieked. He jumped up and pulled a book off a makeshift shelf. "Listen to what your theological better had to say about that, one of our revered early Church Fathers. I quote the famed Justin Martyr on that subject:

"About continence, Jesus said this: 'Whoever looks on a woman to lust after her has already committed adultery in his heart before God.' And: 'If your right eye offends you, cut it out; it is better for you to enter into the kingdom of Heaven with one eye than with two to be into eternal sent fire.' And: 'Whoever marries a woman who has been put away from another man commits adultery.' And: 'There are some who were made eunuchs by men, and some who were born eunuchs, and some who have made themselves eunuchs for the Kingdom of Heaven's sake; only not all are able to receive this.'

"And so those who make second marriages according to human law are sinners in the sight of our Teacher,'" George droned on. "and those who look on a woman to lust after her.'" With that he glared angrily at the couple before his desk. "'For he condemns not only the man who commits the act of adultery, but the man who desires to commit adultery, since not only our actions but our thoughts are manifest to God. Many men and women now in their sixties and seventies who have been disciples of Christ from childhood have preserved their purity; and I am proud that I could point to such people in every nation.'"

His mouth bunched up in a stern pout and he hardened his glare. "What do you have to say to that?" He continued reading before they could respond.

Carl spoke up in response anyway, raising his voice above George's. "I heard a lot of the word "adultery," pastor. Please explain how a relationship between a man and his wife constitutes adultery. Besides, I've heard something about Justin Martyr and the environment in which he lived. There was so much abuse of sex in that society that it couldn't help but affect his thinking on the subject. You mentioned shame. Martyr was afflicted with it as a result of the fall of mankind in the Garden. We all are, to some extent. You certainly are, but we don't blame you. The shame came as a result of the role reversal of Adam and Eve. Instead of behaving in the image of God, they each did the opposite. Eve played a man's role in initiating the eating of the fruit, and Adam played the woman's role in responding to Eve. That role-reversal violated their type of the Godhead."

"Are you trying to suggest that the Godhead includes a woman? How dare you! Eyes bulging, he rose abruptly out of his seat and thrust his hand forward, pointing a shaking finger at Carl. "You're not only disobedient, you're a heretic. You'll stand before a court of your peers, mister, and you'll leave these premises under a cloud of shame. That goes for you as well, Elizabeth. May God have mercy on both of your souls. Now get away from me."

Carl told Jacob about the pastor's confrontation with them, saying that he and Elizabeth stood a good chance of getting banished from the community.

"But that could be a death sentence!" Jacob said. They both sat down, thinking on how they might change the pastor's mind. In the meantime, however, the women flocked around Elizabeth, eagerly trying to acquire the details of their bold and very happy move to go against the pastor's sermon. Elizabeth repeated to them the account of shame people had been burdened with since the fall in the Garden, and the explanation Jacob and Moira had given for the Church's misunderstanding of God's intent for their gendered creation. The explanation included the truth about the feminine gender of the Holy Spirit, a revelation that sent a ripple of shock throughout the crowd.

But mostly the womenfolk were angry at the loss of relationships with their husbands. Leaving Elizabeth, they sought their husbands to tell them the truth. By evening, the entire community was on the verge of mutiny. Sensing this, Pastor George wisely refrained from stirring them further, dropping his objective of casting Carl and Elizabeth from their congregation. For now.

For the next several days, Jacob and Moira happily saw a new warmth and contentment among the people in the community.

God's intervention with the Earthchange was so violent that lives were threatened everywhere. George's survival along with his loyal followers had embedded ever more firmly in his mind the utter sexual depravity of mankind. After all, he had observed, if only second-hand through the media, the unmentionable depravity of the world about him that had bolstered his conviction that there was nothing good about gender. But now he was confronted with a new threat to his survival, at least as a pastor. It was no time to rock the boat.

In his next sermon George departed for the time being from his weekly rant about gender. He decided to return to another topic that had captured his attention back before the Earthchange. The blatant falsehood of the evolutionary theory was largely irrelevant now, but it did demonstrate the corruption that was so rampant in the old days.

"Fraud and abuse without restraint!" George screamed in conclusion of the sermon as his point was made. "What else could we expect from a thoroughly corrupt scientific establishment?" Shaking his head, he waved dismissal to the crowd and sat down, peering at the ground at what might have been one of the many bugs that co-inhabited the area. Had they not been so evil-tasting, they would have been gone by now.

"He's spot on about what he said," Carl said to Elizabeth as they headed back toward the cave. "I wish he'd continue focusing on topics like that instead of the gender issue, but that's probably too much to hope for. Even if he did, he might give some thought about being more up-to-date. The false narrative of the evolutionists has been overtaken by events since the return of Jesus to Earth. But it is interesting. I happened to do some reading on the subject myself. The so-called 'scientists' were not above perpetuating a myth to turn laypeople away from Christianity, and they were blatant about their falsehoods. They disliked the thought of a God so much that they even attempted to brainwash themselves into believing that some day a true link would show up. That never happened, of course."

Chapter Sixteen

One day as Carl opened the shop door, he saw Jacob standing in front of him with his arms outstretched. "Magnificent!" Carl told him as Jacob proudly displayed the completed saw. Beaming with pride, Jacob asked Carl for permission to make something on his own. "It's something I'd like to make for Moira," he said. It shouldn't take too long, and her birthday is in just a few weeks, if I figure right about the time it took for the Earthchange to end."

"Go right ahead, but I suspect the Earthchange might still be going on. At least George hopes so."

Jacob finished his new project one day a few weeks later. *Whenever her birthday actually is,* he thought, *we'll make it tonight.* That evening he snuck his present up to their place in the cave and prepared it for Moira's return. When she came in for the night, he was already in their bed, awaiting her gasp of surprise.

Moira gasped indeed, but her surprise was one of shock and pain as the bed collapsed and a splinter entered her arm, just missing an artery. "What did you do?" she cried.

"I thought I was giving you a gift. I'm so sorry. I'll fix it tomorrow."

"No you won't. Jacob, I love the thought, but you're not mechanically-inclined. You never were. You break things. I'm surprised that Carl hasn't found that out yet."

"Thanks for the encouragement."

Holding her wounded arm, she hugged him. "You have other qualities, darling. They more than make up for your basic klutziness."

Mollified somewhat, Jacob picked up the pieces of the ersatz bed and tossed them out of the cave. *I wonder what that bed looked like,* Moira thought, a touch of mirth entering her mind. *Maybe it's best I'll never know.*

The next morning Carl came into the shed. He looked dubiously at the pile of wood that Jacob had brought in. He couldn't see any function to it, despite his attempt to picture what it would have looked like if assembled. He decided not to ask, figuring that it might be best not to know anything about it.

"You're up and about early this morning," he said to the other man. "Ready to start a new project?" From his countenance, Jacob was more than ready to start something new.

"We'll put your saw to use in making you another tool – something that will give you something in common with the other men. How do you feel about joining a hunting party?"

"I'd be honored."

"Good. We usually take turns at it. Three or four of us go out at one time. We're usually after coyotes, but once in a while we come onto a 'possum, or even a rabbit. They're a real treat, much better than those tough, gamy coyotes. We'll be making you a bow. I'll help."

As Jacob soon learned, there wasn't much wasted of the coyotes they'd caught. Seeing that by the time an animal was given to Carl that the section devoted to organs was an empty cavity, he wondered idly whether the entrails were used as well. He decided that they weren't, a big mistake as he'd find out later.

That evening there was a commotion in the mess hall. After the prayers were given and the community began to eat, Peter held back. He frowned at his plate. Sitting next to him his wife Jane looked over at him, studying his eyes. Her expression turned from placid acceptance to one of alarm. Understanding her attitude, Peter attempted to take a bite. The spoonful never reached his mouth. Instead, his face turned red and sweat broke out on his forehead. Shouting "I can't do this any more!" he jumped up from the table, throwing his fork onto his plate. A sea of eyeballs followed the frantic movement of his head. "Squash!" he continued. "Nothing but squash!" His agonized yell descended into a moan. He brought his hands up to his eyes, wiping away copious tears. Jane stood up with as much dignity as she could muster and took his arm, moving him away from the table. As they left, she picked up his plate and took it over to Jacob and dumped the contents onto his plate. Jacob, troubled by compassion for Peter and guilt over his desire for the squash, forked it over to Moira, who was more than ready to eat it herself.

In the meantime, Jane attempted to comfort her husband. In their less than private conversation, she ended up telling him he was too skinny already and insisted that he can't give it up. In angry response, Peter stamped his foot, grabbed back his plate, and forked his squash from Moira's plate back onto his just as she was about to eat it.

"That's not the first time that's happened," Carl commented to Jacob under his breath. It's a periodic event, as a matter of fact." People began clapping at Peter who, still red-faced, resumed eating with an expression of disgust.

Jacob enthusiastically took to his new task of fashioning a bow. His saw was put to use under Carl's supervision in cutting the dried thigh and leg bones to fashion the arms of the bow. The pelvis was cut and shaped to serve as the hand-hold and arrow rest at the center of the device. Once these pieces were formed, they were assembled together and connected by sinews that had been greased to retain some flexibility and give them a spring-like quality.

He shaped the bone with loving care, sharpening his sheet-metal knife frequently and using it to shave and carve. The shaping task took several days of full-time effort. He frequently compared the emerging shape with Carl's bow. When he was finally satisfied with the result, he set to work smoothing it with a succession of files, from coarse to fine. Where the bone widened out near the center hand-hold, he carved an intricate heart and arrow, inserting the inscription "M+J" in the center. On the opposite side, he carved two hearts that intersected each other. On the top heart he inscribed a "F" for Father, and on the bottom a "M" for Mother. Where they intersected he carved a "J" for Jesus. He strung the bow with a sinew that Moira had furnished. He was admiring his handiwork when Carl came into the building.

"Done?" Carl asked.

"I think so," Jacob replied.

Having observed the progress on the bow with a touch of surprise at Jacob's uncharacteristic precision, Carl had anticipated the next phase of the task. He carried a bundle of slim wooden sticks under one arm and a bag under the other. Jacob peered inside the bag, seeing feathers mixed with what looked like rock shards. "Arrows," Carl said economically. "In the rough. Let's get started on them."

"Dang it," Jacob moaned, two broken halves of a shaft in his hands. He spit out the sinew binding string in his mouth. "I can't seem to get the hang of assembling these things. Doing any better?"

"No. Truth be told, I ended up asking Elizabeth to do the job for me. Women seem to have finer hand-eye coordination, or just better control over their hands. Whatever. Maybe you'd best take these parts up to Moira tonight."

The next morning after breakfast, Jacob and Carl came back into the building together. Jacob proudly held two completed arrows in his hand. Carl immediately picked up a large handful of straw and walked it over to the far end of the building. He continued the process until he was satisfied that arrows shot into the mass would remain there. With a measure of excited anticipation, Jacob picked up his new bow, nocked an arrow, and, when Carl got out of the way, proceeded to draw back the bow.

"Forget that for now," Carl told hm. "Finish the arrows first. You'll have plenty of time to practice after that's done."

When they had finished with the bow and had made a dozen arrows, Carl set up a target in the shop to shield Jacob from the inevitable good-natured ridicule that went with learning to shoot. "No!" Carl called. "That's not the way you do it. Hold on, Jacob." Carl walked over beside Jacob and placed his arms on the other man's shoulders. "You don't face the target," he said, turning Jacob to a position at right angles to the target. He proceeded to instruct Jacob on proper stance, head position and other useful procedures.

CHAPTER SEVENTEEN

A month after his archery equipment had been completed, Jacob joined Carl and two others on his first hunt. At first he followed behind Carl, learning his methods. After a few hours he set off on his own with the intent of adding to the search territory. He caught sight of a coyote, whose track took Jacob into a small canyon formed by a haphazard arrangement of very large rocks. As he turned a corner, he was astonished to see a much larger animal than he had expected, a creature that appeared to be like an antelope. He slowly backed off around a corner of the rock and drew his bow back sharply. Coming back around the rock, he released his arrow, which sunk into the beast's neck, drawing blood. The animal attempted to run away, but after a few hundred yards, trailing a stream of blood that increased in breadth, it slowed and then stopped. Seconds later, its knees dropped and sank into the sandy soil, and then it toppled over, dead.

Knowing that this was the first time a hunter from their community had encountered an animal larger than a coyote, Jacob sank to his own knees and gave fervent thanks to God. After much struggle, he managed to drape the animal over his shoulders and marched triumphantly out of the rock formation. He trudged back toward their camp and called to the others, the nearest of whom told him to shut up and stop scaring away the game. But when he came into view, James stopped cold in amazement. A broad grin came to his mouth and he began to shout, a series of three piercing screams, the signal for the others to come. Jacob received a number of exultant slaps on his backside. They broke camp and, taking turns carrying the animal, returned to the community.

As they arrived at the compound, Jacob dropped the animal, ran to the barn and emerged seconds later with a primitive shovel. He returned to the group and enthusiastically started digging a hole in the soft, sandy soil.

"What's that for?" Carl asked warily.

Without replying, Jacob quickly drew his knife and cut open the belly, proudly scooping the insides into the hole as if he was a seasoned hunter.

"Aw, no! A man cried. Jacob looked up to see them peering down at him with horror on their faces. In their distress, they completely forgot who had bagged the game. "You don't do that!" the same man said, anger in his voice. "We need those parts! We need everything in that animal, you turd!"

Some women came into the meanly staring group. With a sigh of resignation one of them dropped to her knees and began to remove the intestines, handing them up to another woman, who looked with repulsion, not at the entrails but at their coating of dirt. They did their best in a largely-unsuccessful attempt to remove the grit while other women approached the animal with knives and began the process of cutting it up.

"What on Earth are they doing now?" Jacob said to Carl as they both watched the process. The women had slit the intestines and were digging into the poop.

"Looking for seeds. That's where our 'coffee' comes from. Maybe they'll even find something that we'll be able to grow. Wouldn't you like to have something besides squash? I know I would, and you can see that they would, too."

A celebration followed, one in which the others had continued to conveniently forget who had dropped the animal and ignored Jacob. Stung by the rejection, he went alone into the barn, where he decided to finish off a tool he had been working on.

Before Jacob could appraise his work in much-needed satisfaction of a job well-done, his attention was diverted by a loud metallic commotion where the alternator was located.

He loosened the adjustment bolt and pulled back on the alternator, quelling the screeching of the belt, and tightened the bolt with his wrench. He stood back in satisfaction, but as soon as he did the wrench fell out of his hand, almost like it had been yanked away. The falling wrench landed first on the alternator, making abrupt contact with the two wires and shorting out the device. The gravely-injured alternator protested with a shower of sparks that stopped abruptly, to be replaced by thick, black smoke.

Jacob looked down at the black soot coming out of the vents of the now-useless alternator in smoking wisps. The lamp inside the barn no longer glowed, but stood in blank dark accusation of this latest debacle.

Carl chose that moment to come into the barn. "Jacob?" he asked. "Where are you? What happened to the light?"

"Over here, Carl. I guess I'm in hot water again. I fried the alternator."

"Aw, no," Carl responded. "What happened?"

"I was trying to tighten the belt, and a wrench slipped out of my hand and shorted out the terminals."

Carl attempted to maintain civility, but his voice betrayed his anger at Jacob. "You're not having a good day, are you? I don't need to tell you how rare these things are, and how careful you must be around them. As a matter of fact, I do have another one, but that's all. After that, if it happens again, the whole system will be nothing but junk, all that work for nothing. You do understand that, don't you?"

"Yes," Jacob replied sheepishly. Jacob's catch of the big animal was completely forgotten.

"Okay, I'll get the last one. Stand back and watch me do the replacement, but don't touch a thing." He went to a corner of the barn, dug around, and returned with another alternator, which he proceeded to fasten to the structure. He tightened the belt and watched as the lamp in the barn returned to a glow.

"You really did it to the old one," he said to Jacob as he picked the useless, smoke-blackened alternator. He hurled it into a trash heap on the floor.

That night Jacob sought comfort in Moira's arms. He desperately wished for the comfort to include physical solace, but privacy was lacking. Among the numerous eyes on them, many were openly hostile. "I really blew it today," he whispered in her ear. "Are you sure you weren't there behind my back, playing another prank on me?"

"Promise. I'm truly sorry about that, Jacob. It's ironic about that, considering what you did earlier on the hunt. As a matter of fact, the antagonism began almost immediately after your almost-heroic catch of that big animal, whatever it is. That makes me almost certain that Wisdom had something to do with it, maybe because your head was starting to grow."

"Maybe so," Jacob reflected. "I hadn't thought about that."

"Well, seeing as there's nothing else we can do right now, I guess it's best that we try to get some sleep and hope for a better day tomorrow."

As Jacob lay on his mat with eyes wide open and trying to tamp down his misery, Moira next to him began to chuckle.

"What's so funny?" Jacob looked over to her in the darkness. "You're not laughing at me, are you?"

"Yes, in a way I am. But in a good way. Maybe there's a bright side to all of this. Could be that the people here looked up to you – us – more than they should. Maybe we made them a little bit uncomfortable with our knowledge of God. If nothing else, they'll see you as a human being complete with warts, and they'll all be more friendly with you. I was just thinking of that incident you told me that Earl had shared with you. The one that Cindy had told Earl's wife Joyce about on the boat. Apparently when Cindy and Stephen were living aboard their boat at the dock they had a neighbor who was somewhat officious and overbearing. Pompous, kind of like George. Of all the boats at the dock, his was the most impeccably maintained. Neat as a pin, always shipshape. What made it worse was that he was a sailor's sailor. His seamanship was faultless. In fact, every Fourth of July he'd patrol the bay looking for violators of marine law. He'd always catch a drunk or two. Everybody else on the dock respected him, but they were also uncomfortable around him.

"One day," Moira continued, "it dawned on this guy Jack that he had no friends. He tried to correct the situation by having a dock party, so he invited all his neighbors to dinner. He'd supply the chicken. The next day all his neighbors crowded around the dock next to his boat in their deck chairs as he stood above them, presiding over his large, beautiful, immaculate stainless-steel propane barbecue. Wine glass in one hand and lit match in the other, he reached over to open the propane valve.

"But the propane valve was already open. He'd opened it before when he'd interrupted the sequence by opening his wine bottle. The opening took a long time, way too long. When his match drew near there was a loud boom like a bomb had exploded, and the lid of his barbecue took off into space with what must have been close to exit velocity. There he stood, all red-faced, his arms, his eyebrows and much of the hair on his head gone with the lid. His persona had changed somewhat, his scorched shirt bearing ugly witness that he had been stripped of his godhood. But it wasn't all bad, you see. He made some friends that day, as they realized that he actually was one of them. Maybe the same thing will happen to you, Jacob. I truly hope so."

Jacob was able to sleep after Moira's tale, recalling Earl's laughter as he told his friend about the epic event. But the next day wasn't better. In fact, it was unthinkably bad. Elizabeth came running up to the barn where Carl and Jacob were working, red-faced and out of breath. "Jacob!" she screamed. "Moira's hurt!" Startled, both men looked up to see tears streaming down her face.

"How bad?" Jacob asked.

"It's awful! She fell out of the cave entrance and landed on the ground below. Her head hit a rock."

"Is she awake?" he asked, fear distorting his features.

"No," she wailed. "She's not even moving!"

Jacob jumped up and ran out the door. By the time he reached Moira, who lay motionless on the ground, he was out of breath. He didn't notice. What he saw was a large bloody gash on her forehead. With rising panic, he saw an ominous dent in her skull.

Moira never regained consciousness. They buried her the next day as Jacob looked on in denial and anger, grief flooding his being as reality periodically penetrated through. *Why her? he asked over and over. Why not me?* He expected Wisdom to respond, but She didn't. He remained alone in his suffering.

Chapter Eighteen

Elizabeth's eyes followed Jacob's back as he trudged away from the encampment, bent over like an old man. "I wish there was something we could do for him," she said to Carl.

"I doubt if there was anything we could do or say to make him feel any better," he responded. "We've seen that kind of thing happen to other friends. It's like a deep wound, every bit as painful as a physical one. The only thing that helps is time, and lots of it. Remember Frank? He killed himself before the wound could heal."

"Don't go there. He's been a good friend to both of us, and I for sure would miss him terribly if he died too."

"Yeah." Shaking their heads in sorrow, they walked away.

Jacob found a rock and sat down, holding his head in his hands. He wept freely for a time but found no solace in it. He begged God to place him in a distant future, where all the nerves and synapses that connected him to Moira were finally severed. Knowing that the prayer was an impossible one, he stood up and continued his shuffle away from the community. One insistent thought kept recurring as he walked: *Go through the pain.*

"Yes, Lord," he mumbled in desolation.

Back in the community they had forgotten Jacob's terrible misfortune in the wake of a singular event. "Wow!" Melanie shrieked, arm outstretched and finger pointing to the southwest. "Look there!"

Several in the community who had heard her shout turned to where she pointed and gasped in amazement. The object of their focus was shiny like silver and shaped like a disc. It wobbled as it hovered, perhaps a hundred yards away from them and several hundred feet above.

"Is that what I think it is?" questioned her companion. "A real honest-to-goodness UFO?"

Conflicted by opposing desires to approach and flee, the community remained motionless. Before they could react further, the craft shot up vertically and immediately was lost to view.

"What can this mean?" Carl asked his wife. "Can it have anything to do with Jacob's tragedy?"

"I don't know. Let's talk to George about it."

When they approached George, who hadn't seen the object, he refused to believe in the reality of what they claimed to have seen. "You've been quite disturbed about what happened to Moira," he said. "We all have. Somehow that got mixed up in your brains and your minds responded with some sort of delusion. You need to pray that God brings you back to health."

"Maybe he's right," Elizabeth said to Carl as they left George's little corner. "Even now the image of it is starting to fade away."

"Not for me. I know what I saw, and what I saw was something very real and very strange. It's a big universe out there. I guess there are other civilizations besides our own."

Jacob eventually returned from his walk. When he did, Carl and Elizabeth both attempted to comfort him, but there wasn't much they could do or say, and Wisdom was nowhere to be found. Having nothing of encouragement to say to Jacob, Carl changed the subject and gave Jacob an earful about the strange craft with unearthly capabilities. Jacob welcomed the distraction. For a brief time, he was able to get his mind off his loss.

He slowly began to come to terms with his loss as the months went by in agonizing eternities, but his grief never left. He continued to work in the barn, but with a listless attitude.

One afternoon Jacob walked from the mess toward the shed, his head hung down and tears dripping off his chin. *She's gone!* It must have been the hundredth time that awareness had intruded into his head with its consequent stomach-dropping misery. He'd thought that with the passage of time has grief would lessen, but now it had returned with an intensity that he hadn't imagined would be possible. The starkly uncompromising realization sent fresh waves of adrenaline coursing through his body, setting his nerves on edge and clenching his stomach. The thought of forever having lost Moira hit him with the impact of tearing away half of his body, his very essence.

It seemed impossible for him to reconcile his continuing to live after his loss of Moira. What was the point? God had His reasons, of course, but the emptiness of spirit that had replaced Moira seemed too hard to bear.

Wisdom appeared suddenly at his left side. "Hi," she greeted him. His unexpected happiness at seeing Her was tamped down immediately when he looked into Her lovely face and saw the frown and Her eyes glistening with tears.

"Bad news?" he asked. *Go ahead, then. I'm used to it.*

"Kind of," She replied.

"About me?"

"No. About Me. We've – 'We' meaning God – have permitted you misinterpret somewhat an understanding about Our nature. It was something that you didn't need to know, and a more complete understanding of Us would have worked against you, given your particular nature."

"Why now, then?"

"You've grown to the point where it would be better for you to understand more thoroughly who We are. So I'll just let it all out. Jacob, I'm not all there is to the Holy Spirit. I'm just a part, and a small one at that."

"I know that. A long time ago, my old friend Earl in the death camp had shared with me what you had told him about yourself – that you are indeed the Holy Spirit, but that You're more extensive than he could see. Are You trying to tell me now that what you said isn't really true?"

"No. Not at all. What I told him was the truth, but with your limitations of mind and dimensions, you see what I had told him about My nature in a different way than things really are. Actually, I'm an angel, just one of a vast multitude of angels."

"But I worshiped you as God. An angel specifically told the Apostle John not to worship him. It's right there in the Bible, Revelation 19. And, as I recall, Jesus as God was said to be better than angels. And besides, I had pictured you as married to the Father. Jesus had said in Matthew 22 that angels don't marry, which means that they're not gendered. I guess that goes for you too. But you're so beautiful that it would have to be a crying shame if you didn't marry. What gives?"

"All those points are good, and deserve good answers as well. I'll address the last one first. I've been gifted by God with exceptional feminine features, that's true. But the purpose for that is so that the inner beauty of the Holy Spirit, whom I'm privileged to represent to you, would be obvious. And you're stretching things a bit to say that you worshiped me, something you know I never asked for. Our relationship, like that involving Earl and Joyce as well as Moira, was more like that between a mother and her well-favored children, as indeed it was supposed to be. But about that gender business. You've referred to Matthew 22, so you do know what it said. Jesus said there that you yourselves are like angels, ungendered. What do you have to say about that?"

"Well, of course we're not gendered in the spiritual domain. But that holds only for individuals, not the collective Church, which is feminine, so feminine that we'll marry Jesus."

"Jacob, think about what you just said, and remember how Jesus likened you to angels with respect to gender."

"Oh! Now I get it. You angels make up the Holy Spirit, just as we Christians make up the Church. Both we and you are gendered in the collective, and we'll be married to Jesus as you're married, along with the other angels, to the Holy Father."

"That's right, but don't get ahead of yourself. You'll have that marriage in heaven, not here. Then you'll understand how very intimate your relationship with Jesus will be, even at the level of the individual. That's why I could tell Earl that I am indeed the Holy Spirit that he could perceive at the time. To say otherwise would have been truly deceptive, as we angels are so intimately connected to the Father and to each other that in actuality we are the Holy Spirit – all of us. You'll be able to grasp that intuitively when you enter our spiritual domain, to your great joy in your relationship with Jesus."

"So then you weren't actually misleading us. But what about those angels who refused our worship?"

"In their specific missions, they were acting as messengers. In that situation, they weren't involved in representing the Holy Spirit to those humans that they visited. But if you read Scripture carefully, you'll find that at other times angels actually did represent God. Some Bible commentators appreciated that. For example, in the Schofield King James Bible, a commentator said, and I quote, 'In the O.T., the expression "the angel of the Lord" usually implied the presence of Deity in angelic form."

"I understand. I was thinking that with this new revelation I was being taken back to the woodshed."

"Not at all. You'd likened the thought of losing Moira with having half of your essence torn from you. That's very true, as you and Moira were indeed one soul. But that's precisely what happened to My Beloved Father when He released Us – the Holy Spirit – from His own essence. If you give thought to that in terms of your own pain, you'll know intuitively how painful that was for Him, and how very noble was that heroic deed. The best part of that understanding you've just been given is that Father regained in love what he chose to lose, becoming in love one with His divine Partner. That should give you great hope for your future in the spiritual realm, both with Moira and with your own divine Partner, Jesus."

"I do get that, Wisdom – can I still call you Wisdom? —and I'm grateful for the insight. So then I really can see You as I did all along, as the Holy Spirit."

"Yes, I'd be pleased. And yes to your continuing to see Me as you have done before, but now with a deeper insight into My nature. And, I'm very happy to say, you understand in the way I'd hoped you would, which is a whole lot more pleasant to me than it might have been if you'd been someone else."

"Is there a reason, besides understanding the nobility of the Father, of course, that you had to get into the weeds about Your nature?"

"That's a definite yes. Now you can appreciate the happy condition that Moira enjoys, being a part of the spiritual Church, and what you have to look forward to. So buck up, and do your job down here with joy as well."

"Thanks for that, Wisdom. I'll try to do just that. But I have a question.

Sometimes I'm able to get my mind off Moira by thinking about a flying craft some of us saw a while back. Those who saw it said it looked like what they'd heard about UFOs. Was it one? What was it doing here? Does it involve You?"

"Yes and no to what it was and who it involves. To you, at least up to now, it has been a UFO – an Unidentified Flying Object. It's better named a FIFO, which is to say that it's a Fully-Identified Flying Object. I won't say much more about it other than to say that it wasn't an envoy from another civilization like yours. There was no other purpose for it being there when it did, other than a lark. A joyride, if you must know. You'll find out more in due time. Just remember what I said about angels. Think about that a bit. And keep this thought in your heart as well: remember what Jesus told Paul when he asked the Lord to take away his thorn in the flesh: 'My grace is sufficient for thee; for my strength is made perfect in weakness.' Jacob, that applies as well to desolation of heart."

"I've noticed something lately. I'm not the only one around here who's had to put up with some pretty big ordeals. Is there a reason for all this?"

"You know the answer to that. We just talked about it. Look at those people. They're getting harder in body, but softer in heart. It all goes back to nobility and selflessness. And they're relying on God a whole lot more."

"Yeah, well, from the looks of them, they needed a whole lot of nobility."

Wisdom laughed and departed. Jacob continued his walk toward the shed but with his head held higher.

On another afternoon before Carl had returned from a meager lunch the belt to the alternator began again to screech. Jacob plodded over to the alternator, pulled a wrench out of his pocket and without much thought began to loosen the alternator from its mount, intending to adjust the tightness of the belt against the pulley. Distracted by thoughts of Moira, he banged the wrench against a support strut and it fell out of his hand.

Sparks flew, the alternator began to smoke and the room turned dark. *No!* Jacob thought, panic infusing his body. *No! No! No! Not again!* In complete despair, he sat on the ground, his head in his hands.

Wisdom suddenly appeared at his side. "Sorry about your loss," She said, putting a heartfelt hand on Jacob's shoulder.

"Yeah," he replied, looking down in misery at the charred remains of the alternator. "It's my fault, too. I'm already on probation. I wonder if I'll be asked to leave."

"Actually, it's not your fault."

"What? What did you say?" His eyes bulged out in surprise and a smatter of hope.

"I know this community has been down about not making it to the top," She said, glancing over at Jerusalem Peak high above them in the distance, "but lately they've been surviving so well on their own that their heads are beginning to swell again."

"Don't tell me they need another dose of dressing-down."

"You tell me. They've stopped praying for the wisdom to survive. They needed to get pruned back a bit and return to their full dependence on Us."

"Are You saying that – that—"

"Go ahead and say it. You don't need to be delicate about it."

"That You are responsible for this disaster?"

"Yes, I am. And it will be for your good, as well as for a great and permanent blessing upon the community. Some day, someone will show you something you'll definitely want to see, something that will erase your self-inflicted doubts. When you do, you'll witness the power of God in turning bad to good. Actually, this upcoming demonstration will be one of Our more amazing ones." She turned and left the barn after that very enigmatic but promising piece of information.

CHAPTER NINETEEN

No sooner had she left than Carl came through the door. He strode toward Jacob in a cheerful manner, but before he reached his friend he stopped abruptly and stared around in shock. "What happened to the light?" he asked with a foreboding demeanor.

Jacob hung his head in shame. "I did it again, I'm afraid."

"What? You fried our last alternator? You did it again?"

"Yes," he said miserably, forgetting for the moment what Wisdom had said about it being a deliberate act on her part.

Carl responded by stepping over to the ruined device, blackened by the destructive short-circuit. He picked it up, cradling it in a hand like the skull of his best friend. "How?" he pleaded. He dropped the alternator and sat on a bench, elbows on his knees, cradling his head in his hands.

"I can't tell you how sorry I am, Carl. I don't know what to do about it."

"There's nothing you can do. After the last time you did this, they were ready to kick you out of here. Now I doubt if you'll have a choice in the manner. Unless . . ."

"Unless what, Carl?"

He stood up abruptly. "Never mind," he said. He left the building.

Jacob followed him out the door after some delay, in which he attempted to figure out what to do. By the time he saw Carl, he was being dressed down by George, whose eyeballs were popping out in fury. Jacob was too far away from them to hear what George was screaming about. Had he known, he would have rushed up to them and set George straight.

"I've had my eye on you for quite some time, Carl, George told him with malice. Now you've done it. Get your wife and your belongings and leave. Now."

Head down, Carl strode toward the garden where Elizabeth was working. He spoke to her briefly. They both looked toward Jacob, who had just joined the crowd surrounding George. Carl shook his head in warning as he and Elizabeth retreated toward their cave. Shaking his own head in confusion, Jacob went back to the shed.

An hour later, Carl and Elizabeth were embracing their friends in farewell. The entire group around the couple expressed their sadness with tears in their eyes as George and his subordinate leaders stood meanly, hands on hips in silent accusation. The commotion brought Jacob out of the shed, but as he approached the group, Carl shook his head and raised a hand with palm out, warning him off. Surprised, he watched them trudge off to the west out of sight, and he pleaded with God to bless them. After his silent prayer, he saw George approach, a frown of disgust marring his features.

George stood, veins protruding in anger from his red neck and face. "You too. You're nothing but trouble. You're done here. Get your things and get out now."

An hour after his friends' departure, Jacob trudged away from the camp in the direction Carl and Elizabeth had taken. In a fit of anger, George ripped away wire and the now-useless lamp at his makeshift desk and flung the mass toward Jacob. It hit him in the middle of his back. The act humiliated Jacob, but something told him to keep these items. He stuffed them into his bedroll and continued on.

Despite his worry over the lack of food and water, he was relieved at the prospect of seeing his friends again, more so after having finally understood the issue that had cost his friends their place in the community. With a shock of recognition, he realized that Carl had taken the guilt onto himself of the destruction of their last alternator. The nobility that Carl had displayed on his behalf amazed him, and he vowed to find him and help them survive at any cost.

It was nearly midnight on a moonless night when Jacob, tired beyond his ability to travel further, found a sandy knoll on which to lie down and scrunched down to form a hollow. Searching for a thought that would push his despair into the background, he revisited the conversation he had with Wisdom about the unearthly craft that had briefly visited the community. *Why the nudge from Her toward thinking of angels?* He questioned. *What was the context again? Oh, yes, Angels aren't gendered. Like we aren't. But that only applies to individuals. Collectively, as the Church, we'll be the Bride of Jesus Christ. It's the same as with the angels. Collectively – Oh! Wow! I didn't digest that when She told me. Collectively, the angels comprise the Holy Spirit! I remember saying that to Wisdom, but it didn't really sink in.*

"The good ones, that is." Wisdom looked fondly down upon his eyes. "Some angels aren't all that good, just like with you humans."

"I'm missing something. I feel it. What does all this have to do with UFOs or FIFOs or whatever?"

"What you're missing, I fear, is that you see no connection between God and those enigmatic craft."

"I guess. Scripture doesn't have a whole lot to say about such a connection, if indeed there is one. If there was, I'd think it would have been mentioned there."

Wisdom laughed, a cheerful melody. "Jacob, you've been so busy occupied with the femininity of the Holy Spirit that you've missed some very interesting passages, particularly in the historical books. Take, for example, Second Kings Chapter Two. Verse 1 says this:

> *And it came to pass, when the Lord would take up Elijah into heaven by a whirlwind, that Elijah went with Elisha from Gilgal.*

"Doesn't the word "whirlwind" suggest something to you, Jacob? I'll continue on, with verse 11:

> *And it came to pass, as they still went on, and talked, that, behold, there appeared a chariot of fire, and horses of fire, and separated them, and Elijah went up by a whirlwind into heaven.*

"You're right, Wisdom. I'd never read those passages, so I guess I spoke out of turn."

"There's more. I know you've read Ezekiel, but you kind of skipped over some very important information. Actually, several Christians with a scientific bent had latched on to the first few chapters of Ezekiel and made a big deal of it, claiming that it was a helicopter or a rocket ship. More than one fellow had pegged it as a UFO. I'll give it to you:

Now it came to pass in the thirtieth year, in the fourth month, in the fifth day of the month, as I was among the captives by the river of Chebar, that the heavens were opened, and I saw visions of God. In the fifth day of the month, which was the fifth year of King Jehoiachin's captivity, the word of the Lord came expressly unto Ezekiel, the priest, the son of Buzi, in the land of the Chaldeans by the river, Chebar; and the hand of the Lord was there upon him. And I looked, and, behold, a whirlwind came out of the north, a great cloud, and a fire enfolding itself, and a brightness was about it, and out of the midst of like the color of amber, out of the midst of the fire. Also out of the midst of it came the likeness of four living creatures. And this was their appearance: they had the likeness of a man. And every one had four faces, and every one had four wings. And their feet were straight feet; and the sole of their feet was like the sole of a calf's foot; and they sparkled like the color of burnished bronze. And they had the hands of a man under their wings on their four sides; and they four had their faces and their wings. Their wings were joined on to another; they turned not when they went; they went every one straight forward. As for the likeness of their faces, they four had the face of a man, and the face of a lion, on the right side; and they four had the face of an ox on the left side; they four also had the face of an eagle. Thus were their faces; and their wings were stretched upward; two wings of every one were joined one to another, and two covered their bodies. And they went every one straight forward; wherever the spirit was to go, they went; and they turned not when they went. As for the likeness of the living creatures, their appearance was like burning coals of fire, and like the appearance of lamps; it went up and down among the living creatures; and the fire was bright, and out of the fire went forth lightning. And the living creatures ran and returned like the appearance of a flash of lightning.

Now, as I beheld the living creatures, behold, one wheel upon the earth by the living creatures, with its four faces. The appearance of the wheels and their work was like the color of a beryl; and they four had one likeness; and with appearance and their work was as it were a wheel in the middle of a wheel. When they went, they went upon their four sides; and they turned not when they went. As for their rims, they were so high that they were dreadful; and their rims were full of eyes round about them four. And when the living creatures went, the wheels went by them; and when the living creatures were lifted up from the earth, the wheels were lifted up. Wherever the spirit was to go, they went, there was their spirit to go; and the wheels were lifted up beside them; for the spirit of the living creature was in the wheels. And the likeness of the firmament upon the heads of the living creature was like the color of the terrible crystal, stretched forth over their heads above. And under the firmament were their wings straight, the one toward the other; everyone had two, which covered on this side, and every one had two, which covered on that side, their bodies. And when they went, I heard the noise of their wings, like the noise of great waters, like the voice of the Almighty, the voice of speech, like the noise of an host; then they stood, and had let down their wings.

And above the firmament that was over their heads was the likeness of a throne, like the appearance of a sapphire stone; and upon the likeness of the throne was the likeness of the appearance of a man above upon it. And I saw like the color of amber, like the appearance of fire round about within it, from the appearance of its loins even upward, and from the appearance of its loins even downward, I saw as it were the appearance of fire, and it had brightness round about. Like the appearance of the bow that is in the cloud in the day of rain, so was the appearance of the brightness round about. This was the appearance of the likeness of the glory of the Lord. And when I saw it, I fell upon my face, and I heard a voice of one that spoke.

"Pretty interesting, what? Can you imagine the difficulty Ezekiel had in describing something that didn't fit in with the primitive environment in which he lived? And before you start thinking that he was speaking jibberish, note that this same Ezekiel predicted the Jews' return from their very lengthy *diaspora* in the year 1948 A. D., about two and a half millennia from his time."

"I think that pretty well fills in the missing piece, Wisdom. Thanks for that."

Despite the odd nature of the information Wisdom had handed him, he was asleep in seconds.

Chapter Twenty

Jacob awoke in the morning dry-mouthed and depressed. His one consolation, he thought as he picked up his meager belongings, was that maybe now he'd die of thirst and get to be with Moira again. But no sooner had he rounded a dune than he was confronted with an amazing sight. Carl and Elizabeth were sleeping snugly in each others' arms near the lip of a beautiful, crystal-clear lake, like the one he and Moira had slept near on their last day on the trail before they had arrived at the community. Here, too, the lake was surrounded by warm, yellow sand, which itself was surrounded by palm trees gently swaying in the soft breeze. The trees were full with coconuts and dates. He looked closer into his friends' faces. They were both smiling in their sleep.

"Thanks, Wisdom," he breathed. "Wherever you are."

"I'm right here," She said. "What do you think?"

The broad smile on Wisdom's face indicated that her question was purely rhetorical. It required an oblique answer, which he gave Her.

"You must be very pleased with them, particularly with Carl's selfless act of taking the blame on himself for my screwup."

"I told you before, Jacob, that it wasn't your fault. But yes, I am indeed very happy with them. And Carl's nobility in the matter has nothing to do with who actually did the deed, as he thought it was you. In fact, I might just allow them to go up with you when their time on Earth is over. That's beside the point of My being here now – to let you know that while they remain here on Earth, Carl and Elizabeth will be having a dandy time."

"Does that mean that I'm done with the community back there?"

141

"Not by a long shot," She said, laughing. "But that's yet in the future. Here, have a coconut since you seem to like them now." A large, ripe coconut fell from a tree near where he stood.

"See you around," She said, and departed.

Jacob's eyes blinked. When they opened again Wisdom had vanished. He swiveled his head frantically hoping to catch a glimpse of Her. Before he could register disappointment, another apparition appeared before him, one whom he knew very well. The face astonished him. "Moira?" he asked in shock and wonder. His amazement quickly turned to elation.

"Moira! I see you! How wonderful!" he said, his eyes glistening with tears of joy. "I don't know how God did it or why, but I'm so very, very happy!" He reached over and wrapped his arms around her, but they embraced nothing but air. "What's going on?" he pleaded, frowning in confused alarm.

"Sorry about that," Moira responded. "I'm not allowed to be physical around you, at least not yet. But I can talk with you."

"I guess that's better than nothing, but I was so very happy for that short time. You appear just like Wisdom, but I could touch Her. Are you an angel?"

"Not quite, but close. We're pretty much the same in a functional sense, but in a different way regarding whom we are attached to. We spiritual beings who used to be humans are married to Jesus rather than the Father, but, like angels, we're components of a much larger entity you know as the Church. As you know very well, it is the composite Church that is of the feminine gender while we individuals don't exercise that function. Well, not as individuals, anyway. The Holy Father is our Father-in-law. The Holy Spirit is our Mother-in-law. Actually, Jacob, Wisdom was an angel."

"Yeah, I know. Wisdom already got to me with that little tidbit of knowledge. I'm good with that. But why aren't you an angel like Her? That makes me very sad."

"It shouldn't. Like all angels, Wisdom's a component of the

multitude of angels who comprise the Holy Spirit. As you've found out, She's such an intimate part of the Holy Spirit that it really doesn't make much difference. We're much closer together in the spiritual domain than in the material one. We all belong to each other, and experience as much as we wish of others' actions and feelings. As for me, I'm part of the spiritual Church. As Paul said in Ephesians 5 and as I'll say it again, we spiritual Christians are the feminine spouse of Jesus, rather than of the Father."

"Whoa! This is getting complicated." Jacob frowned, and then his face lit up. "Actually, it's not. It's starting to seem beautifully simple as I begin to recall what I had known but not so intimately about this amazing news. But how tragic that I can't touch you."

"Maybe you can touch me a little as time goes on. It just depends."

"On what?"

"On our beloved Husband Jesus. He has the last say in what's best for us both. I still love you, Jacob, and I know that you still love me as much as we both thought we were capable. But you won't understand how deeply love really extends until you become a spiritual being like me."

Jacob frowned again. "Oh, I think you know how much I love you. And how much I've missed you."

"Wait till you enter my domain."

"Well, right now would be a dandy time for that to happen. What's holding me back?"

"Do you know who these people in the community are that you were with?" The question was rhetorical and she continued without waiting for a reply. "The Millennial kingdom of Jesus, the one spoken of in Revelation Chapter Twenty, has already begun. Those people, among others, will remain as inhabitants of Earth during that time, maybe with some exceptions including you. Some of them will be privileged to be associated with Jesus for all eternity after the Millennium, depending on their faith and obedience to Him. Their relationship to Him will be close, just a step down from actual marriage. Remember all those women who belonged to Solomon? It's in First Kings 11::3. I'll refresh your memory:

> And [Solomon] had seven hundred wives, princesses, and three hundred concubines; and his wives turned away his heart.

"You knew about Solomon's wives," she continued, "that they represented the Church that Jesus would – did – marry. Solomon was given so much wisdom from God that he understood that Jesus would marry a congregation consisting of a multitude of lovers, all genderless individually but a beautiful woman collectively. As you know, Paul fleshed out the details in Ephesians 5:31 and 32 and in 1 Corinthians 12. In marrying all those women, Solomon was attempting to represent that marriage which would take place far into the future for him, but which has already occurred for us. But the concubines fit into that picture as well. In fact, you're living with some of the actual ones now. Once the Millennium is over and done with, the chosen among them will fulfill Solomon's prophecy regarding the concubines."

"What's going to happen with me, Moira? Not to be selfish about it, but I'd sure like to be with you. Why did I have to stay behind?"

"You will be with me, and believe me, the phrase "with me" doesn't do justice to the closeness we'll experience together. Like me, you'll be part of Jesus' Bride after you fulfill the mission that Jesus has planned for you. You're going to help these people be chosen of God as concubines to Jesus."

"Why was it you that had to go instead of me?"

Moira grinned at that. "Because you've already established a reputation with these people."

"Yeah, the wrong kind of reputation. If there was a big enough tree around here, they'd want to hang me from it."

"They'll eventually get over the negatives. Perhaps even George. Remember what you've done for them so far." She ticked off some items on her fingers. "You bagged the biggest animal they'd seen since the Earthchange. You've built some tools. And you're beginning to share our real God with them. The last part is by far the most important. You'll be doing a lot more of that in the near future. Of course, I knew pretty well the same things that you do. Although now I know more about God than you." She snickered at that last line.

"Then why didn't you stay here and help me instead of leaving?"

"You know better than that. I didn't exactly plan to leave the way I did, as you should know. But now that I'm where I am, I will be helping you, Jacob, in a much greater way than I would have been able to do down there where you are. You have no idea yet how important it is for Jesus to choose as many concubines as possible, and how hurtful it is to leave the rest behind. A tragedy that we all feel is the loss of the fallen angels. They'd willingly given up the wonderfully intense intimacy that we have the joy of experiencing. We feel very badly for their loss, but they knew what they were doing when they did it. Anyway, back to us. I'll say it again - the wonderful thing is that we can continue to work together," Moira pressed on with a loving stare. "Just like we did when I was in your domain. Maybe the physical intimacy is off the table for now, but we'll be close emotionally, maybe even more so than when I was with you physically."

Moira vanished and Carl came over to his friend. Not knowing what had taken place as he was asleep with his wife, he looked up to his friend in surprise. "What are you doing here, Jacob?"

"I got kicked out too, I guess on general principles. I didn't know that you'd taken the blame for me until I started walking. I can't tell you how proud I am of you, even though it didn't matter to George. But it did matter to me, and more importantly, to God. If you don't believe me about that, look around you. As you can clearly see, our surroundings already are an enormous improvement on our last home."

They were overjoyed about the water in the clear pond before them. Its taste lived up to its visual promise of purity, and they drank the cool liquid until they could hardly hold any more in their stomachs. Had they looked forward to nothing but coyote and squash to eat, they would have refrained from breakfast. The dates and coconuts before them looked so inviting that they couldn't hold back. Jacob had kept his sheet-metal saw and used that to open the coconuts. They stopped only when their insides were at the point of bursting. They looked at each other and laughed in delight. "I guess being cast out isn't so bad," Carl remarked. They laughed again.

Jacob unrolled his mat and spread it on the ground, taking inventory of what he'd brought along with him. Carl and Elizabeth did the same, but only after they carried their belongings beyond a knoll. "Sorry, Jacob," Carl said as they walked away. "I guess we'll be needing some privacy."

"Of course," Jacob replied. But he frowned as he spoke. They had every right to their privacy as a couple. He just wished that Moira was here. He looked up to the blue sky, but it was empty of clouds and of Moira.

A pair of geese flew overhead as Jacob watched the sky, and dropped down onto the pond. *The Earth keeps recovering.* The sight brought another thought into his mind. *I wish I could fly. At least then I'd have something exciting to do. Something to make my life bearable.* Jacob had flown once a long time ago, and recalled the experiences with mixed joy and longing. He'd learned to fly on a little high-wing Cessna 152, and gone on to acquire a commercial rating that turned out to be useless when a hearing problem developed. Several years later an even smaller ultralight caught his attention and that occupied his time for a while. The fragile craft, a Quicksilver MX-2, appealed to his sense of humor, along with its tiny but ear-splitting engine. He figured that the engine had about as much horsepower as an upscale lawn mower, and the thought made him grin. It was small and frail, but its very basic nature got Jacob closer to the true flight of a bird. He recalled the time he came upon some cattle and dropped down to herd them, their frightened eyes bulging out and showing white. He tried it again, but the next time the farmer came out with a shotgun and started blasting away at him. He laughed at the memory. He'd gotten a pilot certificate from the Airplane Owners and Pilots' Association, a practice that they'd soon discontinued after being deluged with lawsuits arising from numerous flights that didn't end well. He continued to chuckle as his mind wandered deeper into the past. In one epic incident according to observers on the ground, the flight path of one ultralight that ended up in its own crater was like that of an angry bee. They thought he was dead until he crawled out of the wreckage and staggered away, repeating the path he'd taken in the air. He ended up falling on the ground. When they came up to him, he was snoring. There was enough alcohol evaporating from his body to start a major fire. Jacob recalled another ultralight episode that he was certain qualified for some sort of evolutionary end-of-the-line award. The craft was a Pteradactyl, a high-wing single-seater that its owner wanted to modify into a two-seater. The man was a braggart, telling all who listened of his prowess as an inventor and a superb aviator. When he was observed next, he was working on some extensive repairs to the craft, hobbling about with his arm in a sling and a leg in a cast. He laughed a bit at the memory, but then he recalled his own debacle. At home it was very windy one day, but he had his heart set on taking off in the ultralight. He'd gone over to the tiny airfield to check on conditions there, and was happily surprised that it was almost calm. Without giving the weather any more thought, he fired up the little craft and took off. What he'd been taught multiple times, some of which were emphasized by shouts, was to avoid wind shears at all costs. He'd heard all that, but didn't visualize the consequences of ignoring that piece of essential advice. He should have, but no. He also failed to picture where the airfield was situated. It was in a bowl, sheltered from the stiff winds that surrounded it that day. Happily, he climbed upward until he reached the crest of the bowl. At that point, if he'd been flying a 747, he'd have continued on his merry way. But no. He was flying something that was equivalent to a gnat. Therefore, the consequence of his failing to heed the warnings hit him like a giant fist, turning him upside-down and flinging him across the sky, batting him back and forth like a ping-pong ball. He reached the ground in one piece after much heartfelt prayer, and hurried back to his car after a little time spent kissing the ground. He relived the episode with a shudder.

Carl and Elizabeth returned to Jacob after a short time. Elizabeth pointed out to the west. "Want to come along, Jacob?"

"No thanks, Elizabeth. You two go along while I try to figure out how to give this oasis some semblance of permanence for us." Elizabeth turned back to her husband and put her hand in his as they walked away on a brief exploration of their surroundings. Rather than do what he spoke about, Jacob's mind turned back to Moira. Before he reached the point of weeping over her, she appeared before him.

"You look kind of miserable, Jacob," she said. "You need to get over yourself. Just a little while longer, and we'll have all eternity before us to share with each other. In the meantime, there's lots to be done, just like you told Carl and Elizabeth."

"Can you give me a clue as to how I can make myself useful with a saw made out of soft sheet metal and not much else?"

"Of course. It's called giving you some specialized wisdom, just like our Holy Spirit gave the Israelites the knowledge and ability to do things like the construction of their wilderness tabernacle. Before we get started with you, strengthen yourself with Exodus 28:3."

Jacob went to the pile on his mat and extracted his Bible, where he found the passage that Moira had directed him to:

And thou shalt speak unto all that are wisehearted, whom I have filled with the Spirit of wisdom, that they may make Aaron's garments to consecrate him, that he may minister unto me in the priest's office.

He looked up to Moira. "Yes, that's right," she nodded. "You humans aren't really as well-equipped in the brains department as you think you are, despite the temptation among some to worship their own abilities. Actually, you're a sorry lot in smarts next to God. Don't get me wrong – I know you intimately, and I understand that you're not exactly that arrogant, but even you can get uppity about yourself at times." She grinned to soften the dressing-down.

"What we're going to do is give you wisdom and knowledge in the art of metallurgy, from the extraction of ore to the finished products. The Holy Spirit gave some of that understanding to Solomon. And, much later, to the Moravians as well, under the Christian Count Zinzendorf. And in between times, of course. But the Moravians were truly special. When they moved to Pennsylvania in the eighteenth century and founded the city of Bethlehem, they did very well. The results were spectacular, both spiritually and materially. Now it's our turn, meaning those of us in the spiritual Church are now doing work that the angels have been doing. When you wake up tomorrow, you'll have an understanding of what to do that you don't possess now. You'll also have some materials that you'll need pretty badly to do what you'll be wanting to do. But you'll have to work pretty hard to get them. By the way, I really enjoyed your ultralight memories."

"What? That was a country and an ocean before our time together."

"Heads up, Jacob. I get the news now, and it isn't fake. I just went back in time and lived those events with you, so now I'm up to speed. I know you like a book. Literally. The thing you should be grateful for is that I know so much about you and still love you." She smiled at him to show that she was ribbing him.

"Yeah, well, if we can't be together, it sure would be nice if I could fly again."

Moira laughed, long and richly. "You just may do that someday. As a matter of fact, you won't believe what you'll be flying. You won't be needing to count the seconds before that beauty gets up to speed."

"High performance? Like a P-51 Mustang?"

"More like a rocket. You'll be pulling some serious Gs with this baby. The only limit will be your ability to withstand the kick-in-the-back performance. Let's just say that it has more horsepower than a locomotive and it's something to look forward to."

"Sid had a high performer once. A Goldwing 1800 cc bike. It was built with the wife in mind. Her seat was like a throne. She could stay on it for hours, listening to the music piped into her helmet. The only downside was when it rained, or got too hot. No roof, no air conditioning. But his wife didn't mind. She liked the adventure. According to him the acceleration was impressive. He claimed that it would go from zero to sixty in around four seconds when he was riding alone."

"Sid had several bikes. He had a Triumph 650 before you knew him. It turned out to be very useful to his faith."

"How so?"

"He rode it to college. He was heading down a thoroughfare toward the freeway, because the college was several miles away. He was late besides, so he was going over the speed limit. A lady heading to work in her car also was late, so she was speeding too. They were heading toward each other when she hung a left in front of him. The sun was in her eyes so she didn't know he was a target. They hit head-on. The crash was so violent that he left his shoes behind when he flew off the bike. He sailed forty feet head-first and headed directly for a fire hydrant. He wasn't wearing a helmet."

"Ouch! It's a miracle he wasn't killed."

"That's the whole point. It was a miracle. He struck a telephone pole with his chin on his way to the hydrant."

"How come that didn't kill him, then?"

"It was a matter of millimeters. He grazed the pole with his chin, not enough to brain him, but just enough to rotate him so that he landed sideways to the hydrant, on the grass between the sidewalk and the curb. He didn't even break a bone. He was sore for a week, but a little pain for a little while and he was fine."

"So you're saying that God was in charge."

"Yes. He was heading off the rails in his faith. He needed to get a jolt. That did it. He's been a real believer after that episode. Kind of like when you got in that wind shear in your ultralight."

"Kind of," Jacob said.

"That wasn't the first time God got him out of a jam with a motorcycle. When he was in high school and had just begun to drive, a friend showed him his own wheels. All two of them. The bike was an old Indian flathead, on its way to the junkyard, but it still ran. As the friend proudly displayed it to him, he asked if he could ride it. Sid and his friend both acted stupid as rocks, because the friend told him to get on and try it out. Well, pebble-brain mounted the steed and discovered, before he even started it, that it was large, in his new perspective large enough to rival a fire-eating, steam-snorting locomotive. Then he discovered that the shift lever was mounted next to the tank, which meant that he'd have to take his hand off the handlebar to shift.

"Oh, by the way," his friend had said in an offhand way. "Careful of the clutch. It's kind of an on-off kind of deal. That's why they call it a suicide clutch."

Sid's forehead was starting to sweat. He was too proud to get off, so he stepped on the starter peddle and gave it a nervous kick. Weak as it was, it was enough to start the beast, which gave off a thundering roar.

"Put it in gear," his friend shouted after a long delay while the sweat poured off his forehead and got into his eyes.

Braving the sting of the sweat, Sid looked down from the top of the steep hill that crested where he stood, blocked out all thought, and stepped on the clutch. The clutch grabbed immediately, jerking the bike into sudden motion, which caused his throttle hand to twist and pour on the coal. The engine screamed as the bike tore down the hill into a sharp left-hand turn. Somehow he survived the turn without falling off and his friend's smile turned into a frown of alarm as the roar of the bike turned into a shrill scream that ended abruptly in silence. The friend ran down the hill and up past the bend, where he saw a man with a hose in his hand and a shocked look on his face. He was staring away from the car he was washing and toward the end of the road where it terminated in his open garage. With foreboding, the friend peeked into the garage where Sid and the bike were plastered against the far wall. But God had plans for Sid, so the poor fellow got off with cuts and bruises. The bike didn't fare so well. Sid did lose a friend, but he lived through the ordeal."

Moira left as Carl and Elizabeth returned from their walk. They were bursting with enthusiasm. "Guess what we found, Jacob! There's a small forest about two miles back there," he said, pointing in the direction from which they came. "Pines, I think. Now we can build some real homes for ourselves. And there's even more – the soil there looks different. We dug some up and found clay. There's lots we can do with that, like make pots to cook with, and maybe some cups so we won't have to stoop down to drink the water."

"That's great news, but with what are we going to be doing the building?"

Carl's face fell, but then he brightened. "We do have your saw. It'll be a start, at least."

True to her word to Jacob, he awoke the next morning to an intricate knowledge of metallurgy that he never possessed before, not even the most basic understanding. Jacob noticed that out of the blue Carl had developed an enthusiasm for woodworking. Elizabeth meanwhile, when she wasn't helping Carl with his task of cutting down a tree, began establishing the boundaries of their homes-to-be. Over the next several weeks they set about their tasks, Carl to his woodcutting and Jacob to his metalcraft. All of them were painfully slow at producing results, particularly Jacob as he dug with only his hands into what he thought would be a promising source of metal ore.

Until his hands scraped over something hard and metallic. Excited, he dug faster, until he was forced to stop from bleeding fingers. It took him several more days, with the help of Carl and Elizabeth, to excavate the sandy soil to the point that they could recognize the object they sought. Amazed, they gazed upon a truck. Digging deeper yet, they found a cornucopia of equipment. The truck obviously had played a role in putting out brush fires, as they found picks and shovels, and a number of other useful tools.

"Guess what might be under the hood, Carl."

"Are you thinking maybe an alternator?" he replied with a smirk.

"Yeah. Maybe we should get it out of here and give it to the community. Maybe then we'll be back in their good graces and they'll allow us to return."

"Gee, Jacob, do you really want to do that? I don't know about you, but Elizabeth and I are content right where we are. Back in the old days, as a matter of fact, we'd have booked a cruise ship to get to a place like this."

Jacob laughed. "No, I wouldn't want to go back either. But we could give them the alternator to make their lives a bit easier."

"Maybe we'd better think that over some. It might be useful here. We'll have to do a lot more digging anyway before we can retrieve it."

"Actually, Jacob, I'm not really as content as I could be. Looking at that truck reminds me of the time we had wheels. It would be nice to be able to drive again, even with the marginal one we used to have."

"What did you have to drive around back in days gone by?"

"We had several at one time or another, but I'm thinking now of our little VW Golf. It looked kind of flimsy, and it accelerated at the rate of a mile-long freight train groaning up a grade. We measured the time it would take to go from zero to sixty. It was over 34 seconds, and when it met a hill, it was like the little choo-choo who could. It would make it to the top, but only if we downshifted. Even then it took a while to do it, and we had to watch the temperature closely. But we loved that little car."

"Sounds kind of basic to be an object of love," Jacob said grinning.

"Yeah, it was mostly the price that endeared it to us. A friend decided to buy a new car and knew it wouldn't fetch much as a trade-in. She sold it to us instead for $150. It was a kind gesture, and we were grateful for her largesse, even though we had other wheels. Maybe in the back of her mind she thought we could eke out from it another year and another couple of thousand miles. Jacob, we had the car for twelve years, and put another fifteen thousand miles on it. It was the best $150 we ever spent. We knew it would go belly-up someday, and we laughed about walking away thousands of dollars ahead of the game when it did."

"So did it go belly-up?"

"Oh, yeah. Spectacularly. We were going up a steep on-ramp to the freeway. About halfway up the engine exploded with a bang, and a cloud of dense black smoke rose from the hood. The smoke was so heavy that I couldn't see the car behind us. I thought it might block out the sun."

"What did you do then?"

"The car did it for us by stopping. I managed to pull it to the side of the road enough to let other cars pass. As they went by, I could see the passengers laughing. We laughed with them. Then we had it towed to a junkyard."

"So after twelve years and fifteen thousand miles, you were only out $150."

"No. The best part is that we sold it to the junkie for $150, exactly what we paid for it in the first place."

"Wow. You really did make out."

They continued digging for a while. Exhausted and sweaty, Jacob paused and wiped his brow. "Take a break, Carl. I'm getting real tired."

They sat down in the shade, Jacob taking a long gulp on a coconut husk that he'd filled with water. "I remember another set of wheels I had once," Carl said. "But this particular vehicle was a real beauty. It was an older English sports car. Maybe it was a bit long in the tooth, and I suppose it didn't rival the performance of a muscle car but its performance was a huge difference from the Golf, and it handled to match. Its greatest asset was that Elizabeth loved it too. We did a lot of traveling on it."

Chapter Twenty One

George was rather proud of himself for the firm stance he had taken in evicting the three whom he considered to be troublemakers. His sermons demonstrated that frame of mind with his incessant flinging of their misdeeds in the faces of the remaining community, painting vivid pictures of the terrible suffering that the miscreants now must be forced to endure. These tirades were unexpectedly effective, even to George. For a while some people even began to acknowledge their own shame in starting to revert to normal marriages and, despite the protests of other elements within the community, they returned to celibate lifestyles. George couldn't help but notice their downcast faces. In reflecting on the probable reason, George's face glowed in triumph.

Despite the loss of their electricity, the community at large maintained a fairly decent outlook at first. Their food, while extremely limited with respect to variety, was almost sufficient to keep them from starvation. Jane, perpetually concerned over her husband's aversion to squash, had been overjoyed to discover that a few of the seeds she had planted recently looked like they were developing into carrots. As the region transitioned from early spring into the beginning of summer, the weather grew more benign and warmer. Yet a general discontent over the celibacy issue began to envelop the community. George's smug self-satisfaction was ultimately short-lived. When rumors began that George had no particular need in that area of life, rendering him quite content in his celibacy, the dam broke. Overnight the camp activities took on the nature of a whorehouse, bringing George to abject despair. He attempted to bring his people back into line, but quickly discovered that his people were no longer his people. Most failed to attend his services, being too busy with their newfound physical adventures.

After a while, things settled down into more stability. Having reclaimed their gendered natures, husbands and wives slept together contentedly. The only dissenter in the congregation was George, whose intense fear over missing the rapture had escalated into near-panic. Over the span of a very few weeks, his own smugness had disappeared, to be replaced by an agonized understanding that even if the rapture hadn't already taken place, he would no longer be included in it. Then a bigger problem arrived on their doorstep, and George was no longer alone in his discontent. The continuing viability of the community came to be at risk.

Several weeks after the three had left, an immense black cloud formed over the community. It was the first cloud they'd seen since the great Earthchange and it quickly turned violent, with wind approaching hurricane strength. The frigid wind forced itself through cracks in the rocks and blew into the living quarters, causing nightmarish living conditions. The blowing dust competed with wind-driven rain to drive the sparse population of wild animals into their burrows and away from the community. Sleepless and perilously close to starvation, they feared for their lives. The only food available to them for the duration of the apparently endless storm was squash.

One evening at meal time Peter reluctantly came into the dining hall with his wife Jane and sat down disconsolately. He stared with disgust at the dinner that confronted him. A cold sweat broke out on his forehead and his Adam's apple started to bob up and down and he swallowed a lot of bile. Holding his mouth, he jumped up and ran outside. Alarmed, Jane followed and held his shoulders while he shuddered with dry heaves. Eventually when the puking began to calm, Jane began to weep. "You can't do this to me," she wailed. "You'll starve to death! You need to keep on living. For my sake, Peter. Please!" She ran over to the garden and plucked up some young and pitifully small carrots. "Here!" she said. He ate them quickly, greatly relieving his wife. They walked together to their quarters. When they arrived in the cave, they searched in the dark for their mats. Stumbling about until they found them, Peter sat and cupped his hands around his head. "I'm at the end of the trail, Jane," he said. "There's nothing but squash, and I get sick just thinking about it. I really can't eat any more. If I managed to get anything down, I'd chuck it up."

Jane had lived for days with the fear over how gaunt he had become. She knew that if she could see him now, she'd be horrified at how pale and weak he was. "Get up," she said sternly.

"What? I can hardly move as it is."

"Get up! she yelled." She tugged at an arm until he complied and stood back up. "We're getting out of here now."

"Where would we go?"

"What difference does it make? If we stay here, you'll die anyway. Maybe George didn't tell us the truth when he told us Carl and the others had undoubtedly starved to death by now. What if he's wrong? At least we could head in the direction they took."

Peter responded by putting his meager belongings on his mat and rolling it up. Jane did the same. Determined not to remain a weak sister, Peter led the way out of the cave and trudged away from the community, guided by the frequent lightning strikes. They were both soaking wet and cold by the time the camp was out of sight, but their spirits were higher than they had been since Carl and Elizabeth had been banished from the community.

The first time Peter fell he spent ten minutes on the ground before he summoned the strength to get back up. A mile after that he fell again. Jane prodded him to no avail. Finally giving up, she lay next to him and fell asleep.

Conditions were hardly better back in the community they'd left behind.

The prolonged absence of electric lighting darkened the environment in the community to the point that there was very little that the people could do except to attempt to procreate. George was utterly devastated. He shut himself off from the rest of the community, spending most of his time pleading with God to rescue him from, in his view, the blatant debauchery into which the camp had descended.

CHAPTER TWENTY TWO

Elizabeth woke feeling the need to accomplish a task she'd been stalling off doing. Walking down to where she and Carl had done their exploring earlier, she dug up some of the clay they'd found and gathered it in her apron. After she'd eaten their breakfast of dates and coconuts, she set about making a pot. As the bowl came close to completion, she slipped and it cracked. She tried to repair it, but it got so messy it didn't look like anything useful. Undaunted, she started over, using more water in the formation. The result was crude but functional. With a look of satisfaction, she set it out to allow the sun to dry it. Later that afternoon she came back with more clay, and by evening she'd set out three misshapen but workable cups.

While she worked the clay, both Carl and Jacob enthusiastically dug a pit in the sand and fetched dead palm fronds which they placed in the pit. While Carl went back to the forest to collect dry evergreen branches, Jacob loosened the bowstring, looped it around an arrow and attempted to create a fire through friction on a stone. He became frustrated and tired from the exertion, but continued until eventually he succeeded in generating a small, delicate fire in the hollow of the stone. He rushed to preserve it with larger pieces of palm fronds. When it was burning steadily, he kept feeding it until he saw Carl return with branches in his arms. He poured the burning fronds into the pit and gratefully watched Carl build a larger fire with wood he'd collected. He and Carl made several trips to the forest, returning with enough wood to keep the fire going for days.

Jane awoke first. She remained still, fearing that Peter had died during the night. Eventually she opened her eyes, surprised to see blue sky above. "Peter!" she said, shaking him. When he responded by moving, she lay back down and wept in relief.

"It's sunny!" Peter said suddenly. He stood up and pulled at Jane. "It's not raining!" he added. They both laughed and started back on their trek with new vigor. Before noon they came into the camp made by the three outcasts, amazed at the beauty of the area. Seeing nothing but the small lake, they dropped their bundles and fell down by the edge of the water and lapped the cool, sweet liquid until they were full. Peter lifted his head and saw the trees. "Coconuts, Jane!" he said. "And there – over there are dates! Suddenly I'm starving!"

Despite their water-filled stomachs, they both gorged themselves on dates. "Well, hello!" a voice said behind them. "Look who we have here!" Elizabeth called. After happy greetings and warm embraces, Jane shared the rapidly deteriorating situation in the community with the three and their hasty retreat from the bleak prospect of Peter's starvation.

"Wouldn't George be surprised to see how we're living!" Elizabeth crowed. "But I'm amazed at that cloud. We can see it from here, but had no idea of its violence or threat. We did think it strange, though, that it seemed to hang around without moving."

"The worst part is that without electricity, our whole community seems to be on the point of despair – oh! I'm so sorry. I didn't mean to bring up a bad subject."

Jacob spoke up instantly. "You need to know that the destruction of the alternator is not Carl's fault. In fact, Carl's a hero to me for taking the blame on himself for something I did. The loss of the alternator is entirely my doing."

"And it's something we should set straight as soon as we possibly can," Elizabeth said. "Jacob found a truck buried in the sand not far from where we are right now. I'm sure it has an alternator under the hood. Not only that, but Jacob got one side of the truck free of sand, and it opened up to show a large assortment of wrenches and other tools."

"I'll get to work on that tomorrow first thing," Jacob said. "Maybe within a week I'll have the hood free and can look inside."

"Can I help?" Peter asked.

"Not if I have anything to say about it," Jane said.

"Yeah, you look like you just came out of an internment camp," Jacob said, looking at his gaunt frame. "You need to put some meat back on your bones."

Peter started to protest, but Jane set him straight. "Listen to the man, Peter."

"You'll have plenty of chance to help out later," Jacob added. "Here, have a date."

"I should be the one helping you," Carl said to Jacob. "I've done a lot of thinking about it. Besides, I've been talking to Elizabeth. Whether an alternator would be useful here or not, we're doing pretty well without it. They're hurting over there, so giving it to them would be the right thing to do."

Two days later, Jacob and Carl came into their camp. Both were wearing wide smiles, and Jacob held up an alternator in his hand. Elizabeth ran over to him with a smile on her face and grabbed it. "I'm going to take it over to the community tomorrow," she said joyfully.

"Not without me you won't," Carl told her. "I'll need to set it up, and I can't trust you to do it. You either," he said to Jacob, who grinned red-faced.

The next day Carl and his wife set out toward the community. "I wonder how they're going to handle it when they see us," he said to her.

"I think they'll be happy to see us still alive. It'll probably give them hope that there's a better world than the one they're stuck in."

"Then there's George."

"There is him," she agreed. The thought of George confronting them darkened their spirits, matching their darkening surroundings.

"It's getting gloomy," Elizabeth said. "It's creeping me out, too. I wonder what's causing it?"

"And it's starting to rain, too," Carl responded, cradling the alternator next to his chest. "Run, Beth. Maybe we can make it there before we're drenched."

They were nearly soaked through by the time they reached the community. Carl ran to the shack for shelter, Elizabeth following on his heels. When they went through the doorway, they were surprised to hear several people speaking. Apparently, with the incessant rain, they were forced to go into this shed to communicate as a group.

"Who's that?" someone said.

"Hello, People," Elizabeth responded. "Carl and I are back for a very quick visit. We have a gift for you." One of the men brought a candle over, his eyes fastening on the alternator. "Hey, people!" he shouted. "They brought another alternator!"

A half hour later, Carl had the alternator installed and the belt tightened. "You don't have a fire," he observed.

"We're out of wood," a man said. "At least anything dry enough to allow a fire."

"We'll be back," Carl said. "Come on, Elizabeth." They went back in the direction they came, spending a night on the trail. As they approached their camp, Elizabeth started. "What's that smell?" she asked herself.

"Smells like cooking meat," Carl said. "It's been so long since we've had meat other than coyote, I can't stop the drooling."

"Yeah, not long after you left Jane saw a fish in the pond," Jacob told them when they met up. "Then there were more, a whole bunch. We managed to catch a few, and gave most of them to Peter. He couldn't get enough. We do have some fish left, so have at them. After, of course, giving thanks to God."

Their thanksgiving to God that evening was fervent.

"We still have a job to do," Carl said after they'd eaten. "The poor people don't have any wood. We're going to have to give them some of ours, at least enough to get a fire started. Those guys are living in misery. It won't stop raining over there."

Jacob felled a tree and the three men set to work sawing it into rounds and splitting it into manageable chunks. "We can thank God for that truck, too," Jacob breathed, wiping the sweat off his face. The vehicle was a fire truck, used for fighting forest and brush fires, and was equipped with shovels, axes and even a chain saw, which actually worked when he filled it out of a can of gas.

When they had created a substantial pile of wood, Carl looked at it doubtfully. "How on Earth are we going to get this wood over to the community?" he asked. "It's going to be hard enough getting it to our camp, let alone the congregation."

"We'll just have to be smart about it," Peter spoke up. "The truck doesn't work, does it?" he asked Jacob.

"No, and it never will, sadly enough," Jacob replied. "But I know where you're coming from. It does have wheels, and axles and there's even a welding torch in the bed. Let's see what we can make do with those parts."

It took them three days to construct a make-shift cart out of an axle and two wheels. "It looks great," Peter said with pride.

"Don't get too happy about it," Carl remarked. "Do you see a horse or a donkey around here? It'll turn us into beasts of burden."

They stared grim-faced at the heavy-looking cart. "Well," Carl finally said, "It's not going to move by itself. Let's bite the bullet and get going." They loaded the cart and manned the handles. It took all three of them to get it going and out of the sand, but it got easier when they reached their trail. Even then, it was slow going. Three days later they entered the compound, exhausted and so bent on finishing their job that they failed to notice the blue sky above them. The dreadful cloud was gone, and its absence was apparent in the faces of the crowd that surrounded them.

"Anybody care to help us out with the cart?" Jacob asked after they'd unloaded the wood. "We're so tired I wonder if we can get it back by ourselves."

They were overwhelmed with eager offers of help. Even some

wives stepped up, asking if they could help shoulder the load. The three men were faced with the sad task of selecting two couples, the downcast remainder waving unhappy goodbyes. With an empty cart they were able to reach the camp within two days. The surprise they found there extended to them all, not just the newcomers. The two couples were astonished at the beauty of the camp, but Jacob and the two others who had been there just days before also were amazed at its transformation.

"Hi," Elizabeth said to the two new couples. Having known them earlier back in the compound, she and Jane needed no introductions. "Glad to see you, Sandy and Dick, and Jim and Martha." She and Jane hugged them all. "Are we going to need to go back?" Sandy said to Jacob. "Do you have enough food that we can stay here? We'd be more than happy to work." The others murmured in heartfelt assent.

"Look over there," Jacob responded, pointing to the palms. "There's coconuts and dates galore. Certainly enough to feed you. And there are fish in the lake. You will have to work, but you're more than welcome to stay. Right, Guys?" Peter and Jane nodded, smiling happily. "And there are other perks to being here, Jane added.

"Yeah," Elizabeth said to them, grinning. "We had a visit. From someone you know, Jacob." They all stared at the lake, which had risen to channel out a stream that spilled downslope. The banks were alive with colorful flowers.

"But that's not all," Elizabeth said. "Come over here." She took Carl's hand and followed the stream down the hill, the others following. "Down there's a small pond," she said, beaming. "And guess what? The water there is warm. Jane and I've been loafing down there, and, believe me, we've enjoyed ourselves doing it. But now we'll be able to share it with our hubbies, which is going to be even better. Oh, sorry, Jacob," she added, understanding the return of his sorrow.

The newcomers' eyes bulged out in astonishment.

That evening the two new couples were more than ready to sleep in the soft sand, having gorged themselves on the bounty of their camp. "Wait just a bit," Jane said, having observed their sleepy eyes. "I'd like to know something about those in the community before you nod off. How are they doing for food? And how is George?"

"George," Dick said bleakly. "George is off the rails. He doesn't eat, not that there's anything to eat anyway, or hasn't been, and he looks like a cadaver. We don't see him much – he pretty much stays to himself - but when we do, he's talking to himself as if the rest of us don't exist. Actually, many of us are feeling sorry for him. But we don't know what to do about it. Maybe since the rain stopped, it just did, by the way, our food will come back. The squash is pretty much trashed, with the rain and all, but maybe some more carrots will come up in their place. I don't know, it's pretty grim.

"Well, guys, it looks like we'll have another trip to make," Carl said. "This time with dates and coconuts."

"Yeah, but you know what'll happen then," Jane countered. "I have a feeling that their knowing there's food here will cause a flood of new arrivals. I can picture the compound becoming a ghost town."

"I know what you mean, but we can't just let them starve," Elizabeth said. "It wouldn't be right."

"Hi," she said softly in his ear.

"Mmm – Moira?"

"Yes, dear. Things are progressing quite nicely for you, I see."

"Well, that's debatable. You aren't lying down next to me."

"Every day that goes by, you're getting closer to coming home. Your real one. In the meantime, I've been hanging out with a couple of your old friends."

"Carl? Elizabeth?"

"No. I won't say any more about it right now. I'm keeping it as a surprise for later, which won't be too long now."

He wondered whether she was talking about Earl and Joyce Cook. Along with Jacob, the couple had endured harsh treatment meted out in the camp in which they'd been imprisoned. It was actually a death camp like the ones in Hitler's Germany, located in the Arizona desert for the purpose of eliminating the "undesirables" of society, including the elderly, sick and those of the Judeo-Christian faiths. Jacob and his first wife, along with their young son, had been incarcerated for the crime of being Jewish. He had lost them there at the hands of sadistic guards. Earl and Joyce were there for having harbored a "useless eater", their adopted daughter Cathy, who was afflicted with cerebral palsy. Cathy had died there as well in a painful, gratuitously-inflicted punishment for her mere existence in that condition.

"Yes!" Moira responded enthusiastically. "They're also looking forward to your being with us. They've been watching you pretty closely, but have stayed away from contacting you. They want the communication to be exclusively from me. I told them I'd be telling you about my meeting them, and they said to say hello for them. You've picked your friends well, Jacob. I like them a lot. When you do arrive, we'll be working together as a team. In the meantime, they've been telling me about some of your adventures when you were with them. I was moved by your situation in the death camp, the one you escaped from with him."

"Yeah, that was brutal. But then I reached Israel and met you, which did wonders for my perspective on life.

"I think about that too, and what you mean to me. But to go on, I thought I might bring you a little closer and more real to us in heaven. I'll fill you in on some things that happened back then to bring America to her knees. Things you probably didn't know."

"Sounds interesting."

"It is. The three government branches were attacked by ruthless thugs controlled by a group of self-styled elites who wanted to condition America for integration into their new global order. In the executive branch of your government a puppet president attained the office through a combination of election irregularities and a growing population of immature, self-centered people who wanted it all and wanted it now." She continued to talk to Jacob about the terrible tribulation the world was forced to endure at the hands of the evil elites.

CHAPTER TWENTY THREE

The next morning the men loaded the cart back up and set off for the community, this time with dates and coconuts. All the men went as a group, planning on changing shifts at every rest.

When they returned, they brought two couples back with them. There were conditions upon that invitation: the food was so welcome it was gone by the evening they'd brought it. The two new couples were assigned to the task of returning to the community with food at least every other day until the mass starvation was mitigated. As Jacob had feared, everyone except George wanted to come to their new home. In response, Jacob told them to be patient, that eventually they'd all be given an opportunity to move, but it would be a gradual process to give the new location a chance to expand gracefully. Jacob opined that two couples could migrate about once every month, at his discretion. They agreed to Jacob's terms, but the look on their faces was pathetic as they watched the empty cart head back to the new camp.

Their return brought another surprise in addition to the astonishment of the two new couples, Mark, Dolores, Jimmy and Pat. "Oh! Wow! Pat exclaimed, looking at the lushness of their surroundings and the cheerful fire burning in the pit. "This is like going from hell into heaven." She immediately went down on her knees to thank God for this unexpected blessing. The rest of them followed her lead.

The surroundings were indeed lush – lusher than when Jacob and the others had left with the cart of food. Grass had appeared, and the palm trees had expanded their domain. "Have you figured it out yet?" a melodic voice above Jacob asked.

"I've just started to ask the question," he responded. "I am grateful, though. And I know that every time we return from the community, things here have gotten more beautiful and pleasant."

"Bingo!   They do have that in common.   When you figure out why, I'll be back."

CHAPTER TWENTY FOUR

Once the burden of carrying food had been removed from Jacob's list of chores and the truck had been completely excavated from the ground, he returned to his favorite task, that of mining for ore. Digging past the hole in which the truck had lain, he hit paydirt. The knowledge of mining that had been imparted to him by Moira allowed him to recognize the hematite ore that he had uncovered. The days that followed bore increasing evidence of that knowledge in the small-scale factory that emerged next to the stream. The equipment there included another fire pit and a clay crucible and primitive chimney within. A large bellows rested in front of the crucible upon a boulder that served as a stool. Beside the fire pit Jacob had constructed a box in which the ore was placed, and next to that was a primitive sluice trough he used to separate the lighter dross from the iron-rich ore. He was most often found laboring beside the ore box swinging a maul to crush the ore into manageable chunks.

The following week Jacob was moved to provide a Bible study, one that would be focused on introducing their growing group to the love of God. He had kept his Bible, apparently the only one in the small community, and prayed daily for both the topic and the ability to present it as God would wish.

"Hey, Mark!" Jacob called out one day as he saw the four pulling their food-laden cart back toward the old community.

"Yeah?" He stopped pulling and went toward Jacob.

"Bring two more couples back with you. And tell them that they'll now have your jobs. When you return, you'll be promoted to cushier tasks. Just saying."

"Thanks, friend. Things are looking better all the time."

Indeed they were. As Jacob looked around, he saw several new trees, all laden with bananas. It caused him to think about what had just happened in the context of what Moira had told him. Suddenly, he knew, and Moira appeared before him again.

"You've connected the dots, I see. Yes, every time that you or someone in your group does something selfless for the sake of others, Jesus tells me with a big smile to bless you. Thanks to you, you're getting a very nice environment.

"Right now we have another gift for you," Moira continued. "One that with your help will make life much easier for your community. Follow me."

Moira eventually stopped in the middle of an otherwise barren field, staring down at a small object at her feet. Jacob rushed up behind her, kneeling to look closely at a shimmering sky-blue and half-round, half boxlike thing with glistening black wings. "What on Earth is this?" he asked her. "It looks natural, but I can't tell whether it's a plant or an animal."

"It's neither," she said, her large eyes moistening in loving pride. "Melinda, there, is a new life-form in-between the two that you are so familiar with. Jesus had me create 'her'" – Moira made air quotes around the word – "and gave me some details as to how He'd like the design to go forward. She's actually not feminine, not truly an animal, so no gender or romance is involved. God had emphasized gender in His earlier creation, intending humans to readily link that attribute to the way mankind was made in His Trinitarian image. But most of you never did get that right anyway, so in this round, God laughingly held up his hands in mock surrender and created a genderless creature."

Jacob frowned in confusion. "But even plants possess gender. I know there is a real usefulness to gender besides the obvious benefits. The procreation of life through the integration of two different DNA strings is supposed to help maintain the integrity of the DNA of the offspring by reducing the influence of bad mutations. That's why incest is considered to be taboo. I remember hearing about how the English royalty was plagued by severe birth defects due to their incestuous relationships."

"I suppose I could be flippant about an answer to that and remind you how human beings have so totally messed up the gender thing that maybe God was fed up with the whole business. The problem you noted with old English royalty was just a small sample of all the weird sexual combinations and body changes that humans have indulged in, to their eventual sorrow. But there's another consideration, more important. Remember, Jacob, that the first humans after Adam and Eve did indeed engage in brother-to-sister marriage and rightly so, for there was no other option for them. Such wasn't a sin at the time, because the fall of Adam and Eve hadn't yet resulted in further mutations to their DNA code. It was only after the passage of time that errors had crept into the DNA code, resulting in the necessity of avoiding incestual relationships. Melinda's a brand-new being, unaffected by the Fall."

"Well, Melinda ought to make the anti-gender folks real happy," Jacob broke in.

Moira laughed, and continued to describe this being to Jacob. "Melinda's so cute that I had to give her a girl name. She's mobile like an animal but limited to moving the wings and getting out of the way of shade and coming together with others of her kind in response to local demands. She's capable of responding to love, but is kind of like what you think of blondes in the brains department. This delightful little creature's joyful purpose in life will be in converting sunlight and giving the product to humans."

"What product?"

Moira's mouth formed a grin. "Guess. What was the community missing the most in the recent past? What caused Carl – and you – to be banished from the congregation?"

"It can't be! Electricity?"

"Yep." Her grin widened. "It's all in the DNA. Like the other two general life-forms, Melinda possesses a rather complex DNA code. The molecular conversion mechanism's something like photosynthesis, but even more complex than that. The process is very efficient, beating your puny engineering efforts by a wide margin. What takes up an enormous amount of real estate the way we used to do it in those ugly windmill and photocell farms is tiny by comparison with Melinda."

"If it's not gendered, how does it procreate? You plan on having more than one Melinda, don't You?"

"Of course. As you know, plants give off oxygen as a byproduct of their "digestive" process. Animals excrete rather more noxious byproducts. Melinda, here has a more pleasant output, somewhat like seeds. These "seeds" have a highly agreeable fragrance, quite different than your output, and, like little animals themselves, are highly mobile. In fact, they're more mobile than their parent. They also integrate very nicely with existing flora and fauna."

"If digestion is involved, what do they eat?"

"They're much like plants in that regard. Basically carbon and hydrogen from water, mostly moisture in the atmosphere. And dollops of oxygen and nitrogen. They're beyond plants in their ability to "fix" nitrogen, so they don't need help with that issue."

"If Melinda is such a great idea, why didn't you just let the community know about it when they really needed it, and at the same time, show yourself to these people? I'm sure they would have liked to know that God is around and thinking about them."

"Jesus is not quite ready yet to reveal us to them. They need to grow more than they have, particularly in their faith in us. You saw the hatred in George's eyes. That has to go, and the only way to do that is to humble him. On the positive side of things, we'd like to help you repay Carl for his nobility in taking the blame for the disaster with the alternator. Show this little darling to him and make him the deliverer of the good news. Jesus loves to change bad into good, and this is one way to take the stigma away from Carl forever. You can't imagine what that gesture on your part will do for his – their - opinion of you."

"Hold on," Moira said to Jacob as he moved to fetch Carl. "Take one of the headlights off the truck and bring it back with you and

Carl along with some wires."

"Can we do it now?" Jacob asked when he returned with his friend. "Show Carl Melinda and her offspring? I have the lamp."

"Yes, certainly we can show him," Moira responded. "They're awake now. Melinda's shedding seeds even as we speak. Free up the wires from the tangled mess that they're in. Take them where the sun's not in shadow from the trees while I gather up these little Melindas-in-waiting and we'll hook them up. They'll know enough to configure themselves to the demand of the lamp."

Jacob watched in fascination as Moira presented the ends of the wires to a young Melinda clone. He saw no eyes on her, but noticed that the shiny black wings moved as the wires came close. Somewhere on the body two holes opened and clamped shut over the wires. Moira pointed to the lamp and he saw it glowing brightly. Overjoyed with God's amazing answer to the failure of the alternator, he wrapped his arms around her and hugged her with all his might, Jesus having allowed the physical embrace to happen that one time.

Carl's eyes bulged with surprise as he watched the demonstration take place without observing Moira's presence. His eyes darted between the group of Melindas and the glowing lamp. "What's going on here?" he asked in Jacob's general direction. "And what on Earth is this blob that's sitting there where the generator is supposed to be?"

"Say hello to Melinda," Jacob told him. Melinda and her companions flapped their little wings in greeting.

"Am I going insane?" he asked.

"It's a very long story, Carl," Jacob replied. "And you wouldn't believe it anyway. Just accept that the contraption works and don't ask too many questions. Maybe some day I'll have a chance to fill you in with the big picture, but for now you just need to know that it's a new life-form, a device very recently created by God. It demonstrates, among other things, that He's still around and loves you very much. Melinda has siblings or offspring, I don't really know which. A lot of them. We can use them to electrify all sorts of things, including lighting for our camp. If we have the know-how and smarts, we might even be able to make a heater and stove. Maybe even a refrigerator, but I'm not sure we'll be able to make the parts for that. One thing I do think that we'll want to make our first priority – a water pump, so the women won't have stoop down to extract water from the lake."

"God is with us," Carl said with conviction. "For whatever reason it's not ours to know, we aren't with Him on the mountaintop. But now I'm certain that He loves us."

"Actually, Carl, I think that I do know the reason. As you suspected, the rapture has come and gone. But this community still has a special place in His heart. Many in this community have been selected to remain as humans and live here on Earth during the Millennium, the thousand-year reign of Christ on Earth."

"Where are you getting this, Jacob? Has God Himself spoken to you?" Carl said this in anger, resenting Jacob's apparent arrogant attitude.

"Yes, actually."

"What?"

"Carl, while you were out, I had a visitor. Somebody I've known very intimately. My wife Moira, in fact."

"That can't be true!" Carl shouted. "She's dead!"

"Just her old material body. She's been resurrected, and now she's very alive in her spiritual form. She gave us – you – the gift of Melinda. And yes, she's told me a lot about what's going on with your life, now and in the future."

"But if we're going to remain in our bodies here on Earth, then we won't be with Jesus and the Church. We won't be married to Jesus."

"Eventually, at the end of the Millennium, the community will be with Jesus."

"But not part of Jesus' wife?"

"Sadly, no. But they will be loved by Him in a very happy

relationship. Remember the account of Solomon in the Bible? It's in First Kings Eleven, I believe. Solomon had 700 wives and 300 concubines. Solomon's concubines represented the multitude who would return to Jesus at the end of the Millennium, just as the wives represented the Church that Jesus would marry."

"You seem to be saying that we're not going to hell."

"Yeah. Where they'll be going is a lot better than that."

"I can live with it. Particularly since this enforced celibacy won't be necessary."

"It never was."

"You keep saying 'they'. What about Elizabeth and me?"

"Your future is still up in the air, as far as I can figure. Don't fret. Wherever you end up, you'll be very happy, I'm sure. Both you and Elizabeth."

On Wednesday evening Jacob began his first Bible study. It was well-received. Those who came to the gathering among the palms were far more enthusiastic than with the study George had held in the community mess hall. The fact didn't please him. George's recent humiliation weighed on his mind and depressed him, but there was a possible silver lining: George's ego may have diminished to the point where his character was strengthened. Jacob prayed for this. He waited for several minutes past the time he'd set for the invitation, and eventually all the couples in this new community had showed up. Thrilled with the turnout, he dove with enthusiasm into his first topic.

"I know you've read your Bibles religiously, so I don't think I'll have to cover what's in there as unfamiliar stories. But to be certain of that regarding the topic I'd like to discuss tonight, is everyone here familiar with the account in 1 Kings 3 of Solomon's prayer to God for wisdom?"

After noting a unanimous chorus of assent, Jacob continued. "Then let's dig right in," he said. "You know from the story that God, in seeing that Solomon's prayer was given selflessly in a desire to please God as King over Israel, gave Solomon wisdom in great abundance. The amount of understanding that he received from God, in fact, was so enormous that it's likely that no mortal person before him or since had so much. You also know that through the Mosaic Laws God intended men and women to be paired together in a one-man, one-woman marital relationship."

Jacob paused shortly for effect. "So why, then, as noted in 1 Kings 11:3, did Solomon accumulate seven hundred wives and three hundred concubines?"

The question was met with silence. "To answer that," Jacob said, "we need to turn to Ephesians 5, keeping in mind the understanding that God had given Jacob of His nature. Would someone please read Ephesians 5:31 and 32?"

Sandy responded, her frown suggesting that she didn't know where this was heading.

> *For this cause shall a man leave his father and mother, and shall be joined unto his wife, and they two shall be one flesh. This is a great mystery, but I speak concerning Christ and the Church.*

"Judging by your frown, Sandy, you do indeed think this is a great mystery." She blushed at the ensuing laughter, but nodded with a smile.

"Your concern is understandable," Jacob replied, "because our Church leaders hardly ever touched this passage. When they did, they treated it as meaning that such a marriage would be in name only and without procreation. But that violates the intent of Scripture, as suggested in John 2, Isaiah 54, Galatians 4:27, and Romans 7:4. Take Romans 7;4 first, which says

> *Wherefore, my brethren, ye also are become dead to the law by the body of Christ, that ye should be married to another, even to him who is raised from the dead, that we should bring forth fruit unto God.*

"This definitely suggests procreation of one sort or another, although I have no idea regarding the specifics. This thought is amplified in Galatians 4:27," Jacob continued, "where Paul is describing the implications of the Church's marriage to Jesus in the spiritual domain."

For it is written, Rejoice, thou barren that bearest not; break forth and cry, thou that travailest not; for the desolate hath many more children than she who hath an husband.

"That particular passage in Galatians came from Isaiah 54, which I see as a happy sequel to that well-known passage in Isaiah 53 describing the Jesus who suffered for our salvation."

Sing, O barren, thou who didst not bear; break forth into singing, and cry aloud, thou who didst not travail with child; for more are the children of the desolate than the children of the married wife, saith the Lord. Enlarge the place of thy tent, and let them stretch forth the curtains of thine habitations; spare not, lengthen thy cords, and strengthen thy stakes; for thou shalt break forth on the right hand and on the left, and thy seed shall inherit the nations, and make the desolate cities to be inhabited. Fear not; for thou shalt not be ashamed, neither be thou confounded; for thou shalt forget the shame of thy youth, and shalt not remember the reproach of thy widowhood any more. For thy Maker is thy husband; the Lord of hosts is his name; and thy Redeemer, the Holy One of Israel; the God of the whole earth shall he be called. For the Lord hath called thee like a woman forsaken and grieved in spirit, and a wife of youth, when thou wast refused, saith thy God. For a small moment have I forsaken thee, but with great mercies will I gather thee.

"What a beautiful passage!" Martha exclaimed. "I never made that connection with the Church."

"It describes the marriage between Jesus and His Church as a joyful, meaningful one rather than just a figure of speech. Remember too, that the marriage that Jesus attended in Cana, according to John 2, involved Jesus' very first miracle. That fact is significant, as is the joyful character of that passage. Jesus must have been looking forward with great anticipation to His own future marriage.

"Is that why Jesus never married on Earth during His first advent?" Jim asked.

"Yes! Very perceptive, Jim. He was already betrothed to His future wife, the Church. The significance of all these passages is that the Church is a composite of many people. According to 1 Corinthians 12, all these people in their spiritual form fit together as components of a much greater body, like our own organisms and components are part of our entire being. Carl, would you please read verses 12 through 30 of that chapter?"

As Jacob continued, those in attendance began to fully grasp the magnificent love in God's inclusion of gender in His creation.

"Hi again." Moira appeared in front of Jacob as he was attempting to fashion a heater for George, the lone remaining occupant of the old community. With progress in mind, he had been extracting copper wire out of the remains of some dashboard wire from the truck, no longer useful for its purpose and, thanks to Melinda and her companions, no longer necessary. The rectangular grate on which he would mount the wire sat nearby, complete with the stones he'd struggled with for days to mount as insulators. Startled but pleased, he tried again to wrap his arms around her and grabbed nothing but air.

"That's pretty slick, Jacob," she said with a cheerfulness that she didn't feel, knowing his loneliness without the intimate companionship they had shared. His transition from happy wonder to disappointment at this new reality unnerved her as well. Attempting to get out of that mind-lock, she looked at his project. It didn't look like much, but she admired his grit for making do with what he had on hand, knowing the pitiful limitation on materials and tools available to him. And, of course, his pitiful limitation of finesse as well. "Did you think that up yourself?" she asked in a forced attempt at approval.

"Yeah," he said, a smile returning to his face. "I'm planning on making as much use as possible from Melinda and her friends."

"Good for you. I'm happy to see you show compassion for George. You're going to return to your first love, Jacob. When you first came to Israel and met me. Remember? You were on fire for God and wanted to share your love, particularly to give them an understanding of the Holy Spirit. You can do that again, only now you have even more ammo for the job. Show them how I fit into the Church, now spiritual, and our relationship, individually and as a composite, with our common Husband Jesus. Keep explaining to them how as individuals we're genderless components of the Church, but as a whole we are gendered indeed. Let them know how a couple of passages in Scripture – you know which ones - from Jesus and Paul were misinterpreted so horribly wrong and shallow that the Church on Earth thought the spiritual realm didn't possess gender. You can also tell them right from the horse's mouth, me, that gender is very important here in the spiritual domain. An enormous number of my fellow Christians were very surprised to find that out when they arrived here."

Her mouth turned up in a grin of delight. "I have another surprise for you," she told Jacob. Another lifeform. But you'll recognize this one, because it isn't a new development. Look over there."

Jacob turned his head toward where she pointed and gave a shout of joy. "Cows!" he exclaimed. "And they're standing on grass! Fresh grass!"

"Yes," she replied. "Now you'll be having some milk as a change from the coconut water. They're a pair – male and female. Pretty soon they'll be having some little ones."

"So then we'll be having meat?"

"No. Those days are over. You'll be moving on soon. Those that are here will be living on plants, but God is enhancing the taste of vegetables, and most people who remain here will be happy with the closest things that are like meat, such as avocados and artichokes."

With that, Moira departed.

CHAPTER TWENTY FIVE

Jacob and Carl pulled the cart toward the old community, Elizabeth at Carl's side. The cart, the food on it and Jacob's newly-fashioned heater spoke to the trio's fears that, given George's stubborn nature, they wouldn't be returning with him. In case George's certain starvation rendered him unfit to walk, the cart would also serve as a stretcher to carry him back.

The dark cloud was gone when they reached the old area. In fact, the sky was blue and the sun shone hotly above them. Except for the odd stillness, the space around them looked more livable than it had when they had dwelt here. Seeing no sign of life, they went to the caves and called his name. When no response was forthcoming, Jacob climbed into the lowest cave and peered inside. After his eyes had adjusted to the darkness, he saw a still form on a mat.

"George!" Jacob said, gently shaking his shoulder. The person stirred, and an object in his emaciated arms let out a screeching howl. A furry cat jumped out and bounded for the cave opening. The animal looked healthy and well-fed, leading Jacob to the conclusion that, like God had done with Jonah by supplying a gourd for his comfort, Moira or one of her cohorts had given the cat to George as a kind of compensation during his time of misery and want.

"Bring up some water, Carl," Jacob called down from the cave entrance. "And a couple of bananas and some dates. George is in a bad way."

Elizabeth came up with Carl, bringing more food. George sat up to eat. He was ravenous. After he had gobbled up his fill, he glared at the three people. "You could have just left me alone to die," he told them. "You've deserted me," he accused. "To the last person. What's the point of my living if you've gone away and God Himself has rejected me?"

"God hasn't forsaken you," Elizabeth said softly. "Either have we. In fact, we came here to take you back with us."

"Why would you want me around? You obviously didn't want to listen to my preaching. I guess my cat's gone too." A tear dribbled down a cheek. "I guess God didn't care for it either. I've gone as far down as one can go."

"Then you have nowhere to go but up," Jacob told him. "It looks like your ego has left you as well. Which is a move on the 'up' side. Your messages weren't that bad either, except for your attempt to take away our gendered natures. What you never could get into your thick skin is that this attempt of yours rubs against the very core of our existence as God had made us. In His own image, I might add."

George thrust his chin out at Jacob. "Are you still going on about God Himself being gendered? In direct opposition to what the Bible says?"

"But the Bible didn't say that," Jacob countered. "It implies it in one area – the 'He' references in John's Gospel, but that wasn't the case in the original version. The versions we have were corrupted in that area by people like you who thought sex was so evil that it should be banished altogether. People have tried to reason with you about that but you wouldn't listen. There's a wealth of reasons, all from the Bible itself, as to why we think the Godhead is gendered. We've given them to you, and I'm pretty sure you remember some of them. We've also talked to you about why so many of us thought that sex was evil, or at least impure. We'd acquired all that trash with the transgression of Adam and Eve, a baggage of false guilt. I won't rehash all that now, except to say that the biggest problem is that you don't understand why the issue is so important, although you yourself made it important, in a truly negative way. It's important because the love of God goes way beyond the kind of benign but remote affection that we associate with the Greek word 'agape'".

"You're going to suggest again that God possesses love with the flavor of 'eros'. You make me sick. I want my cat back." George began to weep.

In response to George's distress, Elizabeth went out of the cave in search of the pet, suspecting like Jacob that Moira had something to do with its presence with George.

"The thing about 'eros', George, is that it involves possession in a romantic sense. Eros goes way beyond just sex as most people view the word. It includes the harmony between husband and wife, making them one flesh as God intended for them. A big part of that harmony comes from their mutual ownership."

Elizabeth returned with the cat. George greedily opened his arms to receive the pet and clutched it to his breast. He petted it until it began to purr. A beautiful joy lit up his face.

"Look at you and your pet, George. As you see it, the cat is yours. It belongs to you, and your love in return belongs to it. That's the kind of love that God wants to have with his Bride, the Church. It's an extended form of eros, like the love between parents and their children. It's a beautiful kind of mutual ownership. Agape love, as most Christians understand it, can't begin to compare with it, and it's the kind of relationship in love that God has within the Godhead and what He wants with us."

"Maybe you're right or maybe not, but so what?" George pushed back. "I don't see the point in your insisting that God is gendered. I love my God the way He is."

"Okay then," Jacob said. "If you love Him the way you say you do, and you're a pastor, I'd suppose you have a calling to share that love. I'd like to love Him too. Tell me about Him. What's He like that makes you love Him?"

George glared at him, supposing that he was being mocked. But he was a pastor, and he indeed saw himself as having a calling from God. "First off, if you'd been paying attention to my sermons when you were here, you'd have heard that God is omnipotent, omnipresent, and omniscient. Which means, of course, that He is all-powerful, all-seeing, and all-knowing. He's so much grander than us that He deserves our worship. We must love Him because He's worthy. He's the most majestic, worthy Being in the universe.

And, since He's our Creator, we must appreciate Him all the more, because without Him we wouldn't exist."

Jacob stared at George in disbelief. "Not once did you mention His love toward us, or of our love toward Him. Of course, God deserves our worship, but where's the love in that? I didn't ask why we should worship Him. I asked about loving Him."

George attempted to regain the initiative. "Don't forget that God demands that we love Him," he said. "He said that in Deuteronomy 6, and Jesus repeated that in Matthew 22. He also demands our obedience. You put those two together, and guess what? If we love Him, we must be obedient, and if we're obedient, we must love Him. How can we do otherwise?"

"So you're saying that we must control our minds to the extent that we insist on loving God. That it's an intellectual exercise that needs our constant self-reminders of all the good things God does for us."

"Yes, of course." He spoke as if he had a Q.E.D. moment, that such followed naturally.

"That just doesn't work," Jacob responded. "Remember what Jesus called the Greatest Commandment as He echoed Moses' words in Deuteronomy 6:5: 'You shall love the Lord your God with all your heart, and all your soul, and all your might.' That's less of an order from Him than a promise. Loving God intellectually doesn't cut it, and never can. You must imprint on Him possessively, like a partner in marriage. Your soul must become one with Jesus' soul. That's possible only when you understand Jesus at a deeper level than you can obtain from the genderless view of the Godhead that you've been taught. Only as you see the gendered nature of Jesus and the Godhead will you perceive the intrinsic harmony of gender-based functional differentiation."

"You worship God your way, I'll do it my way," he pouted.

"You don't understand, George. Your way doesn't work. You can't even love God intellectually, because you don't really understand who God is. If you want to love God, you need to know Him in more detail than you do. As it stands now, you – and a great many of your fellows – don't have any idea of the functional relationship that exists between the Father and the Holy Spirit. If you don't understand that, or even the nature of the Holy Spirit, how can you truly love God?"

"You aren't married, George," Jacob added, noting that George was about to stop his ears. "But you must have some understanding of the relationship between married spouses. Does a lack of mutual understanding support a fraction of what love means to them? You're well-read in the Bible, so you know from Ephesians 5:31 and 32 that the marital relationship defines the union between Jesus and His Church. If you do go to heaven, how will you handle that?"

"It's called a marriage, but we have no idea what that entails. Intimate, yes. Loving, yes, in an *agape* way. But romantic, no, definitely not. Scripture just doesn't support that view."

"Oh, but you're wrong, George. The Song of Solomon says otherwise. So does Romans 7:4. So does my late wife Moira, who has given me just a glimpse of what heaven must be like. Not only will it be romantic, but it will be procreative, as that passage notes. But there's more in Scripture. Take, for instance, Isaiah 1:21." Jacob reached for George's Bible and read from that passage:

How is the faithful city become an harlot! It was full of justice; righteousness lodged in it, but now murderers.

"Or how about Jeremiah 3:1?"

They say, If a man put away his wife, and she go from him, and become another man's, shall he return unto her again? Shall not that land be greatly polluted? But thou hast played the harlot with many lovers; return again unto me, saith the Lord.

"And, of course, God told Hosea to marry a harlot as an example of Israel's unfaithfulness to Him. All these passages present Jesus as our lover in a far more intimate way than mere *agape* would suggest. The notion of *eros* instead of *agape* is confirmed in Ephesians 5:31 and 32, which puts our relationship with Jesus in the context of that between Adam and Eve:

For this cause shall a man leave his father and mother, and shall be joined unto his wife, and they two shall be one flesh. This is a great mystery, but I speak concerning Christ and the church.

"How can that be?" George said. "You put Jesus in the Old Testament with those passages from Isaiah and Jeremiah. You're confusing the Father with Jesus."

"You know better than that, George. John 1:18 tells us that no man has seen the Father at any time. The God of both Testaments who showed Himself to the Israelites many times was none other than Jesus, as He Himself declared in John 8:56 through 58." Jacob turned again to George's Bible and read the passages to George:

Your father, Abraham, rejoiced to see my day: and he saw it, and was glad. Then said the Jews unto him, Thou are not yet fifty years old, and hast thou seen Abraham? Jesus said unto them, Verily, verily, I say unto you, Before Abraham was, I am.

"Maybe, if the thought of an intimate kind of love embarrasses you, you'd be better off not meeting Jesus in heaven."

"No! Don't say that!" Startled at George's sudden outburst, the cat jumped off the bed, amplifying George's panic. Elizabeth returned the cat to George's grateful arms.

"Thank you, Elizabeth. But all of you, please leave me alone for now," George said, subdued. "I need to process what you've told me."

They left George alone for the night. Returning the next morning, they found him in abject misery. His weeping rose in volume as they entered his space. His shaking became so profound that the cat was startled into clawing its way out of his arms. Elizabeth rushed over and knelt in front of his tear-marked face.

"Can we help, George?" she asked, the concern in her voice lifting his red eyes toward hers in a silent plea.

"I – I think I understand," he said. "But then I've done a terrible thing. A terrible thing to God and to you. I've lost everything now, even my pride."

"Here, have a date," Carl said, reaching out to George with the fruit. Elizabeth looked at him strangely. The sharpness of her stare softened when she realized that the lame offer was all that Carl knew what to do in this awkward situation. Nevertheless, George accepted it in appreciation.

"Your pride was worthless anyway, George," Elizabeth replied. "It had to get lost to get you right with God. In fact, that's the best possible thing that could have happened to you."

His shaking subsided with Elizabeth's soft, reassuring voice. He chewed on the date and held out his hand for more. "Perhaps now you can apologize to God and ask Him to help you become the pastor He wants you to be."

"Do – do you really think He might still want to use me?"

"Why don't you ask Him? I think we'll leave you for a while, and let you talk to Him alone."

George closed his eyes and began to converse with God. Carl placed some dates onto his outstretched hand, and they left.

The next day they brought George down from the cave and placed him onto the cart. As the three trekked back to the new community with George in the cart, Jacob looked down at the man, who had maintained a downcast countenance. "I've been conducting a Bible study in your absence," Jacob told him. "I'm not a talker, George. Not as eloquent as you, and I'd appreciate it if you'd resume your position as our pastor when you get well enough to handle it."

"Really?" George's eyes brightened. "You mean it?"

"Of course," Jacob replied. The remainder of their journey became happier.

CHAPTER TWENTY SIX

"Hi, Jacob. You're looking good. Almost makes me want to come back to Earth and grab you."

"Could you?" Jacob grinned hugely with delight at the prospect.

"I said 'almost'. I've got a good gig where I am. Patience, Jacob. It won't be long before you'll be able to see for yourself. In the meantime, I have another present for you. The three of you did good with George. We were especially pleased to see that you had given your Bible study back to George. I know you were reluctant to do that. But don't worry - he's grateful to be useful, and he's come around to a much more loving understanding of God. He'll do well."

"I just hope he doesn't revert back to his old obnoxious self."

"Not likely. He had a life-changing confrontation with himself. We helped with that, of course."

Jacob grinned at her. "Why am I not surprised at that? You spoke of a present. I don't see anything."

"The gift is named Charlie, but "he" isn't here. Grab your canteen and come along."

Moira walked alongside Jacob for several miles. Despite repeated questions from him, she refused to tell him where they were going. Presently they reached the top of a hill where they could see the shimmering blue water of the Mediterranean below. Another hour brought them to the shore, where Moira pointed down to an area of quiet water protected by a little cove. "There's Charlie," she said.

"Where?" All I see is a green blob."

"The blob is Charlie. Keep looking."

As Jacob watched, the blob slowly formed a bubble in its midst. The bubble grew to engulf the entire thing, and as it kept expanding the surface of the bubble ate into the solid green mass and began to display a beautiful iridescence. Blemishes like little pimples appeared in a regular pattern on the surface. Eventually the bubble rose from the surface of the water, but as it lifted it dropped some tiny seeds back in the water. An opening appeared in the midst of one of the blemishes and the bubble drifted off with apparent purpose, propelled by exhaust from the hole that the blemish had created.

"Where's it going?" Jacob asked.

"Nowhere special. That particular Charlie doesn't have anything to respond to. Poor Charlie will eventually drift off to who knows where and probably end up on some barren stretch of ground." She appeared to be grieved by that, but her expression brightened. But there are other Charlies, and if you handle things right they'll be quite useful to you. They respond to music, Jacob. We made them that way. When sound waves of a certain type impact their surfaces, they'll come down to ground near the point where the sound originates. They particularly like "Amazing Grace", which I know is one of your favorites. They also like a number of your other favorites. I had a hand in the selection," she said with a grin.

"The bubbles rise because their insides are filled with the hydrogen that they've extracted from the seawater," she continued. When they land they stop living. That's okay, no need to feel sorry for them as they're not really sentient beings. But when they die, their DNA has been programmed with a new twist, the addition of very specifically controlled decomposition. They decompose, but in a very orderly manner such that the hydrogen recombines with oxygen in a non-combustible way to create water and carbon dioxide. The carbon dioxide dissipates into the air to promote the growth of the plant life that you need. See how new blobs have formed and bubbles are starting to form in them? Let's go back to the community and you can call them down."

As they trod back, Moira describe to Jacob how they'd be useful to the group. "Together they'll eventually form an oasis representing a significant freshwater source, which will be badly needed in the future."

"That's an incredible design. Makes my little heater a cobbled-up piece of junk."

"Don't say that, Jacob," she replied. "I'm very proud of you for what you've been doing with so little at your disposal. And it's still something George can use until he gets a little meat on his bones. It's just that we have far more to work with, including an enormous common mind. But now that you've finished with the heater, you'd best set to work making a water pump."

"But why do we need this water so badly? You've created some lakes on your own, as I recall. Clever as these creatures are, you seem to be able to summon water at the snap of your fingers. Why can't you keep doing that?"

"Because it's a lot more fun to set things in motion and watch them happen on their own. Besides, we have better things to occupy ourselves with. Like bringing your communities up to speed on your natures. We'd really like you – all of you – to be a tad more loving and selfless."

"Communities? Plural? Are there more of them besides us?"

Moira laughed, a musical melody that amplified her beauty. "Oh, yes, Jacob. If you thought your group was all there is, you're off-base. It's time I gave you a bigger view of things. Take a walk with me."

Moira led him around a knoll, where he was shocked to see an elegant, smooth-surfaced building in a muted beige color, its architecture much more compatible with the surrounding countryside than anything he'd ever seen of man's efforts to create beauty through his own aesthetic skills. While ultra-modern in appearance, it also blended amazingly well with the natural environment in which it was ensconced. "So that's what real architecture is all about!" Jacob exclaimed. "Is naturally artificial even a valid expression?"

"Get prepared for a bigger surprise," Moira responded, pointing a finger toward the building. An opening appeared. What resided inside the opening astonished Jacob. "What?" he questioned in disbelief. "That's a UFO. Or what Wisdom called a FIFO. A flying saucer. What on Earth is that doing here? Are there aliens here, too? From another planet?"

"Most humans have had a strange and mistaken view of FIFOs, induced by their unjustified materialistic mindset along with their near-worship of individualism. And that's when they even acknowledged the possibility of their existence. FIFOs have been around for a very long time, as those who've read the Bible and thought about what they were reading were forced to conclude. Of course, that's not saying much, because those who've thought about what they were reading have always been in precious short supply. I guess I'd have to include myself in that condemnation when I was alongside you as a human. Believe me, Jacob, this spiritual realm is a real eye-opener. About this FIFO business – for starters, the occupants of these craft are anything but aliens. They've been angels throughout history, but since Jesus has taken over on Earth, we of the Church have been privileged to use these vehicles as well. Even I have an 'occupant' license," she said with a laugh. "Well, anyway, on a bright side of things, how'd you like to go for a ride? I might even let you take the controls once in a while."

"You bet!" he replied. They went together toward the craft. A ladder appeared beneath it as they approached. She invited him into the craft and climbed in after him.

"I'm an occupant now," he said as he entered the device. Does that make me an angel?"

"Ha ha. Not yet, but you're getting close. Almost as close as me and the rest of us who make up the Church."

"But why would angels – and you – need to tool around in a machine, when you seem to do very well flitting here and there without help from any device?"

"Good question and I'll give you an excellent answer: it helped angels interface with humanity in a way that wasn't overtly religious. Besides, it's lots of fun," she added with a grin. "I've been told that the look of shock on a person's face when he first encounters one has been a rich source of laughter on the part of a good many angels."

"That puts a new slant on the meaning of angels."

"You forget what you already know. In the collective sense, angels comprise the Holy Spirit, just as we Christians in the spiritual domain comprise the Church as a body. Individually, we don't amount to much, but the real action is in the collective sense, just as Paul tried to tell the Churches. He was particularly open about that in his first letter to the Corinthians. Here, let me give you an excerpt:

> *For to one is given, by the Spirit, the word of wisdom; to another, the word of knowledge by the same Spirit; to another, faith by the same Spirit; to another, the gifts of healing by the same Spirit; to another the working of miracles; to another, prophecy; to another, discerning of spirits; to another various kinds of tongues; to another, the interpretation of tongues. But all these work that one and the very same Spirit, dividing to every man severally as God wills. For as the body is one, and has many members, and all the members of that one body, being many, are one body, so also is Christ. For by one Spirit were we all baptized into one body, whether we be Jews or Greeks, whether we be bond or free; and have been all made to drink into one Spirit. For the body is not one member, but many.*

> *If the foot shall say, Because I am not the hand, I am not of the body; is it, therefore, not of the body? And if the ear shall say, Because I am not the eye, I am not of the body; is it, therefore, not of the body? If the whole body were an eye, where were the hearing? If the whole were hearing, where were the smelling? But now has God set the members, every one of them, in the body, as it has pleased him. And if they were all one member, where were the body? But now are they many members, yet but one body.*

"Yeah," Jacob replied. "We kind of blew that one, not comprehending that we have a collective identity that's more significant than our individual selves. Couldn't think outside the box the misguided clergy stuffed us in. We were so off-track that most of us couldn't figure out the enormous functional difference between the individual and the aggregate, leading us to think that Galatians 3:28 meant that there was no such thing as gender in the spiritual domain."

The vehicle, which was as elegant as the building that housed it, gave him a sense that he, himself, was an alien from another planet. Moira sat at the controls and motioned for Jacob to sit beside her. She deftly maneuvered the craft out of the building and into the sunlight. "Brace yourself," she said, and they rose above the ground.

"We won't be able to make any sharp turns or accelerations with you aboard, but you'll have a lot to see anyway."

The acceleration, while fairly mild under her graceful command, continued until they were traveling over an ocean at a shocking rate. Presently, after the trip which was all-too-brief to Jacob's mind, land reappeared and they descended over what looked like a community somewhat similar to the one to which Jacob belonged. Their craft hovered above a crowd. The look of shock on the upturned faces evoked a grin from Moira and a laugh from him. "Thought you'd like that," she said to him.

CHAPTER TWENTY SEVEN

Moira guided the craft a short distance away from the settlement, where it rested out of sight behind a knoll. "Let's go," she said, standing up and heading toward the exit. "I have some people I'd like you to meet."

As they trod across a dirt field, she spoke her intent. "I won't be seen by these people," she began. They're holding a meeting right now. They have a pastor, James, who's giving them a sermon, much like George did with you – us. Much of what he says will explain itself automatically to you, maybe even give you a laugh. Just go in and sit down on a bench, as if you belong there. When he's finished, go back to where we landed unless something intervenes."

As they approached the community, Jacob sensed something different than what he'd expected to see, not exactly out of place, but not completely in harmony with what he'd gotten used to in the gathering he'd been associated with. It eventually came to him: a large, crudely-woven tent stood in the center of a clearing. When he reached the tent, he marveled at the weave, wondering how and when that same material could be made available for his own people.

"Where did they get the cloth for the tent?" he asked Moira. But Moira was no longer by his side. He continued on inside and found a bench inside the tent. "We have a right," James said as Jacob sat down. Eyes glanced his way, but if there was any surprise, it didn't register on their faces. "We have expectations and they haven't been met," James continued, his volume on high. "And as far as I can see, we've done all we can to worship Him. We love You, Lord," he spoke to the sky. What more can we do for You?" A multitude of hands raised in fervent, worshipful agreement.

"Hi," he called to a man who walked nearby after the sermon had ended. The man had been deep in his own thoughts, and the greeting surprised him. He turned to face Jacob and peered into his face, a question in his eyes. "Who are you?" he asked.

"I've been living over there," Jacob replied noncommittally, pointing vaguely in the direction of some trees in the distance. "I haven't been able to find anything to eat. I wonder if you people might have a little food you might be able to share."

"Of course we do," the man said kindly, extending his hand. "My name's Louie."

"And I'm Jacob," he replied shaking his hand.

"Follow me," Louie told him, walking toward another tent. He opened the flap and ushered him inside. They came to a chubby but attractive woman. "This is Lois. I know, Lois and Louie. You can't beat coincidence." Lois smiled warmly and shook Jacob's hand. "Jacob here is hungry. Can you dish him up something?"

"Sure thing," Lois said, and turned toward what looked like a kitchen area. But there was a hint of a frown on her face as she left them and walked by a man whose face showed displeasure toward her.

"Lois is my wife," Louie told Jacob. "She's a fine woman. A treasure, really. I don't know what I'd do without her." As Lois returned with a plate, she was accosted by the man who had given her the stink eye. "What are you doing, Lois?' he said sharply with a nasty expression. "We've already had lunch. Nobody needs more." Lois walked past, ignoring him, and handed the plate to Jacob.

"If you don't have enough to go around," Jacob said, "I can make do on my own."

"Sit," Lois replied. "Eat. We don't turn away hungry strangers."

"Will you both sit with me?" Jacob asked, sitting at a wooden bench in front of a wooden slab table.

"Yes, sure," Louie said as he and Lois sat beside him. "Don't mind Jimmy over there. He's kind of a worry-wart."

"But what he said – are you short of food as well?"

"Kind of. We're okay with some foods. Chicken, as you can see." Jacob looked down at his plate and the drumstick made him drool. "And eggs too, of course. But we're mighty short of fruits and vegetables. I'd give anything to bite into a nice big hunk of squash." Jacob laughed so hard that tears came to his eyes. "Perhaps some day I can help you with that," he told them. Their eyebrows jumped up at that. I can't say any more about that right now, but maybe my coming here won't be the burden that Jimmy implied." He looked over toward Jimmy, who was watching him with a glare. "You might want to let Jimmy know what I just said before he gets a stroke," Jacob added.

"What has Jimmy off the rails is the apparent change lately in our circumstances," Louie said. "We're believers. Charismatics, truth be told. Have been even before the Earth started to rock and roll. After this thing that happened to our world," he continued, waving his arms in an all-encompassing motion, "God helped us out. Gave us water, and chickens and other things that let us continue to survive. One night Jimmy there got a message from God. A communication. Jimmy learned how to make a weaving machine right then and there, supernaturally from the Holy Spirit. And how to spin the grass fibers into twine. I saw you looking at the tent. We have other ones, giving us couples real privacy. Then more people got zapped by the Holy Spirit, with gifts of all kinds. Knowledge, the kind that's made our lives much easier. I guess we got kind of used to receiving these gifts, thanking God and all, but things had dried up lately in the gift department. We worship God with all our might, singing to the Holy Spirit and yearning for answers, but nothing seems to happen. The worst of it is that our water is getting scarce. We have wells, but the water level in them is getting lower at an alarming rate. That's truly a survival issue."

It was dark by the time Jacob returned to the craft. Moira was there, waiting for him with a loving smile. They entered the craft silently as Moira sat at the controls and Jacob sat beside her. Light from the instruments shone on her beautiful face, giving Jacob a painful yearning for her.

They traveled miles in silence until Moira finally spoke. "Learn anything?" she asked him.

"Oh, yeah," he replied. "Lots. They seem to have a different problem than we did. More like they want things from God more than anything else, like maybe they think of Him as some kind of cosmic Santa."

"Good assessment," she replied. "That's precisely what's holding them back – a very shallow, infantile relationship with God. They have good hearts but don't see the big picture about God. Anything else?"

"Yes, something very positive, if it can be pulled off. They seem to have things we'd like to have, and we seem to have things that they're desperate for. Like squash, if you can believe it." They shared chuckles on that thought. "Would it be possible to start up a trade with them?"

"How? By flying saucer?" She laughed again. "That's off the table for now. It would be too easy for them, make them more focused on the Santa aspect of God. But maybe something can be arranged. Both you and they share a habitable land bridge that bisects the sea we traveled over. You're on one side, and they're on the other. Maybe a boat's in your future. Or theirs. Or both of yours. Or maybe something else. We'll see." She looked at him with a smile. "Actually, your different needs have come about by design. Yes, trade is definitely on the table." "By the way," she added. "I was watching you running around frantically before you came up to the craft. Were you really trying to steal a chicken?"

"Yes, I guess I was," he admitted. "I can't believe how good that chicken at lunch tasted. And how much it would have been appreciated if I could have bagged one and returned home with it."

"Sorry, Jacob," but first things first. I don't want your group to know about this trip, not yet anyway. And you don't want them to be lusting after chicken and thinking of nothing else when there's so much more work to be done to get the trading underway. I know about your mindset with the bird – you were thinking of others, and the thought is appreciated." When they landed, she gave him a loving look and disappeared, craft and all.

CHAPTER TWENTY EIGHT

The lips caressing his ear woke Jacob. The pleasant sensation caused him to smile. For a moment he thought that Moira might have returned to him. The sound of heavy breathing amplified his joy. But there was something off about the breath. When he opened his eyes, he stared in shock. The creature, he saw in astonishment, was a horse. Moira stood behind the animal, a wide grin on her face.

"Sorry, Jacob, I couldn't help myself from laughing. There's two more a little ways away. You have enough grass in the area to support them, and plenty of water besides."

"What are we going to do with them?"

"They're here for a reason. You wanted to establish trade. These animals will get you from here to there and back."

"I don't know anything about horses, how to take care of them or ride them, or – anything."

"No, but Carl does. We gave him a big dose of wisdom in animal husbandry. You'll laugh when you see how capable he is. But you'll be helping him out with some woodworking skills to go along with the metallurgy. He needs a wagon, and the sooner he gets one, the sooner you'll be on the road to helping the community you saw. I've named it 'Jacobville', by the way."

"If you've been naming communities, what's ours?"

"Other people have done that. They're calling it 'Moira City.' I'm touched."

Jacob's memory of western movies, along with the knowledge that Moira had given him, enabled him to complete a two-wheeled cart that was much lighter and suitable to be drawn by horses than the makeshift cart fashioned out of the wheels on the buried truck.

The biggest problem he faced was with the new wheels, which resembled those that graced scenes from the old American West, hubs, spokes and all.

While Jacob was busy making the new cart, Carl and Elizabeth were occupied with the horses. Elizabeth was ecstatic about learning to ride the painted horse. Carl leaned into his new craft of caring for the horses and teaching two of them to operate as a team with the old cart. Elizabeth was gone for hours riding the paint, which she called 'Donna'.

It took them four weeks to prepare for their journey. As the day neared, they loaded the cart with food that would be the least perishable, which included coconuts, dates and, of course, squash.

"Hey, Peter," Carl yelled. "Got a job for you, if you don't mind."

"Yeah, what?" Peter asked as he approached the other man.

"We need help in loading this cart," Carl responded. "See that patch over there?"

"So?" Carl's mouth turned upward in a futile attempt to suppress a grin as he watched Peter's Adam's apple bob up and down at the site.

"We need some of that – the ripe stuff – to go with us. They're hungry for it. Mind bringing some over?"

"They can have it all," Peter said with a sour face. Despite his discomfort, he headed toward the patch of squash. Carl's conscience got the better of him when he saw Peter pinch his mouth in a suppressed retch.

"Hey, Peter," Carl called. "Hold on. I was just funning you, and I'm sorry. I'll take care of the squash if you'll bring over some more dates."

"Nah," Peter replied. "Some day I'll have to learn to live with it, if only to improve my reputation. I might as well start now."

Carl looked at Peter's retreating back with a new-found respect for the man.

The squash they selected had hard, heavy rinds that would keep the contents from spoiling during the trip. But their most valuable cargo was a number of the little seeds that hopefully would turn into the blobs that Moira had named "Charlie". An ongoing question in Jacob's mind had been answered by their voyage in the flying device. He had wondered at the time why, with all the water God had given them, they might even need the remarkable little watermakers. Now he realized that the need was urgent in Jacobville, and he happily anticipated the joy the little blobs would deliver to the water-starved community.

The travelers met with obstacles their first day out, and Moira was nowhere in sight as events unfolded. Jacob swore that he could see Donna the paint sneer at the two horses lugging the wagon. That suspicion was confirmed in his mind when he saw the brown mare Jamie snort in response and come to a quick halt, which caused Jack the grey stallion, who wasn't doing much upstairs, to strain in his harness until he stopped as well. Jamie remained in a snit until Elizabeth rode ahead on Donna until they were out of sight. Even then, Jamie tried to bite Carl's hand as he attempted to soothe her. Carl, out of patience, began to yell at Jamie, which only made her attitude worse. Ears pasted back, she stomped a hoof onto the ground and set her leg in a position of stubborn immobility. After an hour of yelling, the recalcitrant horse began to move. But the awkward manner in which the cart had stopped had put a twist on the fragile axle and caused it to break with the resumption of movement. "Whoa!" Jacob shouted in alarm as the cart abruptly tilted. Fortunately, Carl had brought some of his woodworking tools along for just that kind of event, and he set to work immediately to repair the damage. They were still working on it when Elizabeth had returned, wondering what had held them up.

"Better park your horse away from these two," Jacob told her. And we might as well bed down here, as it's almost night anyway."

Moira came into their camp as they were finishing their meal. "Uh-oh," she remarked. "Had a tad of trouble, I see."

"Yeah, and maybe you did too good of a job on their brains, at least with the womenfolk. Donna and Jamie aren't exactly the best of friends. A little more placid would have been good."

Moira laughed musically. "I've already taken care of that. They'll get along fine tomorrow. See you around."

The next day was more productive, and by nightfall they'd traveled an appreciable distance. They were in much better spirits as they prepared the evening meal.

The trio reached Jacobville two weeks later, to the surprise and warm welcome of the townspeople. "Horses!" Louie exclaimed as he approached them. "What a grand event! Do you think that they might produce some more?"

"Hello again, Louie," Jacob said, reaching for his hand. "Here are two of my friends, Carl and Elizabeth. They're a couple. As for the ability of these horses to reproduce, I haven't thought about that. But I suppose they can, and if they do, we'll see that you eventually might get some offspring. But right now," he continued, pointing to the cart, "we have something more immediate to give you."

Carl had already moved to the top of the cart and started handing down some of the items to Louie and Lois, who eagerly accepted them and handed them over to other townspeople. "That's squash!" Louie exclaimed as Carl handed him a gourd. "Wow! My tummy's gonna have a good time tonight!"

"Good thing Peter didn't come along," Jacob said to Carl under his breath. "Might have disgraced himself by barfing on the squash and ruining some appetites."

"Actually, Jacob, Peter's acquitted himself well with the squash. He was the one who loaded the cart with it."

"Mm," Jacob said noncommittally.

After dinner, Jacob gave a demonstration of the little Charlies, to the awe of the assembled community. Their expressions of gratitude brought joy to the traveling trio. The excitement over having abundant water continued on through the night. When Jacob turned the conversation to the possibility of trade, they were enthusiastic over that as well.

Jacob and the others remained in the community for three days, enjoying the peoples' generous hospitality. On the third day they loaded up the cart with trade goods. They were happiest with the chickens, which were enclosed in a sturdy wooden cage. Second in favor among the remainder of items was the cloth. They anticipated the delight on the faces of their friends as they looked forward to replacing the palm fronds with the more permanent privacy the tents would provide.

CHAPTER TWENTY NINE

The travelers were met with enthusiasm on their return. People crowded around the cart, eagerly examining the contents. They were most fascinated by the chickens, Peter chief among them.

"You'll be first to have a chicken dinner, Peter," Jacob told him. "Put some meat on your bones." Peter responded with a drool.

George came to the cart, knelt and gave thanks for the bounty. "Bless this little community," he continued. "We're grateful for your wonderful generosity, Lord, and thankful for the love You've shown us in connecting our little communities." He left for the place he'd made after that little dialog with God.

"Notice how he didn't embellish on what he had to say?" Carl said to Jacob. "I'm impressed by that."

"Me too. He's becoming a real asset to us."

Not long after they had returned, Donna gave birth to twins, a pretty little filly that looked a lot like her mother and a husky brother having a solid rust color. The new arrivals occupied much of Elizabeth's time, with Carl furnishing help with time he could spare from his other duties.

Development at Moira City continued to expand. A farm was established to grow grass for the horses and expanded beyond their immediate requirements in anticipation of an increase in the herd's size.

Over the next several months the two communities continued their relationship with each other as well. Early on, Carl and Elizabeth brought grass seed to the other community and taught them to plant it in preparation for a gift they had planned. The water-producing Charlies had provided the community with enough water to start a reasonably-sized farm in addition to supplying their everyday needs. They would continue to multiply, permitting an expansion of its crop acreage, which had begun to include bananas and squash as well as coconut and date palms.

Once the horse twins were weaned and had gained weight, the couple returned to Jacobville with them in tow, along with a cart full of trade goods. Almost immediately the other group returned the favor. Having begun with the motivation of trade, the people began to assimilate into each others' groups, forming new friendships and romances. The most surprising of these new relationships was the love that had developed between George and his romantic partner Betsy from the other community, a serious-minded lady who had devoted much of her life to the reading of her Bible. Attracted to each other by their mutual interest in Scripture, they exchanged interpretations of the passages of their interest. Betsy's interpretations softened George's understanding of God, which Moira was quick to note and encourage. Together they brought love front and center in the community's perception of God, a development that God Himself was quite pleased with.

Jacob's enthusiasm with trade led him to an idea for innovation. *Why not build a boat?* he asked himself. *It would hold a lot more than a cart. And, if it had a sail, it would be easier as well.* The problem was that Jacob didn't know how to build one, and didn't know how to sail if he ever got it built. *Maybe Wisdom will teach me those things,* he thought. As his excitement over the prospect grew, he became all the more determined to do this thing. He moved his sparse belongings to the shore, as well as the tools he could take without causing problems in the community that he left behind.

As he started on the project, Wisdom gave him a few tips but at Moira's request held back on many of the critical insights pertaining to shipbuilding. "What, you want to get a laugh at poor Jacob's expense?" She asked Moira, frowning at her unexpected and rather dark levity.

"He'll get over it. He has a good sense of humor, you know. And I'm not talking about just a laugh. When's the last time you had a real belly-laugh? As You Yourself know, he has a couple missing brain parts when it comes to executing the finished product. It's in his DNA. Besides, we can help him big-time afterwards."

"Can't do it," Wisdom said. "I have more of a sense of humor than you do, Moira, but to Me, kindness and love trump the pain we'd give him."

"Well, okay then, give him the smarts he needs to get the boat built. But I guarantee that he'll find a way to mess it up anyway. He's great with some things, but with projects like that it's what he does."

"Okey-dokey," Wisdom said, smiling with a beginning anticipation of what might turn out to be an epic event. But She had mixed feelings about the project. She refused to go forward in time to see the finished item, as She wanted it to be a surprise. She hoped that he would show Moira up as being wrong about his lack of talent in boatbuilding.

Moira entertained no such hope. She rubbed her hands in glee as he started to work on it.

For weeks his excitement over a boat drove Jacob to work until he was about to drop. First, he had to cut down some trees, which he did with the chainsaw and gas can that he'd found in the buried truck. Then he had to drag the trees close to the shore. Fortunately, he had a horse to help him with that task. He rode the horse bareback every evening to return to the camp for dinner and companionship, becoming an expert rider in the process. As he'd sit by the fire at night, he tended to brag a bit about his accomplishments. His camp audience hung on his every word, looking up to him somewhat more than Wisdom considered to be appropriate. Everyone there, She knew, was eager for large-scale trade to begin, but he was carrying things too far attempting to cash in on it somewhat prematurely.

Moira listened to him too, but her take was different than Wisdom's. She'd peeked ahead in time, just a little, but it was enough to send her into hysterical fits of laughter.

Ideas would pop into Jacob's mind about how to proceed, but

their orientation was a little off, to Moira's profound delight. He knew that the boat needed to be built around a keel and ribs. He spent much time fashioning the keel, and it ended up looking pretty good. Next came the ribs, which didn't work out quite so well. He'd shaped them okay if straight boards were truly okay, but curved boards would have been much better. Even then they may have worked out to some extent, but he attached them to the keel horizontally rather than at an angle to the vertical, which made the affair look like outstretched oars. He did perceive, if somewhat dimly, that the assembly didn't look quite right. Nevertheless, he proceeded methodically to begin shaping the boards that would attach to the ribs.

After working for an inordinate length of time on the first board, he sat on the sand and wiped his brow. After some reflection, he decided that this part was way too tedious. Besides, it had already taken much more time than he'd originally estimated to get this far. *Let's get this show on the road,* he thought, and decided that instead of making planks, it would probably be acceptable to use whole logs. Further effort eventually revealed the essence of the craft: a log cabin without the roof. Even he could tell that this wasn't the result he was looking for, but he doggedly continued until the structure was completed. He then stepped the mast, which was another log considerably thicker than necessary for its function.

It was then that he suddenly realized something that had slipped his mind. He was supposed to place the keel on top of logs, which would have permitted him to simply roll the boat into the water. Up to this point he intended to get the boat into the water by himself. He'd wanted to make sure the craft actually worked before he had an audience, but now he knew that he had no choice: it would be necessary to enlist the aid of those in the camp.

Having smeared asphalt on the bottom to seal the craft from the intrusion of the sea, he was ready for the movement into the water at noontime one day. Reluctantly, he mounted his horse and went back to the camp, where he asked for strong bodies. There was more enthusiasm for the task than he thought he'd get, which buoyed up his spirits a little. With the help of a roller log next to the "bow" (one side of the foursquare trapezoid) and a lot of grunting on the part of the struggling men, the "boat" inched toward the water. As rollers were added, the task became easier. Eventually, it achieved flotation, albeit somewhat awkwardly. The logs on one side of the craft appeared to be larger than those on the other. At least that's what Jacob supposed gave the object such a decided tilt. It looked exactly like what it was: a waterborne derelict.

Wisdom wept with compassion for the poor man, now red-faced in his extreme embarrassment.

Moira also wept, but hers were tears of uncontrollable hilarity.

An idea came to Jacob as to how he might resurrect this awkward situation. "Help me find some rocks," he called to the men looking on. "It's just a matter of applying some ballast. We need some rocks, the bigger the better."

Several men wandered off in search of rocks, returning to the boat and handing them up to Jacob one-by-one. The number of rocks required to level the boat was considerable. A slight correction was noticed, but the amount of leveling was miniscule compared to the reduction in freeboard, which was now just inches above the waterline. The onlookers frowned with concern as the boat settled further into the water. The added weight was making itself felt along the tar-plastered logs situated above the ribs. As a rock was dropped onto the growing pile, the tar in one place finally gave up the ghost and popped out of the crack between two logs. The inevitable happened: the boat sank beneath the surface, except for one poorly-fashioned corner, which stuck up like a sore thumb to accuse its builder of workmanship that lacked goodness.

After the crowd left to return to their camp, Jacob overheard one man say to his wife, "That was the best show I think I've ever seen. Even before the Earthchange." Like all the rest, their laughter continued to float on the air after their receding backs.

The debacle was so complete that Moira stopped laughing and frowned in concern for him. She approached Wisdom, who had buried Her forehead in her hands.

"We'd better do something for Jacob, and quick." Wisdom agreed, and in response She implanted in Jacob's mind a much more vivid understanding of what was required to fashion a workable boat, one which would make its builder proud. In the process, She had Jacob fashion several valuable tools before he attempted to start anew on the boat itself. Among these tools was a circular saw that appeared in the bed of the truck, which by now had been completely extracted from the sand in which it had lain. Horses tethered to a central pole would be used to power this device, which would be extremely useful in preparing proper planks for the skin of the boat. Another item of importance was a trough which in heated water would be added to soften the immersed boards enough to permit them to be bent without breaking.

At that point he began to salvage the logs of his first attempt, removing them from the derelict and cutting them into planks. He had to make many dives to remove the rocks until the boat was refloated, but the effort trimmed his body up, to Moira's loving approval.

"I thought you were a hunk before, but look at you now. Makes me almost want to get physical. Almost."

"Thanks for coming back to comfort me, but how can I get over all those people laughing at me?"

"People? There are angels up there with front-row seats, who were whooping too. In fact, it's not just the world, Jacob. The entire universe was laughing!"

"Gee, thanks a lot. It couldn't be worse. I know you, Moira. You had a hand in it. Why'd you do it?"

"It brought back memories. Loving memories. You'll get over it. If it's made you more humble, that's a good thing. Not only that, but in such a colorful display of the human condition, you endeared yourself to many spiritual beings, including me. But then, you endeared yourself to me long before, when I loved to tease you. It brought me closer to you. At any rate, you'll have an epic welcome when you get here."

To Jacob's credit and Moira's appreciation, he never called it quits and walked away. He wanted to, particularly during the evening dinners where he was forced to endure the constant ribbing of the others in the community. But the jibes were good-natured, as he eventually came to realize. Even the sign planted on the shore next to the water that read: *Houseboat for sale. Cheap. Very Cheap.*

After the passage of much time, during which trade via the land routes with the other communities had taken hold and started to increase, Jacob completed his second boat. Wisdom and Moira looked at the finished craft with admiration. This time when the community turned out to observe the launch, the laughter was replaced with renewed respect. Having been instructed by Wisdom on the basics of seamanship, Jacob set sail for Moira City with two other able-bodied men.

His boat returned laden with an abundance of foodstuffs and other goods. The trade by sea became so successful that Jacob constructed a facility to fabricate more boats. The communities prospered.

CHAPTER THIRTY

After his humiliation and near-death, George was soon perceived within the community as possessing a very welcome warmth and humility that portrayed a true change of heart. Despite the reservations of a few, he was reinstated as community pastor by popular acclaim. In his tentative position as a probationary pastor before being officially installed, he had already given some presentations about God that were far more loving and accurate than those oriented toward his fixation with group celibacy. These new sermons were so kind and knowledgeable that people eagerly awaited Pastor George's next offering, a confession and presentation of his view of where the community stood with respect to the Rapture they had so earnestly hoped for and had appeared to miss.

"We, and I'm talking about all of us, here and those with Jesus right now, didn't know the actual sequence of events that led up to the Rapture. Friends, I'm pretty sure that this Rapture has come and gone, and we just didn't make it. I'm afraid that much of our fault in missing it is squarely on my shoulders, and I'll have to live with that for the rest of my life, hopefully not for eternity. At any rate, I owe you a profound apology, and I hope you will forgive my past failures as a pastor." There were murmurs of acceptance from the large crowd who had gathered that Sunday to listen to him.

"Now let me explain to you a little about that Rapture that we appear to have missed. As Scripture suggests, the Rapture and the Second Coming of Jesus Christ are two separate and distinct events. The Scripture verses that are thought to describe the Rapture are First Thessalonians 4, verses 13 through 18, and First Corinthians 15, verses 51 through 53. Possibly the most direct implication of the Rapture is given in the Old Testament, in Leviticus Chapter 23. You'll find there that the Rapture is implied in the fifth feast, the first of the Fall feasts. I'll let you read the passage yourselves as an exercise. Let's now examine the New Testament passages. The passage in Thessalonians has Paul saying this:

> But I would not have you to be ignorant, brethren, concerning them who are asleep, that ye sorrow not, even as others who have no hope. For if we believe that Jesus died and rose again, even so them also who sleep in Jesus will God bring with him. For this we say unto you by the word of the Lord, that we who alive and remain unto the coming of the Lord shall not precede them who are asleep. For the Lord himself shall descend from heaven with a shout, with the voice of the archangel, and with the trump of God; and the dead in Christ shall rise first. Then we who are alive and remain shall be caught up together with them in the clouds, to meet the Lord in the air; and so shall we ever be with the Lord. Wherefore, comfort one another with these words.

"Notice that those who are Raptured are with Jesus forever, as spiritual beings. Paul pins down this notion of their spiritual form in the Corinthians passage:

> Behold, I show you a mystery: We shall not all sleep, but we shall all be changed, in a moment, in the twinkling of an eye, at the last trump; for the trumpet shall sound, and the dead shall be raised incorruptible, and we shall be changed. For this corruptible must put on incorruption, and this mortal must put on immortality.

"There is precedence for understanding these passages as the Rapture. One can be found in Genesis 5, where Enoch was taken by God, apparently without dying. Also, according to Second Kings Chapter 2, Elijah the prophet was taken up alive by God in what was described as a whirlwind.

"As for the timing of this Rapture relative to the Tribulation, generally thought to be the final seven-year period of the seventy weeks spoken of by Daniel in Daniel 9 verses 24 through 27, there were four schools of thought posed by Protestant theologians. The first was called the pre-Tribulation Rapture, to occur before the Tribulation began; the second was called the mid-Tribulation Rapture, to occur at the midpoint of the Tribulation, three and a half years after its beginning; the third was called the post-Tribulation Rapture, to occur at the end of the Tribulation; and the fourth was called the pre-wrath Rapture, to occur somewhere between the beginning and the end of the Tribulation before things got really bad.

"I would think what actually took place was the pre-wrath Rapture which took place before the bowl judgments of Revelation, as it seems to be most in line with what Scripture in general says about events that preceded Jesus' Second Advent. Also, according to Leviticus 23, you'll note when reading it that the feast associated with the Rapture precedes the second Fall feast, which is the Day of Atonement, which is usually linked to the Great Tribulation of Revelation. Actually, the upheaval we experienced during the Earthchange was so violent that the pre-wrath Rapture was very close in time to Jesus' Second Coming, foretold in Leviticus 23 as the last of the feasts, where booths were established to represent Jesus dwelling with us. While it was quick to those close to God, it must have felt like an eternity to the others. That includes me, and I'm pretty sure to all of you as well. I also think that the pre-Tribulation Rapture view was rather too self-serving, as it would have gotten Christians safe and sound before the real evil hit the world. Its freedom from pain is probably why it was so popular. But I don't know what actually happened. What we do know," George continued, looking up toward the Jerusalem mountain, "is that we missed the boat regardless of which view actually came to pass.

"Paul was pretty specific about saying that the Raptured go to heaven and start their new lives as spiritual beings. Many have anticipated that they would return to Earth with Jesus at His Second Coming as He took over the world. We know from the example of Moira that they can return to Earth as spiritual beings, and interact with us humans. We also have a good idea that Jesus resides over there," he said, pointing to the Jerusalem Mountain. "He, of course, is in His spiritual form and will be forever, but remember those passages in Luke and John where the resurrected Jesus appears to the Apostles in human form, and is capable of eating and drinking and appearing solid, although He can come and go without the use of doors. He may rule in Jerusalem, or go between Jerusalem and His Father's side. He's definitely ruling the nations according to Revelation and Daniel 2, even as I stand here speaking. Daniel 2:44 and 45 have a lot to say about Jesus discarding the rule of man on Earth and replacing it with His rule.

"The bad news is that Jesus has already married His Bride the Church, and we aren't part of that blessed group. There's good news though, as I see it. You might recall from First Kings Chapter Eleven that King Solomon acquired seven hundred wives and three hundred concubines. I think his having done that may have been a sin, but I also am convinced that he was attempting to represent Jesus in His loving relationship with Christians."

"Oh boy!" Jane breathed in Peter's ear as George caught his breath. "As they say, there's nothing like a reformed alcoholic, in this case a reformed gender-denier. As I look around, I see a lot of surprised faces."

"It may be that Solomon's representation in that respect was more accurate than most Christians have understood," George continued. "Perhaps, to our great joy, we ourselves might just be those concubines whom Solomon represented, and perhaps after the Millennium is over, we'll be legitimized by our inclusion in that spiritual Church. In the meantime, our life here is good and it seems to be getting better every day. We should be encouraged by the promise that we Christians who have remained behind are loved by God as well as those now in heaven. We who are here for the duration of the Millennium have the honor to personally receive Jesus' necessarily firm but loving management of our lives. Perhaps this time here on Earth is kind of a restoration of Adam and Eve's condition before their fall from God's grace. Just maybe we're being given a second chance during the Millennium to straighten out our relationship with Jesus, and to love Him fervently as He commands. At least I know from Scripture that there has been a group, probably very large, who didn't get to go either here or in heaven. Those were the people who ended up accepting the mark of the beast noted in Revelation Thirteen, verses 16 through 18, to avoid starvation or torture. Revelation Fourteen, verses 9 through 13 is possibly the saddest passage in Scripture. Those who accepted the mark were doomed to everlasting alienation from God, as that passage very straightforwardly asserted. I feel for the Catholics who were so heavily influenced by their idol Augustine. They were misled by him, and the error was far from trivial. But perhaps, because they didn't see Revelation as something to be interpreted literally, God might have cut them some slack. Some of them might even be among us.

"The mark itself could not be understood by Augustine, as he didn't have the benefit of modern technology to figure it out. The Book was closed to him, as foretold in Daniel 12. His time on Earth was off. That wasn't his fault, but what was his fault was his arrogance about his own mental ability, so he thought he could understand what was closed to him. The result is that he allegorized key passages of Scripture. We were able to perfectly understand it, as the technology was in-your-face before us, and at least we knew what it was when it was adopted as policy. Thank God for that!"

The next Sunday George gave a sermon in great depth, but it was well-received, being considerably kinder in its presentation than his earlier messages. He spoke from the Book of Ephesians, focusing on Chapter Five, the love chapter. His sermon addressed Paul's great mystery of Jesus' marriage to His Church, emphasizing the Church as a body belonging to Jesus fulfills the precursor words of Adam in Genesis that declared Eve's body belonged to him to create a greater whole, one flesh formed of complementary others that harmonized together as one complete being. Carl and Elizabeth hugged each other in joy at George's budding understanding of this truth, and of their having already begun to live it. Jacob observed that and, while he felt sorrow over losing Moira in that way, he was genuinely happy for the couple. His thoughts shifted to the meat of the sermon, speculating on the greater happiness the Church would experience with Jesus as spouse.

George's messages of hope were so enthusiastically received that word of his preaching spread to their trading partners in Moira City. Despite their initial disappointment in realizing that they would remain on Earth for at least the Millennium, there was a vast general relief within both communities at no longer anxiously awaiting an event that wouldn't be coming their way, at least not for some time to come. They already were happily occupied with their part in restoring the Earth to a beauty even surpassing the one inhabited by the prime couple, Adam and Eve. Every advance they made was a delight sufficient to maintain a joyful enthusiasm toward the tomorrows to come.

PART THREE

AFTERMATH

Preface to Part Three

Observing the rapid completion of his mission on Earth, God at last prepared to bring Jacob into His lovely Bride, the spiritual Church, where he would be re-united with his loved ones, including his beloved wife Moira, who preceded him on the journey from Earth to Heaven.

In the spectacularly beautiful spiritual domain, Jacob will link up with Earl and Joyce in addition to Moira, and with Carl and Elizabeth, the close friends they had made during the time when they were influencing a small congregation of somewhat harsh and unhappy people who regarded themselves as devoted Christians. Together they will participate in thrilling projects of a cosmic nature on, above and beyond the Earth as guided by Jesus Christ.

But first they all will meet their beloved Jesus face-to-face as their collective Husband, to be awed by His amazing beauty of character. Now that they will be in their spiritual *personas*, they will have the ability to see Him in all His glory, to be awestruck by the depth of His nobility.

CHAPTER THIRTY ONE

"Hi, honey," she said to Jacob one night as he lay on his cot.

"Moira! I didn't expect you." Jacob gave her a smile of delight. "How wonderful to see you. Can I give you a hug?"

"I'd like nothing better, Jacob. I've missed you as well." They clung to each other with fervor, expressing their mutual love.

"I just wish that we could stay together like this forever," Jacob murmured in her ear.

"We can," she said.

"What?" he asked, shocked. "I don't believe what you just said!"

"Get used to it. We'll be spending more time together. I've come to take you home."

"Wow! Together again at last! You have no idea how much I've yearned for you to tell me that." His adrenalin level soared with the joyful news. But then the implication of that hit him. His expression of joy turned into a frown. "What are going to do? Shoot me?"

Moira laughed at his consternation. "Nah. As a special case, you'll be Raptured, like you wanted to be so many long months ago. I'll be tagging along for the fun of it.

She grasped his hand. "Actually, I'll be bringing you back with me. Ready?"

"Of course! But can I say goodbye to Carl and Elizabeth and my other friends?"

"No, Jacob. That's not how it works. You're not departing on a cruise ship, waving goodbye to the crowd on the dock below. They will miss you and wonder what happened, but they'll also be comforted by other angels. Let's go." She tugged on his hand, and soon they were surrounded by space as they headed for a distant light."

Odd, he thought. *I'm not suffocating. I'm not even cold.* His confusion ended abruptly as they reached the light and entered into the loving embrace of heaven itself. As he looked at Moira, he saw her anew in her spiritual form. *Have I changed too?* he wondered. *I must have,* he thought as Moira entered his domain, far more intimately than he'd ever experienced. *We are truly one now.*

"Yes we are," Moira said without speaking. "This is just the beginning. There's more – much more."

"Greetings, Jacob." Jacob looked in awe at the new figure who'd arrived and entered their domain. He instantly recognized Him as Jesus, gasping at the inner beauty of his Lord. He radiated pure love, which washed over him in sight and sound, like a musical symphony conducted next to a turquoise lagoon surrounded by tropical palms filled with colorful birds. "I just wanted to stop in to say hello and let you know how treasured I am with your presence. We've been waiting with much anticipation for your arrival. You're here now, never to depart. Welcome!" Jesus departed, leaving Jacob bereft for a moment.

"He hasn't really left, Jacob. He'll be with us always. He wants you and me to spend more time alone, getting reacquainted with each other in our spiritual form. She hugged him again, expressing her joy that they were together again, this time forever. "Let's walk around," she told him. "There's so much to see."

"It's all so beautiful, Moira. The colors – they're so vivid! And everything seems to be in its place, like a garden. And the birds! Their colors are so beautiful!"

"Yes. And no weeds!"

"I had no idea that heaven would be like this. I could stay here forever!"

"You will, of course."

"Will it always be like this? Strolling leisurely within such spectacular beauty?"

"Would you like it to?"

Jacob gave the notion some thought. "Actually, I could see myself getting a bit tired of this stroll – maybe after a couple thousand years or so."

"I'm happy you said that, because there will be plenty for us to do, to keep active. We'll have the joy of serving our Husband Jesus and seeing the fruits of our work ripen into beautiful creations."

An uncomfortable thought entered Jacob's mind. Moira picked up on it immediately. "I know, Jacob. It must be confusing to be a male and thinking of Jesus as our Husband. You yourself spoke of that back on Earth, and you had no trouble conceiving of it, because you differentiated us as components of the Church, and the composite Church herself being the Bride of Christ. Now that you're confronted with the immediacy of that situation, you're a bit put off by it. Just remember that you and I are just tiny cogs in the workings of the Church, a vast body that's married to Jesus in the collective. If that bothers you, it shouldn't, for several reasons. First, ego doesn't belong here in heaven."

"Don't worry about that. I'm perfectly content just being with you, insignificant as we may be in the grand scheme of things."

"Very good. Second, just being a small part in a vast body, we'll still experience intimacy with Jesus, much more so than, say, our fingernails would have experienced and appreciated our lovemaking back on Earth. We'll all participate in that intimacy and be fully aware of it, but it won't have the same connotation to us individuals as it did in the material world. You'll maintain your notion of your own masculinity while the Church as a composite experiences her creative union with Jesus.

"Hi, you two!" Moira said as they continued down the flower-edged pathway.

"Earl!" Jacob exclaimed. "And Joyce! I knew you must be here, but it's still a surprise to see you. And with two working arms.

Joyce, how does it feel to have legs again?"

"Wonderful! Hi, Moira."

"You know each other?" Jacob asked. "You'd never met back on Earth."

"You might recall that I had mentioned meeting them," Moira said to him. "I was interested in knowing all about the man I loved. All I had to do was go back in time."

"Things are different here, as you're beginning to understand," Joyce replied, adding specifics. "Jacob and Earl knew each other. In fact, they went through hell on Earth together at one point in time. Earl knew from Moira's spiritual essence that she had been one with Jacob, and he recognized that immediately when they met. He introduced me to Moira, and through her to Jacob as well. Since then we've been together a lot."

"So you know all about my experiences after getting out of that awful death camp?" Jacob asked.

"Completely. And your adventures with Moira as well. Including your growing love for each other. So let's call each other close friends, because your experiences – all of them – are now mine as well."

"You're right. As a matter of fact, I recall one of your darkest moments as though I had witnessed it myself: lying in the hospital bed after the accident, realizing that you'd lost your legs. Oh – wait a second! I also recall you listening to 'Magpie', your nurse, and her telling you about jumping off their bike with a sore butt!" Jacob laughed at the shared memory. What happened to Buddy? And Cathy?"

Holding hands and skipping together, Buddy and Cathy chose that precise moment to join their group. "Hi!" they communicated in unison. "We're an item now," Cathy laughingly told Jacob. "Well, at least the very best of friends. We spend most of our time with Earl and Joyce as well. It's such a blessed freedom to move as we wish, now that we're no longer encumbered with our disabilities."

CHAPTER THIRTY TWO

"What joy! What freedom! And now you're here beside me!"

"And you beside me! I've been waiting long for this, my darling Jacob. But, truth be told, my love, you've hardly experienced anything yet. Wait 'til you spend some very quality time with Jesus."

"Let's take care of that right now. Hello again, Jacob."

"Jesus! Our Lord! How beautiful You are! I'm still amazed – but that intensity of my feeling troubles me. Should I have that feeling, being a male? I'm still a male, aren't I?"

Jesus laughed merrily. "That's okay, Jacob. Just keep in mind what Moira told you about that. I feel the same way toward you. But you already know the situation here. You've talked about it enough. In fact, you were rather fixated on it, as I recall. Yes, you still are a male. You could exercise it as well, if you chose to throw away your new nature as a spiritual being. I don't think you'd want to do that. As you already know, here in the spiritual domain you're a component of a female, and a very beautiful one at that. Collectively, the Church has a feminine gender, and is extraordinarily gorgeous if I may say so. Your participation in that femininity is different than it was in the material world. You'll still experience that gender, but in a deeper, more profound way, as you're already one with your others in the spiritual Church in a manner that is closer and far more intimate than you experienced in the material world. Here in this domain you've already merged with your former lover Moira, and you understand even now that the intimacy that you sought on Earth through the partial merging of your bodies is more complete and permanent here. Your focus will center on Me, but you and Moira are now naturally one being. As you merge with more and more beings like you, and through Me your composite One experiences unity of a magnitude beyond that possible in the material domain, you will understand with an unsurpassable joy how blessed are your new circumstances, and how exciting the adventures will be of our creative acts that follow."

"Thank you, Jesus, for your wonderful nature. I already know freedom from pain. Strange, I never knew that I had so much."

"Most people are surprised at that when they arrive here. Much pain, both physical and mental, is suppressed for the sake of survival and the maintenance of rationality. I do say, though, that you had more than your share. It made you a better person."

"I have so many questions to ask! We're talking, but then we're not. What gives with that?"

"It's part of the greater unity here, although you already had a taste of it with your communication with Moira in the material domain. We don't need to communicate by sound, but more directly through the mind. It could get confusing if you didn't have your new ability to maintain separation of thought in the presence of multiple simultaneous dialogues. But you do have that ability."

"I'd always had it in the back of my mind that I'd lose something in the spiritual domain by not being able to love Moira the way I did on Earth. Now I know that I didn't lose anything, but gained much. I now possess You in a way that I couldn't back then, but I didn't lose anything with Moira either, as we're now as close together as it's possible to be. But I have another question. Am I the last person to arrive as part of the Church? Is your Bride complete now?"

"No and yes. You weren't the last one to come in, and yes, the Church is now complete. The last to come in were a couple you were very fond of. Say hello to Carl and Elizabeth."

"Wow! I didn't expect that!"

"You should have – you'd thought about it. You thought they deserved it, and I agree. As a matter of fact, I'd say you two couples should merge right now."

Satisfied that they were comfortable and happy in their new

integration, Jesus occupied Himself with preparing for a group-merge of the entire Church. The Church's gender would play a significant part in this event to come.

"Oh!" the entire Church exclaimed as one, having experienced Her first group-merge, an ecstatic event that convulsed Her with the force of an electric shock. As a unit, She embarked on a singular creative adventure in which individuals and smaller groups set out on their separate objectives.

Each of these were filled with the knowledge of and desire for the pursuit of their separate tasks that would contribute to the whole creative event. Jesus looked on with joy as the conductor of this beautiful symphony of action.

Jesus' objective in this event was to restore a canopy of ice around the Earth. Unlike the original globular canopy that enclosed the entire planet before the great flood, this one was to be a band that encircled it as a belt around the equator. The band of ice would consist of individual angular pieces that would collectively refract the sunlight to create narrower bands of vivid colors for the appreciation of those who were Earthbound and remained for this millennium in the material domain. He added a special treat for Jacob and Moira.

"Well, look who's here!" Jacob exclaimed to Moira. The two rushed over to welcome Carl and Elizabeth. "Looks like you've been given the same objective as us," Moira commented with pleasure. "I'll bet we make a good team."

CHAPTER THIRTY THREE

Jesus called His Church together once again. It wasn't a command, but rather a common desire within His spiritual Church to participate in His companionship. When they had merged with Him, He told them that the communities scattered around the Earth had become sophisticated enough to manage trade with each other that extended beyond their immediate environs, almost becoming international in nature.

"The communities are becoming so large and comfortable," Jesus continued, "that egos are beginning to swell. Pride is showing its ugly head again, and if we don't step in, the rivalries that are beginning to form will expand into open warfare. Other problems are starting to show, such as attitudes toward sex that don't belong in a one woman, one man bonding relationship reflective of Us and of My beloved divine Parents. It's time that we embarked on a very important task, that of maintaining order and love through the establishment of nations to be governed internally by laws and governed externally by a judicial system whose members are composed of those among you who have the particular interest and emotional suitability to serve in that manner."

Some members of the spiritual Church immediately signaled telepathically to Jesus their desire to participate in that way. Jesus acknowledged their wishes. "Very good," He communicated back to the entire group. You do realize, don't you, that the positions are more sedentary than most." It was a rhetorical question, needing no answer. "Furthermore, all of you previously had careers as lawyers. The job involves having to put up with my extensive repertoire of lawyer jokes." The group laughed at that, the greatest mirth coming from those who were to be granted judicial posts. "These jobs won't necessarily be permanent," Jesus continued. "Some of you will want to be more active and creative after a while. That's fine. So we'll need to have more participants in this in a standby mode. Keep in mind that this will go on for an entire millennium, so we'll need to keep rotating you into those positions. You all may end up being involved in this endeavor." In response to the comforting thought that the positions might be temporary for each, many more signaled their willingness to participate in the judging of the humans on Earth.

"While we're all here together," Jesus added, let's fully merge and enjoy some intimacy with each other." Gasps of pleasure sounded throughout the Church. Many openly responded with joyful expressions of creative impulses supported by Wisdom-induced knowledge of the paths toward the accomplishment of their new objectives. The merging continued for an indefinite length, to the great blessing of the happy participants.

"How very wonderful," Jacob said to Moira after the merging had ended.

"We'll have more," she responded. "Many more. They're all quite wonderful. Did you see our task to come?"

"Yes, amazingly so. I also know how we'll be accomplishing it. Intimately."

CHAPTER THIRTY FOUR

"Jesus, I'm privileged beyond measure to be speaking to You face-to-face."

"No need for formality, Jacob. You're not only part of My Wife, but we're also friends."

"There's something I've been thinking about. Who thought up the idea of FIFO visitations?"

"I did. Why do you ask?" Jesus, of course knew what was on Jacob's mind, but He enjoyed being conversational.

"What about the Gulf Breeze incidents? Where You – or someone – kept hounding that poor man with an endless string of sightings."

Jesus laughed, a rich, booming sound. "Just because I'm God, can't I have a sense of humor? You humans were taking yourselves far too seriously. I wanted to lighten things up, as well as being loving."

"You call that loving? That guy almost tore his hair out in frustration. But it is funny to think about. It was so over-the-top from the usual sighting."

"You should have seen those who were in the craft. They were reduced to uncontrollable laughter, which I enjoyed as well. But the 'victim', as you seem to think of him, was so caught up in his own independence that his ego needed a little pruning back. It ended up being a win-win event."

"I don't see some other events as being funny. You really gave the Apostle Paul what-for, didn't you? At least that's what Your Word implies in Acts 9."

"I did indeed, because of My love toward him. He was on the wrong mental track, but it wasn't his understanding at fault. He couldn't help the way he was brought up. What really needed correction was his ego, his self-satisfaction of the head knowledge he'd acquired. Even more, his righteous anger was directed toward My beloved people. That couldn't continue."

"You obviously did a good job. He must be among the most dedicated Christians of all time."

"We gave him an incentive, and it wasn't all negative. We took him on an awe-inspiring look-see into Our spiritual domain. It blew his mind. From that time on, he knew which side his bread was buttered on. Still, with the help of My beloved Holy Spirit, he was very courageous and very faithful."

"I gathered that from Paul's mention in Galatians 1 about having received his knowledge of You in special way, and then in the next chapter about a fourteen-year time period, the same period he noted in Chapter 12 of his second letter to the Corinthians about a person who was taken up into the third heaven and shown wonders beyond imagination."

"You were quite right. And congratulations on your perception. But then I know how thoughtful you were in reading and digesting My Word."

"Every bit of which was absolutely true. But I had a lot of help from Earl and Joyce. They really knew what to say and how to say it."

"I know. Wisdom, of course, was behind it all. She had much joy in seeing your understanding come together."

What I could never understand is why so many lost people didn't read it in enough depth to understand or trust in it. Especially when they gave so much more thought to the daily newspaper."

"All those souls, and I loved every one!" He wept briefly, but His countenance brightened when He looked at Jacob. "You do understand. You've read Paul's letter to the Romans. It's right there in the first chapter, as you well know, and it's quite simple. They didn't want to. Mostly because of their egos and the sins they were so happily engaged in. In that state of mind their sins kept growing and their hearts kept hardening. They just didn't want a God to get in the way of their pleasure and perceived self-importance."

"So they ignored what stared them in their faces: the amazing detail and accuracy of the prophecies. Moses and David. Ezekiel and Daniel, not to mention You.'

They got around that too, by claiming those prophetic passages to be written after the fact."

"But the Dead Sea Scrolls, Jesus! They were dated to before the prophecies came true."

Jesus laughed ruefully. "Their minds didn't extend far enough to see that. There's an old saying you had that's largely true, that a bully is a coward. Here's another one: a selfish mind is also shallow. It has to be, to swallow all the inconsistencies in the brainwashing the godless have been handed. Even then, the utter uselessness of that false information should have clued them in that something was wrong somewhere. The fact that none of the information that attended Darwin's theory was useful in providing further insights into details of living systems should have caused them to wonder about the theory itself. But, again, they wanted to believe what they wanted to believe. But let's go to a happier topic, which is what I've planned for you and your closest companions."

CHAPTER THIRTY FIVE

The group of four, Jacob, Moira, Carl and Elizabeth, worked harmoniously together, leading them to identify their small collective the Sandies in memory of the lush oasis they had encountered after leaving the first community. Although they had no part in that experience, Earl and Joyce joined that group as well. It expanded yet further with the addition of Buddy and Cathy, who in this spiritual domain occupied with great joy their new, fully intact bodies.

The eight Sandies set out to obtain chunks of water and fashion them into the appropriate angular shapes as they froze in space above the Earth's atmosphere. It was a happy task in which they cooperated so well together that they seemed to consist of one organism.

"Moira!" Jacob exclaimed as he placed a chunk neatly among others, "Look down below. Notice that the continents don't look the same as they did in the globes we used to use in high school? In fact, I can't recognize the Americas anywhere."

"There was a pole shift, Jacob, like what happened in Noah's Flood. Remember the coal they found in Antarctica before this latest Earthchange? None of the science "experts" could figure out how it got there. Their paradigm that excluded a violent Flood prevented them from applying common sense to the question. Well, that's Antarctica that you're looking at now right down below us. It straddles the Equator and you can see how green and lush it's becoming. Now that most of the ice has melted, evidence of an advanced pre-Flood civilization has been exposed. Unlike the other continents that have taken God a lot of work to restore and still need more loving care from us, its late residence at what used to be the South Pole with its cover of ice prevented its trashing by the misuse of technology. That's North America down there where Antarctica used to be. It's already covered in ice."

"Looking to the north, I see a landmass spreading across the North Pole."

"Yep, that's South America. It's getting an ice cover as well."

When the quartet had finished their objective, they returned to the ground below, in the midst of the Antarctic continent. Looking upward, they grinned in pleasure at the sight of their handiwork. Their eyes were greeted with the sight of a band of light from the ring that now encircled the Earth. Its colors were stunning and included variations not known in the post-Flood rainbows seen in the old Earth.

"Now what?" Carl asked, not expecting an answer.

"Something even more fun," Jesus responded. "How would you like to overlook the creation of a community on the Moon?"

"Wow!" Jacob said enthusiastically. But what do You mean by 'overlook'?"

"The actual work will be done under your supervision – you Sandies - and supported by the knowledge you'll be given."

"Who'll be doing the work, then?"

"Those left on Earth during the Millennium. Some of them will be your friends in the community you left behind. I love them too, Carl. If you want to understand where they stand with Me, recall what Solomon did as recorded in First Kings Chapter Eleven. As you well know, you here with Me are My wonderful loving Bride. Those who remain on Earth for now are presently My concubines. A little less intimate, but still very dearly loved by Me. Some of them will eventually come into your group – the spiritual Church."

"Are we going to be able to go in our so-called FIFOs?"

"Not really necessary, as you already know from your spectacularly colorful work on the Earthring without them. They were really good only for reminding those on Earth that there just might be Someone who was bigger than them. Even then, the paranoia got too great.

Remember how the nature of those 'occupants' was so radically misinterpreted as technologically advanced beings and still alien? People just couldn't get over their materialistic mindset. On the other hand, while they may not be all that useful to you, the people who drove them were greatly amused with the experience. Sure, that might be another fun thing for you to do, so yes, why not? Have at them."

"I can't wait! But are they really no longer useful?"

"Not at all. The stay-behinds in your community will get the use of them, and not too long from now. It will continually be amazing to them how rapidly under My governance they'll be able to recover the knowledge and technology they had before things took a turn for the worse. After that, they'll continue on beyond that point – way beyond. They'll get much of the technology behind the craft used by the angels, but of course, being limited to the material plane, they won't be able to perform the maneuvers they've seen the angels do. They'll still get the best joyrides they'll ever have this side of heaven. They're going to build a sustainable community on the Moon in preparation for a longer journey to Mars and beyond. It will be a very exciting and adventurous time for them all. But before they do that, they're going to be doing some final cleanup on Earth. Even that won't involve much drudgery, as they'll be given some rather interesting tools to help do the job."

Jacob spoke up. "I don't want to sound like a malcontent, Jesus, but it's starting to sound like the Left-Behinds might be getting more adventure than us."

Jesus laughed, a rich baritone. "Moira, let our beloved friend here get a glimpse of the truth of the matter. I know what you're thinking as well, that it could be a joyful experience for Carl and Elizabeth as well. Yes, they'll do some wonderful reminiscing about the fun they had on their Goldwing as they maneuver on a level impossible with an Earthbound vehicle. I'm going to give them a chance to do just that, and you'll be right there with them, enjoying the experience."

CHAPTER THIRTY SIX

Moira took Jacob by the hand. "Come," she said. With Jacob in tow, she pointed beyond the sky to a tiny red dot. "Hold on," she said, and grabbed his arm. The dot rapidly grew larger. "I want to take a detour," she said again, pulling him in another direction. The red planet maintained a constant size as they circled around it. When it was behind them Moira resumed heading outward. Mars shrank back to a dot and the sun took on a small, feeble appearance. An enormous planet loomed large ahead of them and began to dominate their field of vision. As it grew in front of them, another planet appeared off to the side. Jacob thought he knew the solar system pretty well, but he didn't remember this one. They changed direction again, heading toward it. As it loomed nearer, other, smaller objects began to appear. As their trajectories appeared to encircle the planet, Jacob supposed them to be moons. But there were a multitude of them. They soon revealed themselves to be gigantic, odd-shaped boulders. The numerous boulders circled a large planet at various distances from it. The planet itself was engulfed in clouds and radiated heat. Jacob pulled on her hand, trying to understand what made him think of the sight as beyond strange. "Moira," he said, "aren't we between Mars and Jupiter?"

"Yes," she said with a grin.

"There wasn't a planet here before. Just the asteroid belt. What's that planet doing here, and how did it get here?"

"It's confusing, isn't it? The rocks we're going through are still asteroids, but now they're circling the planet as satellites."

"But the planet. Where did that come from?"

"The Earthchange. Now you're seeing a sample at the cosmic level of the cause of all that chaos on Earth. This fella came very close to the Earth, disrupting it in a planetary catastrophe just like what happened during Noah's flood. Remember what Jesus said about the end of the age in Matthew 24. I'll repeat it;

> *But as the days of Noah were, so shall also the coming of the Son of man be.*

"Wow!" Jacob exclaimed. "Jesus was exact in that comparison with Noah."

"Truly so. Humans never really grasped how very profound and deep is the Word of God in Scripture. Jesus named the planet Nibiru as an offhand nod to Zecharia Sitchin and his Twelfth Planet theory. It careened around the solar system until Jesus put it in this "missing planet" slot. It fits perfectly, as Jesus planned."

"Yes, I see. Apparently like this Nibiru, the object in Noah's time did the same thing until it eventually achieved a stable orbit and became the legitimate planet we now know as Venus."

"Venus?" Carl questioned, surprised. "You have to be kidding!" Carl and his companion Elizabeth had been tuning in to their exchange as they moved away from Earth. He was still in the vicinity of Earth, but the group was so spiritually close that their thoughts transcended the distance between them. Jacob and Moira welcomed his intrusion.

"That's the attitude Carl Sagan had when Immanuel Velikovsky wrote about it," Moira responded. "But it was primarily because Velikovsky involved God, more than the oddity of the event, that incensed Sagan about Velikovsky's assertion. Sagan attempted to debunk him because Velikovsky borrowed facts from the Bible to support his thesis. True, a secondary issue was that the mere thought of Venus starting out by being birthed by Jupiter was so implausibly lurid. It sounded like the kind of stuff that you'd find in the tell-all rags in the checkout aisle of the supermarket. But, as the saying goes, truth can be stranger than fiction. Regardless, based on his hypothesis about Venus, Velikovsky made some important predictions about the nature of Mars and Venus that Sagan attempted to refute, but couldn't. Every one of them, including the high temperature of Venus, was found to be true.

"But," she continued, "Nibiru, under Jesus' direction, reached its stable orbit much sooner than Venus did. Venus had several encounters with the Earth and its inhabitants, each serving some purpose in God's plan for mankind."

"Yeah," Jacob assented. "The Exodus of the Israelites from Egypt, and Joshua's long day for two."

"And indirectly, involving Mars during Isaiah's lifetime."

"The moons of Nibiru, the old asteroids. Where did they come from originally? How did they get there?" Jacob asked her.

"Another thing that Venus did during Noah's time was to completely destroy a planet. Those rocks make up the asteroid belt. They're all that remain of it. Nibiru is a replacement. Someday we'll be doing some terraforming on it. That will be a later project after our work on Mars and Venus and several other tasks we'll be taking on while it continues to cool. Maybe we'll keep some of the biggest rocks around as moons to Nibiru, create some interesting uses for them.

"So say goodbye for now to Nibiru. We won't be going there for quite a while."

"It's hot."

"Quite. We'll eventually get to exploiting it, but not for several more millennia. Venus will be habitable sooner than this one. But first there's Mars. Let's go there." She placed her hand in his again, and they moved back toward the red dot in the sky.

They threaded their way past the lifeless rocks, leaving Nibiru behind. They returned to the emptiness of space as they continued toward their objective. As they approached, the dot grew and took on the round shape of a ball. Closer yet, it identified itself as the planet Mars. "First, a little background as to the scale of things," she told her companion as they stood off the surface. "Our Left-Behind friends won't be Earthbound, but they'll merely be visiting, witnessing, or sometimes at most patching up those things that God created in the past. Like Mars here. We'll be creating, Jacob. Doing things like the Holy Spirit did in response to the divine Will that resulted in the reality represented by Jesus. Now we'll be doing the same kind of things in response to our own beloved Jesus. Creating. Bringing in a new reality from nothing. But first repairing, on a far grander scale than would be humanly possible. "We'll be handling the big stuff," she continued as the red dot rapidly increased in size. "The Left-Behinds like George and his group will be handling the smaller tasks after we prepare the planet for them. We'll be using some of the big rocks that we encountered back there."

"Take a look at the planet underneath your feet as we move around it," she said as they approached. Everything okay?"

Jacob gasped in surprise. "There's a volcano here, a very big one. Huge, in fact. And the surface! It looks like the surface of half the planet is gone. And the enormous rifts. I see one that rivals the Grand Canyon on Earth, maybe even surpasses it in depth. No, everything's not okay. There's even a bulge on one side, like something was trying to get out. The planet's devastated."

"Now for another history lesson, in a little more detail than you've had so far," Moira replied. "Mars used to have an atmosphere. It even had water. It was farther from the sun than Earth, but still habitable under the right conditions in places that were more benign than others. There was no volcano like Mount Olympus there. There were no rifts, or a surface missing over half the planet. Then came a comet, small but very fast. It hit Jupiter, passing through it and continuing on to hit Mars. Jupiter itself responded by ejecting an even larger mass which we now know as Venus, molten and deadly, which careened around the other planets like a drunken billiard ball. Its orbit was unstable, bringing it perilously close to Earth. So close that it destroyed the beautiful globular canopy around our planet, which we so recently restored in ring form."

"Having gone through the Earthchange with our friend Nibiru, I can picture Jesus allowing that to happen," Jacob said, interrupting her narrative.

"He not only didn't prevent that catastrophe, He actually caused it. Deliberately."

"Of course. He always has a good reason. But go ahead with what you were saying."

"At that time as you're aware, some angels broke off from the Holy Spirit, having decided in disobedience to take wives of human women. Satan attempted through them and their lust to corrupt the blood line from Adam to Jesus, as He had to be both fully God and fully human for His sacrifice of Himself to be effective toward our collective salvation. These fallen angels did corrupt mankind, except for Noah and his family, and also our collective character in the process, turning our world into a hellhole of violence, hatred and disobedience to God. God had had it, and did something about it. It was drastic. People all the way in time up to Jesus' return downplayed the effects of the Flood, but it was a huge event and very violent. Just like our recent Earthchange."

"Wow. I get the picture. That explains the bulge on one side of the Red Planet."

"For sure. It's called the Tharsis Bulge, by the way. But it doesn't explain the rest of the destruction on Mars. Eventually Venus, still in an unstable orbit, came very close to the red planet here, almost colliding with it. The two objects almost broke apart, but not quite. The atmosphere of Mars was ripped away, and along with it went half the top layer of the planet's surface. Fissures formed and the volcano erupted. Mount Olympus is the largest volcano in the solar system. Then the errant object wandered off again."

"To return to Earth later."

"After trashing Mars. What a mess. Are we going to fix it?"

"Yes. Unlike Venus and Nibiru, Mars is cold, so we can work with it now. That will be one of our first tasks, and it's and exciting prospect to me. I think it will be to you as well. Does what you've seen and I've told you satisfy you that we'll all be doing important and adventurous work?"

"Yes. I'm overwhelmed."

"So am I," Carl said. "Things here are getting very interesting too. I'll tune out for now. Goodbye."

"You should have known there'd be enough adventure to keep us all entertained, my beloved," Moira said to Jacob. "We're not going to be sitting around for eternity being bored out of our minds. But you're a neophyte here, so it's natural that you'd have questions like that. As you're just beginning to see, heaven's much more real than the very limited material world, and there are passages in Scripture that point to the greater joy that we'd have in heaven. I envy you a bit for that, in a good-natured way, because you have so much ahead of you to discover, all joyful. I guess there's a lot yet for me to discover as well. Let's do that ourselves. It's time to head back to Earth and get to know more of our wonderful new body, the Church. We have many friends to meet, old and new."

"What about the other planets?" Jacob asked as they reached Nibiru and threaded their way back through its new moons.

"Jesus has big plans for them as well," Moira responded. "There is so much here that we'll be occupied on construction for a very long time."

"But not forever."

"Well, yes, forever. We're no longer restricted by the speed of light. Even if we were, we now have interdimensional doors through which we can cross if we want to take shortcuts. Very significant ones, as a matter of fact."

"So travel is no barrier."

"Gee, Jacob do you see one?"

He laughed. "Sounds pretty exciting."

"You don't know the half of it. And all of our accomplishments will be to Jesus' glory as He showers us with His love in return."

"I'd like to know more about the Earthchange from the perspective of heaven," Jacob said as they arrived back on Earth.

"You will. And guess who's involved."

"Who?"

"Look over there, she said, pointing at a couple coming their way.

"Stephen and Cindy Miller!" Jacob exclaimed.

"Yes, among others. They arrived in heaven early enough that they actually were able to participate."

"Hi, you two," Stephen said enthusiastically as they came near.

"Hello back to you. I'd like you to meet my wife Moira," he said, his arm planted on her shoulder.

"The three laughed. "We've already met," Moira told her husband. "But I see someone over there I'd like to know better."

Earl and Joyce Cook drew near, looking in the direction of Moira's interest.

Joyce followed her eyes, which rested on a lively girl. "That's Cathy," she said. "And Buddy's holding her hand."

"They're an attractive couple," Moira murmured. "Did you say they were afflicted with cerebral palsy?"

"Yes. God sure cleaned them up nice, wouldn't you say? They deserve an eternity of happiness after what they've been through. I witnessed some of Cathy's abuse at the hands of the guards at that horrible death camp. The memories would still be painful if we weren't up here and able to see the beautiful outcome for us all."

"Amen, sister. What about Buddy? Was he tortured and murdered as well?"

"Absolutely. Earl and I lost track of him when we escaped with Cathy on Cindy's sailboat, but we learned about what happened to him here in heaven. In fact, he arrived at the death camp and had been killed well before we got there. We went back in time to see what had happened to him , and believe me, it's not something either of us want to remember. Let's just say that he and Cathy are in a much better place now, and have all of eternity to enjoy it."

Joyce poked Earl, pointing to another couple. "There's Magpie, holding her husband's hand. We need to go over and re-acquaint ourselves with her and meet her husband."

Earl poked Joyce back, turning toward Stephen and Cindy. "We need to apologize for the trouble we got them into," he said.

"I already know what you want to say," Stephen said to Earl. "You want to tell us how sorry you are for getting us to into the Murder Motel. Do you see us weeping? You just got us here sooner than we expected, and we should thank you for that. "Hey, by the way, congrats on getting your arm back."

"Thanks. Same to you for making it to this beautiful place. Can you imagine being anywhere else?"

"No, but I suppose that's where our governmental movers and shakers are right now. And those guards! Actually, just thinking about that gives me the willies."

"Do you miss your sailboat?"

"Not at all," Cindy spoke up. "Not now with our free use of a FIFO. What a crazy ride that is! We took her over to Mars the other day. It was like going to a museum, only a million times more fascinating."

"We went there ourselves, but just our spiritual selves traveling between dimensions and moving around the odd rock here and there. Next time we'll try a vehicle, just for a change."

"Yeah," Cindy said. "It may not be necessary, but that makes it even more of a blast! I wonder what my old therapist Maggie would have said about it, her being a biker and all." She looked at Joyce, smiling about their shared memories of their recovery in the hospital, and their outspoken therapist who helped them through such a difficult time.

"Hey, I'm right here," said Maggie, who was holding on to a man's arm. "And I'll second that comment. The FIFO is a great ride, better even than the epic adventures we had on the bike. And since we've gotten all spiritualled-up, poor Bob here can't give me a hard time with the back seat any more. He even looks at me wrong,

I'll just step outside and continue on without him. He knows that, too. Don't you, Bob?" She gave him a jab in the kidney for old times' sake as the others laughed. "By the way, what happened to you, Cindy, after you left the hospital? I imagine that you returned to your sailboat."

"Meet my husband Stephen, Maggie. And a hello to you, Bob. Your adventures with Maggie made our ordeal in the hospital much more manageable. Yes, I did go back to the boat, and yes, we continued to sail her, all the way until we got into trouble with the authorities with you aboard," she said, turning toward Cathy to address her directly. "As I'm sure you remember, we made our final journey on her with you."

"Wow," Buddy spoke up. "That must have been a great trip! Cathy told me a little about the boat's last voyage. But it was such a painful experience for her that I'm pretty sure she didn't tell me everything. Was any part of the trip fun at all?"

"It was for a little while. Then it got very bad for all of us. The aftermath of the trip was even worse. Much worse, being the end of the line for Stephen and me as well after Cathy was murdered. But, of course, it sure turned out okay. We're here, and that's all that really counts."

"But what happened to make it turn bad?"

"The government nabbed us and sank our boat. Then they took us to their death camp, complete with the evil guards. Both men and women, they were all evil. It's still a vicious memory that I really don't want to relive. If you want to go back in time and see what happened as the terror unfolded, have at it. But I don't think you'll want to see what happened to me. It's pretty gruesome. One thing you'd probably like to see in detail is what became of Joyce and Earl. They were at the death camp with us and went through a pretty awful time as well. But they survived at the hands of a lovely Lady you know as Wisdom, who created a devastating earthquake that knocked down the camp and allowed Joyce and Earl to escape. Their adventures afterwards were pretty awesome. As a matter of fact, their escape brought them into contact with another wonderful guy you've already met, Jacob over there with his lovely wife Moira. Jacob and Moira's life together was very adventurous too. Jacob's journeys took him to Israel on a boat that also sank at sea, but he survived that to meet Moira, an Israeli who gave Jacob another round of adventures. But let's turn this conversation around. What happened to you after we left the hospital?"

"You'll be surprised about this, but Bob and I were at that same death camp in Arizona as you, maybe a little earlier."

"Oh? How did you end up there?"

"After you all left, hospital policy began to deteriorate. It became obvious that the elderly patients weren't being given the care they needed to recover from their various ailments. More of them began to leave in body bags, and those who didn't were starting to get treated with indifference that quickly morphed into outright abuse. I tried to put a stop to it, but the trouble actually began at the top, so you can guess how effective I was. I quit, but not too long afterwards, they came after me. And Bob too, because I guess they figured that I'd told him too much. Which I most certainly did. He had to put up with all those earfuls I handed to him."

"Which I'm glad you did," Bob spoke up. I'd have handled it poorly if they'd dragged you away and left me behind. As it was, I tried to wrestle you away from that big guy who held you, but he must have had a lot of training to handle guys like me."

"And an evil mind," Maggie added. "They all were as bad as humans can get."

They were interrupted by a group invitation to spend time with Jesus. Happy to have something better to think about, they rushed to His side, eager for some quality time with Him. Moira looked at Jacob, then toward Jesus, content in the knowledge that they had all eternity to experience this joy.

More than content. Excited beyond an Earthbound soul's imagination.

www.ingramcontent.com/pod-product-compliance
Lightning Source LLC
Chambersburg PA
CBHW071308250626
47159CB00004B/1347